"Crime to make you laugh out loud… warm and witty…delving into the dark side of the west of Scotland. I look forward to reading more Queste adventures."   Alex Gray's Books of the Year, *The Times*

"*The Dead Don't Boogie* is classic noir effortlessly transposed from the mean streets of Chandler's LA to 21st-century Glasgow. Dominic Queste is an engaging new hero with a unique voice."   **Mason Cross**

"Fast-paced, funny and frightening – Dominic Queste's first outing supplies it all."   **Lin Anderson**

"If you like your humour black and your detective novels hard-boiled, *The Dead Don't Boogie* is a cut above the rest."   **Theresa Talbot**

"A white-knuckle, wisecracking thrill-ride."   **Caro Ramsay**

"The plot rattles along at break-neck speed. This is modern pulp fiction at its best…fast-paced and flippant."

Alastair Braidwood, Scots Whay Hae

"Dark noir at its finest…compulsive reading. One of the best crime novels I have read in a long time. Hugely enjoyable."   **Mark Leggatt**

"Queste is an inspired creation…Perfect for those who like their prose sharp, plot twists sudden and characters sassy."   **Neil Broadfoot**

"Scotland's answer to Sam Spade, with quips, a femme fatale, and a body count to keep even the most bloodthirsty crime fan satisfied. Undoubtedly his best work yet."   **Matt Bendoris**

"Fierce, all too believable."   *Daily Mail*

"Effortless prose."   *Crimesquad*

"Tense, dark and nerve wracking."   *The Herald*

"A gory and razor-sharp crime novel from the start ... moves at break-neck speed."   *The Skinny*

"Doug Skelton has been hiding his talent for long enough. High time he shared it with the rest of us."   **Quintin Jardine**

Also by Douglas Skelton

Fiction

The Dead Don't Boogie

Open Wounds

Devil's Knock

Crow Bait

Blood City

Non-fiction

Glasgow's Black Heart: A City's Life of Crime

Dark Heart: Tales from Edinburgh's Town Jail

*Indian Peter: The Extraordinary Life
and Adventures of Peter Williamson*

Bloody Valentine: Scotland's Crimes of Passion

Deadlier Than the Male: Scotland's Most Wicked Women

Scotland's Most Wanted

Devil's Gallop

A Time to Kill

No Final Solution

Frightener (with Lisa Brownlie)

Blood on the Thistle

TAG –
YOU'RE DEAD

Douglas Skelton

CONTRABAND ⊖

Contraband is an imprint of Saraband
Published by Saraband,
Suite 202, 98 Woodlands Road,
Glasgow, G3 6HB,
Scotland
www.saraband.net

ISBN: 9781910192726
ebook: 9781910192733

Typeset by Iolaire Typography Ltd.
Printed and bound in Great Britain by Clays Ltd, St Ives plc.

10 9 8 7 6 5 4 3 2 1

Prologue

The mobile phone was cheap and nasty and basic, but that didn't bother me.

It didn't offer internet access or even have a camera. That didn't bother me either.

What really bothered me was that it was sitting on the coffee table in my living room and it wasn't mine.

I froze, listened for the sound of someone moving in my flat. It's not a big flat. If a fly sneezes at one end, I'll still say 'bless you' from the other. I heard a car pass in the street. I heard music playing somewhere. I think it may have been One Direction. I heard the click of heels as someone climbed the stairs in my tenement building. I heard nothing disturbing. Unless you count One Direction.

My breath had stilled, so I exhaled and then inhaled before I lifted the phone, turned it over in my hand. Someone had come into my home and left it behind. A burglar wasn't likely to lay his phone on the table while he rifled my valuables – it wasn't much of a rifle, to be honest, unless you like CDs of film music and DVDs. And the flat was undisturbed. Maybe not tidy, but the mess I'd left was untouched. Everything was where I'd dropped it.

That meant the phone was left here deliberately.

I thought, who?

I thought, why?

I thought, who?

I know I thought that twice, but I really wanted to know.

And then it beeped. A text. It wasn't loud, but it made me start.

v

It wasn't my phone, but something told me the message was for me and I pressed OPEN, read three words:

Hello, Mr Queste

Hello yourself, I almost typed, but then the phone beeped again. Another text. Four words this time.

You have been selected

No thank you, I thought. I don't know what you're selling, but I'm not buying. Whatever was coming next wasn't good.

And then it came.

Two words. Capitalised for added emphasis. Not that they needed them.

FOR DEATH

I'll be honest, I felt my skin crawl. I now knew what this was about. I knew this was no prank. I knew that whoever sent these texts was very serious indeed. He had killed before.

Right then, another question sprang into my mind.

How the hell do I get myself involved in these things?

Chapter One

I find it hard to refuse an attractive woman when she asks for a favour.

I find it damn near impossible when we're both naked.

Let me tell you, that doesn't happen very often these days. Hell, that's never happened often, because even though I'm no Quasimodo, I'm not exactly catnip for the ladies. You can count the number of women I've been intimate with on one hand and still have fingers to spare should you feel the need to make an obscene gesture. In fact, for a long time the closest I came to sweaty bedroom action was changing the duvet. So I was very grateful that Ginty O'Reilly had seen fit to end a dry spell that made *Lawrence of Arabia* look like *Waterworld*.

I'd met her after her ex-husband, a former boxer nicknamed Tiger, had introduced me to his fist when I found him in the home of a recently murdered woman. Tiger later wound up hanging from the yardarm of a tall ship, but that's another story entirely. Ginty and I seemed to hit it off, though. She was tall and slim and blonde. There's a Raymond Chandler line about a blonde who would make a bishop kick a hole in a stained-glass window. If the bishop met Ginty, that stained-glass window would have more holes than Marlon Brando's vest. I was punching way above my weight, but she didn't seem to notice. Don't get me wrong, she wasn't some high-toned kind of gal from the West End. She was an East-End hairdresser who, when pressed, was capable of bleaching a barnet with the kind of industrial language that would shock Quentin Tarantino.

She was also no doe-eyed teenager looking for any kind of permanent arrangement, which was fine with me because I don't think I'm a permanent arrangement sort of guy. For one thing, I like my own space. For another, the work I do calls for some pretty unsociable hours. But more importantly, I have a streak of Celtic melancholy that can emerge when the wind changes direction and I wanted to shield her from that. Call it what you will – depression, self-pity, a dark side – it's not something I wished anyone to see, let alone Ginty, who was one of those people who liked to see the bright side of life, despite her having been round the block a time or two.

So we saw each other once or twice a week, if I wasn't working. We went out for lunch, dinner, to the movies. We did all the things pals did and a few things pals didn't do, like rolling around in bed. That's what had happened that night. We'd had dinner in Frankie & Benny's at Springfield Quay – our sophistication is the envy of the trendy set – then headed across the car park to the Odeon where we ignored this week's clutch of superhero movies (all that testosterone and rippling muscle makes me feel insecure) in favour of a comedy in which lots of people puked, urinated and farted. Ginty and the audience laughed like they were watching something funny. I didn't. Still, the fact that I'd done the manly thing and taken her to a film of her choice earned me brownie points. It's all about the giving with me.

Suffice to say that later we were cuddling in my bed, having sated ourselves. John Barry's 'The Beyondness of Things' was on the CD player and the beautiful melodies were both soothing and sad at the same time. Some people think Barry was only about Bond music, but the real heart of the composer came through in his gentler moments. It was raining outside, for a change, and the street light outside my bedroom window cast a pale glow through the drawn drapes as I lay on the bed with Ginty's head resting on my chest, my fingers stroking her hair, listening to the sinister opening chords of 'The Fictionist' give way to another gently romantic melody. I was happy, which was not something

I was used to, despite my tendency for smart-arsed quips. The rain caressing the window, the soothing music and my recent exertions combined to make me contemplate slipping softly into the sleep of the just-after.

'Erasmus,' Ginty said. Her voice was low and throaty. It turned me on just to listen to it. But then, I'm a guy. I get turned on when I squeeze a melon. And Erasmus isn't my name, it was simply something I said the first time we met and it stuck. She knew my real name, of course. She just preferred to call me Erasmus.

'Present,' I said.

'Would you do something for me?'

'Well, if it entails dressing up and/or swinging from the light fitting, you'll need to give me fifteen minutes.' I thought about that again. Who was I kidding? What was I – an athlete? 'Maybe half an hour.'

She laughed in a slightly derisive way. 'No, but hold that thought for an hour or two,' she said, rather unnecessarily I decided. 'I need a favour.'

'Go ahead. But don't think I didn't notice that slight on my manhood. I'll think of a snappy comeback, don't you worry. Once my breathing returns to normal.'

She raised her head from my chest and propped her chin on one hand. She wasn't smiling. I loved to see her smile, but there was something in those blue eyes that told me this was serious. 'So what's the favour?' I asked.

'It's my cousin, Sam. Sam Price. I think he's in trouble.'

I almost said that trouble was my business, but I restrained myself. I could see this wasn't the time for my usual nonsense. 'What kind of trouble?'

She bit her lower lip. Normally that would drive me crazy, but Ginty was right, it would take another hour or two.

'I don't know. All I know is that he's disappeared. He's not turned up for work, he's not seen his family. His sister has a key to his flat and he's not there. She told me it looked like he'd been gone for days.'

'What does he do?'

'He's a butcher, has his own shop on Dumbarton Road, near Partick Cross, but it's been shut for two weeks. He had two assistants and they say he gave them a month's pay and told them not to come in.'

'He sacked them?'

'Not in so many words, but they've not seen or heard from him since.'

'Is he married?'

'Divorced.'

'Girlfriend?'

Ginty shook her head. 'Don't think so.'

'Does he have money problems?'

'Not that we know of. The shop is very popular – he was a good butcher, won prizes for his steak pies.'

'Does he gamble? Drink? Take drugs?'

Something registered in her eyes. 'He doesn't take drugs, as far as I know. He takes a drink, but who doesn't?' I was about to say my mother, who condemned alcohol while shovelling Valium down her throat, but this was no time to depress Ginty. Or me.

'I sense a "but" coming,' I said.

She took a breath. 'Sam was always…' She looked for the right word and found it. 'Dodgy.'

'In what way?'

She hesitated. I could tell this wasn't easy for her. Talking about your family's shortcomings never is. 'He's not crooked, exactly, but he's not exactly straight either. He's…'

'Dodgy,' I said.

'Yes. He's not into anything heavy, just petty stuff – receiving stolen goods, that sort of thing.'

I understood. To some people I was pretty dodgy too, but that's because of the company I keep. And some of the things I've done in the past don't bear too much scrutiny, even by me.

'Will you have a nose around? Please, Dom? For me?'

She'd used my real name. This was seriously serious.

4

'Okay,' I said, but there really had never been any doubt that I'd do it. 'I'll look into it. But you have to know, your dodgy cousin may have dodged into something heavy, which is why he's on the lam.'

A laugh began in her eyes and then made it to her throat.

'What?' I said.

'I can't believe you just said "on the lam". You're such a tough guy. You should be in black and white and wearing a fedora.'

Her laugh finally erupted as I pushed her onto her back and loomed over her. I made a show of leering at her body. Believe me, it was no hardship. Unlike me, she'd kept herself very trim indeed. Again, I wondered what she saw in me. 'Listen, sister, I don't work cheap. You gotta pay the freight.'

She smiled, made a show of patting her chest and stomach, looking for pockets. 'I don't have any loose change on me right now, Bugsy. Can I pay in kind?'

'Well…' I looked at her nakedness again, licked my lips in an exaggerated fashion. 'You know what I like at times like this.'

She wiggled closer to me, one hand running down my chest to where I was sucking in my gut. 'Oh, I know what you like, right enough,' she said, her voice even throatier than usual.

I leaned in, kissed her. It was a long kiss, all lips and tongues. I pulled away and said, 'So what are you going to do about it?'

She rolled her head back, her long neck inviting me to run my mouth along it, but I had something more important in mind.

'Okay,' she said with a slight sigh. 'You want jam or marmalade on your toast?'

Chapter Two

Sam Price's sister Mary was a forty-something, small, box-shaped woman with close-cropped dark hair iced with grey, kindness in her eyes and lines on her face that showed she laughed a lot. She didn't laugh when she spoke to me, though. She maintained a typically Glasgow veneer of breezy chatter, but her concern for her brother's wellbeing was almost palpable. I saw it in those kind eyes, I saw it in the tightening of her mouth, I saw it in the tension as she sat on the edge of her armchair, leaned over the oblong-shaped coffee table between us and poured the tea. I liked her. If I hadn't been doing this for Ginty free of charge then I would've been doing it for Mary free of charge. I'll never be a millionaire.

Her two-bedroom flat in Chancellor Street was bright and airy and filled with cat ornaments. Big ones, little ones, glass ones, china ones. One was life-size and so realistic I thought at any minute it was going to get up and claw the settee. Or spray my leg. I've had bad luck with cats in the past. They seem to see me as their territory, for some reason. Come to think of it, two dogs have peed on my leg, one while I was talking to his owner in a park. All those trees and he chose me. As a metaphor for life, it was pretty telling.

I'd barely settled into the comfy armchair in her living room before typical Glasgow hospitality came to the fore and she asked me if I wanted a nice cup of tea. Of course I did, no-one wants a horrible cup of tea. I didn't say that, though, because smart-arsed Dominic Queste had to be left at the door. She was too pleasant a lady to have to put up with that. She served the tea in what I knew would be her good china – little cups with delicate handles that I feared would snap off as soon as I touched them. Saucers, too. My good breeding came to the fore, and I resisted the impulse to pour the tea in one and slurp it.

There was a selection of biscuits, including Blue Riband. I didn't think they made them any more. Even so, I bypassed them and picked up a Penguin. I haven't had a Penguin biscuit for years, and biting into the thick chocolate and tasting the raisiny goodness took me back to my childhood. I pushed the memories away though. It's too early in the story for depression to set in.

I sipped my tea and decided it was time to get down to business. 'So, Mrs Lennox…'

'Mary,' she corrected.

'Mary,' I said, 'when did you last see Sam?'

'Two weeks ago. He was over here for his dinner, brought me a nice steak pie from his shop. He's known for his steak pies.'

'So I hear.'

'Won prizes for them, so he has. Learned the art from our dad. It was his shop and our grandfather's before him.'

'So it's a family business?'

'Aye, but looks like it'll end with Sam, though. I've only got one kid, a lassie, and Sam was never blessed. It's a shame, because those steak pies are special. They come from all over to buy one of Sam's steak pies. One customer all the way from Bearsden.'

'Really?' I've made snappier comments, but I couldn't think of anything to say. Bearsden isn't exactly the ends of the earth, it being just a few miles to the northwest of where I sat. But then, it did seem to be a bit far to travel for a steak pie, even if it was a prize winner. 'Did he seem unsettled in any way? Did he tell you something was bothering him?'

She thought about this. 'He wasn't his usual self, right enough. Don't get me wrong, son…' *Son*, I thought. I was older than her. My Peter Pan skincare regime was obviously still working. '… he's no that outgoing at the best of times, my Sam. He was never a sullen boy, but he was quiet. That was one of the things that used to worry me about him, being so quiet. You know – with the lassies. But I didn't need to worry about him on that score – he was never short of a girlfriend, was Sam.'

'He's divorced, isn't he?'

'Aye,' she said, and for the first time I saw something like bitterness in those kind eyes. 'That was a big mistake, so it was. She was never the one for him. Cassandra. I mean, who calls their wean Cassandra? She was from Yoker, for God's sake.'

Yoker, the frontier country where the city of Glasgow gives way to Clydebank. I once knew a guy who rented a flat in a tenement on Dumbarton Road. It wasn't a slum exactly, but his weekly rent included all the rats he could kill. It's been gentrified now – or as gentrified as Yoker can get – thanks to a housing association. Yoker's not a bad place, but I knew what she meant. It was unlikely any local mum would have named her daughter Cassandra thirty-odd years ago.

Mary was warming to her theme now. 'I reckon she made it up, cos she's an uppity cow. Sorry, son…' I shrugged to show her I was unconcerned by her bovine slur. 'I'm telling you, show me a wean called Cassandra in Yoker and I'll show you a wean that gets her head shoved down a cludgie so often she'll think she's a toilet brush. Course it's all changed now, hasn't it? I mean, the names they give wee yins these days. My lassie's called hers Kandi. That's with a K and an I. I mean, Kandi! What sort of name is that?'

Someone who perhaps has a future in the adult entertainment industry, I thought, but kept it to myself. I had to divert Mary from her deliberations on the science of child-naming. 'She live in Glasgow?'

'Who, Kandi?'

'No, Cassandra.'

'Aye, she married again. Some bloke from money, lives up Lenzie way, I think. She'll be happy now. God knows she wasn't happy with Sam – and she made his life miserable, too.'

'In what way?'

'She had ideas above her station, that lassie. Fancy notions.

8

Wanted Sam to expand the business all the time, open new shops. She wanted to be a millionaire, so she did. But Sam, he was happy with the one shop. Best thing he ever did was getting shot of her.'

'Did he leave her?'

'No, she walked out on him. She said she couldn't abide a man who had no ambition in life, who didn't want to better himself.' Mary snorted. 'Better himself! As if having a flash motor, wearing a Pringle jersey and voting Tory was bettering yourself.' She looked at my cup. 'Need a refill there, son?'

'No, I'm fine, thanks.'

'Have another wee biscuit. It's okay – I'll no charge you for them.'

I smiled. 'No, I'm okay, thanks. Has Sam been seeing anyone recently?'

'Never mentioned anyone special. He's no a monk, he goes out with lassies, but he's never said there was anyone in particular. He's still a good-looking man, so he is. Looks after himself. Goes to a gym. Doesn't smoke, doesn't drink much. A wee whisky now and then, maybe, but he doesn't go out and get steaming.'

'You said getting a girlfriend was one of the things that worried you about Sam. What else was there?'

She laid her cup down on the silver tray resting on the coffee table. She moved a crystal cat ornament sitting beside it. It didn't need to be moved, it was just something to do with her hands.

She asked, 'What did Ginty tell you about Sam?'

The word "dodgy" sprang to mind, but I kept it to myself. 'Not much. But I'd like to hear it all from you.'

She didn't look surprised. 'Aye, she was never comfortable around him. Can't say I blame her, after what she went through.' I assumed she was talking about Ginty's deceased husband. Mary didn't look too comfortable with this side of her brother either. 'He was quiet when he was a lad, like I said – still is, to an extent – but he was also a bit of a tearaway. Nothing serious, but he ran with a bad crowd.'

'How bad a crowd?'

Her face crinkled. 'I suppose you'd call it a gang. They fought, they stole things. Sam grew out of it but I know he was still in touch with some of the others. Ginty never took to that. You'll know why.'

I knew why. Her husband had been something more than a tearaway. 'Did Sam hang around with anyone in particular?'

She thought about this. I couldn't decide whether it was because she was trying to come up with a name or if she was debating with herself whether she should share it with me. 'There's this one guy, really bad news, so he is. Always was. Tank, they call him, cos he's so big, you know? Anyway, he worked at the shop when my dad still had it. Him and Sam were both apprentice butchers. Sam used to say that Tank was good with the meat, had a future, but he was always out to make a quick buck, you know?'

I nodded. I knew.

'Tank gave up the butcher's, went his own way.' She paused. 'It wasn't a good way, son, neither it was. Broke my heart to hear he was back in the picture and palling up to Sam again.'

'Has Tank got a second name?'

'Milligan. God knows what his real first name is. He's always been Tank, far as I know.'

I'd never heard of Tank Milligan, but that didn't mean anything. My knowledge of the city's low-lives was vast but far from encyclopaedic. I knew a couple of guys who might've heard of him, though.

I asked, 'You said "back in the picture" – was Tank out of the picture?'

'Aye, he was away for a long time…'

'Jail?'

'No, abroad. America, I think. Anyway, he came back – must be six months ago now – and him and Sam started talking again. I've warned him time and time again about that bloke, but all Sam would say is "he's all right when you know him". Well, things I've heard about him…the more you know him, the less all right he is, you know?'

'What have you heard about him?'

She lowered her voice, as if what she was about to say would frighten the cats. 'Bad things. He's no right in the head, that Tank. He hurts people, you know? And he likes it. I didn't want Sam to have anything to do with him, but he wouldn't listen to me.'

I thought about this. I'd have to find Tank, have a word. 'Did Sam have any money worries?'

'Not that he mentioned.'

'His shop was doing okay?'

'Aye, roaring business, so it was. He won prizes for his steak pies.'

I'd heard that somewhere before, but I pressed on. 'But he seemed subdued of late?'

'Aye, subdued, that's right. Like there was something over his shoulder and he didn't like it.'

That sounded interesting. Something over his shoulder was a good way to put it. Sometimes Glasgow folk can surprise you with their phrasing. Whatever that something was, Sam Price had chosen not to share it with his sister. But everyone needs someone to share things with. I had a two-fisted, campaigning Glasgow priest called Father Francis Verne and the Sutherland brothers, two ex-cons with hearts of gold. Who did Sam share his worries with? Certainly not his ex-wife, by the sounds of it. This Tank Milligan, perhaps? Or was he the something over his shoulder?

I asked, 'Do you know if Sam used social media at all? Facebook, Twitter, Instagram?'

'Is that they things where people show off photos of their dinner?'

'Yes, something like that.'

'Naw, son, he wasn't into any of that. Self-obsessed nonsense, so it is, taking your own photie all the time and telling people you've had a nice shite…' She stopped short, realised what she'd said. Her hand shot to her mouth and she blushed. She actually blushed. 'Sorry, son, that just kind of slipped out.'

I smiled, waved it away. 'Do you have a photograph of Sam I can have?'

She nodded, reached down the side of the cushion on the armchair – the area in my house I like to think of as the Bank of Queste when I need some spare change – and pulled a colour print free. She held it out to me across the table. 'Ginty told me you'd want one, so I printed this one out. It was taken a month ago, down the coast during that good spell of weather we had. He was out with my lassie's kids – a wee day out, you know?'

I looked at the face of the man staring back at me. It looked like Ayr beach; I could see the sandy shore stretching all the way to the dark line of cliffs that formed the Heads of Ayr in the background. He was a good-looking man, maybe in his late thirties, with a thick head of black hair which, like his sister's, was showing grey. His face was square, his jaw firm but beginning to bulge with jowls. He was smiling at the camera but I thought I saw something in his eyes. A shadow. As if something really was just over his shoulder. Something he didn't like.

I laid the cup and saucer down on the silver tray and stood up. I thanked Mary for her hospitality. Then I thought of something else.

'Do you have a key to Sam's flat, Mary?'

She stood up. 'Aye, right here.' She moved to an old-fashioned wooden sideboard, the kind your granny used to have and removal men would ask danger money to shift nowadays. She picked up a keyring with a plastic fob bearing a photograph of Edinburgh Castle and handed it to me. 'The Yale key is for his flat, the other one is for the shop down at Partick Cross. I thought you'd want both.'

I thanked her again, moved to the door, but she stood in front of me and stared me straight in the face. I saw fear in those kind eyes.

'Find him, Dom,' said Mary, and for the first time I heard the desperation in her voice. 'He's my brother. He's my family. I know he's no perfect and I can't shake off this feeling that he's involved in something he shouldn't be. But he's never done anything like this before, not disappear.' She reached out, grabbed my hand, held it. 'Please. Ginty says you're really good at this sort of thing. Please, find my brother.'

I wanted to say I'd find him. I wanted to reassure her. I wanted to sound like a man who always does what he says. Solid. Dependable. In short, I wanted to be Simon Templar, the Saint. Roger Moore's TV version, not Val Kilmer's big-screen effort. But I couldn't do it. Ginty's sales pitch aside, I knew that I was successful only some of the time. Sometimes people disappear for a reason. Sometimes it's of their own choosing. Other times, it's not.

'I'll do what I can,' I said.

No halo appeared above my head.

Chapter Three

Sam Price lived in a ground-floor flat on Gardner Street, not far from Mary's home. This Partick street is built on a very steep hill leading to – wait for it – Partickhill, and whenever I see it I expect Steve McQueen to come flying over it in that Mustang Charger from *Bullitt*. I'm disappointed every time. Glasgow is not renowned for its action scenes, despite my best efforts.

I brought my old Ford to a halt and kept it in reverse gear in case the brake failed and it decided to go off on a downhill race all on its lonesome. I climbed some steps to reach the front door of the tenement and punched the code Mary had given me into the controlled entry panel. Glasgow's sandstone tenements were originally built with the entrance ways open, but the city, life and the world had changed since then. I'm not sure the crime rate is any higher these days than it was over 100 years ago when these streets were built, but the fear of it is certainly greater.

I was just about to turn the Yale lock when the heavy door leading to the street opened and a man of about seventy appeared carrying a cloth bag, which I guessed was filled with groceries. He gave me a quizzical stare as he moved to the door of the flat on the other side of the corridor, a keyring in his hand. His face was lined and weathered, his nose bulbous, his eyes sharp and suspicious. He had a scar on his chin and bags under his eyes that could house a family of four. The face wasn't so much lived-in as condemned. His grey hair was thinning, but expertly combed with a parting as straight as a Roman road. He was broad-shouldered and had the build of a manual worker. It was autumn, but it was warm outside and the sleeves of his plaid workman's shirt were rolled up to show off muscular forearms. His right arm bore the purple shadow of a tattoo under dark hairs. He laid his bag down and it fell open to reveal bread, milk and a daily newspaper. Just call me Sherlock.

He sized me up. 'Help you, pal?'

I gave him my most appealing smile, held up the key. 'Just going to have a look around.'

He leaned against his doorframe, crossed his arms, making his muscles bulge against his sleeves. I'd bet he gets many a heart fluttering at the senior citizen's club.

'Oh, aye? And who would you be, when you're at home? Because, son, that's no your home.'

'I'm looking for Sam Price – he lives here.'

'Aye.'

He waited.

I said, 'I take it you've not seen him, have you?'

'No for a week or two. But you've still no told me who you are, son. And see, I'm wondering if I should be calling the law.'

I took a step closer to him and he shoved himself upright again. I saw his fist was clenched. He was an old geezer, but I'd bet he could still pack a punch. I did not want that punch packing my way. I held my hands up in what I hoped was a placating manner, tried my smile again. 'No need for that,' I said. 'His sister, Mary, gave me the keys. She's worried about him, so I'm having a wee nose around. Do you know his sister?'

'Aye. Nice lassie.'

'What about Sam? You know him?'

'I've lived here for over forty years, son. I know everyone up this close.'

'What can you tell me about him?'

This was on old trick. Most people like to talk. Most people like to feel they're in the know. I'd detected a note of pride when he said how long he'd lived here and that he knew everyone in the building. The more I got him to talk, the more he'd trust me. Never fails.

'Look, son, I'm no telling you nothing until you tell me who the hell you are, clear?'

Never say never.

I sighed, reached into my inside pocket, took out the little wallet that held my bank cards and credit cards. I slid my driver's licence out of its slot and handed it to him. 'The name's Dominic Queste,' I said as he studied the photograph on the card and then my face.

'No a very good photie, is it, son?'

'Is anybody's?'

He conceded that with a jerk of the head, handed me the licence back. 'Okay, son, just checking. You can't be too careful, no with the way things are these days. The name's Jack Stewart.'

My eyes flicked over his shoulder to the nameplate on the door. A little oblong of plastic, tartan background, the name J. Stewart printed in white. He held out his hand. I held out mine. He took it. I winced. He had a grip like a garbage crusher on the Death Star's detention level. When he released me I resisted the impulse to shake the circulation back into my fingers.

'Unusual name you've got there,' he said.

'I borrowed it from a friend. Just trying it out.'

He smiled. 'That right?' Then he asked, 'So what are you, some kind of private detective?'

'In a way. I'm a friend of the family and I'm doing this as a favour. So, what about Sam Price? What can you tell me?'

He seemed to have accepted me because I saw his fist had unclenched. So did my colon, because I really didn't fancy going toe-to-toe with him, even if I did have a good twenty years on him. Getting my arse handed to me by an OAP would not be good for my self-esteem.

'As I said, no seen him for a week or two. He's a quiet lad, good neighbour. And he brings me sausages from his shop. You know he's got a butcher's, down the Cross there?'

I nodded. My next port of call.

'Now and then he's brought me one of his steak pies. Makes

them himself, right there in the back of the shop. Won prizes.'

Some day, I thought, I have to try one of these steak pies.

'What about visitors to the flat here? You ever see any?'

He thought about this. 'He didn't have a stream of people stop by, no. There's been a big bloke dropped by, seen him twice this week, looking for Sam. First time he just gave the door a battering. Must've had the security code to get through the main door.'

'What did he look like?'

'Big fella, he was. Wouldn't like to clean out his litter box, know what I mean? I didn't like the cut of him. You get a feeling about some people, don't you? I spoke to him but he just ignored me and walked away, which I thought was all kinds of rude. I mean, at least you've made an effort to explain yourself, have a wee chat. I don't sleep much these days – when you get to my age you like to stay awake as long as you can – and this one night I heard this noise and I looked out and he was trying the door. I told him to get the hell away or I'd call the law. He just gave me the look, you know?'

I knew what the look was. I've seen it a few times myself. It was the Glasgow look, the one that told you to back off lest you get given your head in your hands to play with. The big guy was Tank Milligan, I presumed.

'There was the occasional woman, though. He's a good-looking sod, is Sam. Keeps himself fit.'

'Any woman in particular?'

'There was one. She was a looker, but a wee bit tarty, you know? Like one of they footballer's wives. All blonde hair and...' He dropped his voice, glanced up the stairs to ensure no-one could hear, '...a chest you could play keepy-uppy with, if you know what I'm saying?'

I did, but I was too much of a gentleman to discuss it further. 'Did she have a name?'

'I'm sure she did, but I didn't hear it. She would come bustling in here in her high heels and then bustle out again, sometimes late at night, if you catch my drift.'

I'd've caught his drift even if he hadn't emphasised it with a wink. All boys together here.

'She been by since Sam's been away?'

'Came by the other day. She had the security code too, but Sam's front door there's as far as she got. She gave the letterbox laldy, then looked through it, like maybe Sam was in there and giving her a wide berth.'

'You speak to her?'

'Aye, I came out, told her he'd no been home for a week or two. She never said nothing, just nodded and left. I'm telling you, she's no bad but she's no as young as she thinks she is. I could see it when I got this close to her, you know?'

'None of us are, Jack,' I said. 'She come by car or taxi, did you notice?'

'Car,' he said, 'one of they fancy jobs.'

'Any idea of a make?'

'Ah, son, I don't know about cars. I can't even drive, me. Never had the need. Lived in Glasgow all my life – the bus and the underground do me just fine. A taxi if I'm pished and feeling flush. All I can tell you is it was blue and so low down on the street it'd scrape its undercarriage if it hit one of they speed bump things.'

I thought about this. Tank Milligan had been by. And a mystery woman. Gangsters and blondes. All I needed was a tough-talking cop and I'd feel right at home. I thanked Jack and he told me that if there was anything I needed I was to just give him a shout. I'd made a pal. The old Queste charm had done it again.

As he bent to gather his shopping together, I twisted the Yale, opened Sam Price's front door and stepped into the hallway beyond.

I smelled fresh cigarette smoke in the air.

I don't smoke.

Sam Price didn't smoke.

I wasn't alone in the flat.

You astound me, Holmes.

18

Chapter Four

Jack Stewart across the way was a powerful-looking man, but the guy I found puffing away on a coffin nail in Sam Price's living room was big enough to generate his own gravitational field. He wore a double-breasted suit that hadn't come off a rail and must've given the tailor who made it RSI. The body underneath was packed with more muscle than all the *Expendables* movies put together. His shirt was a brilliant white, his tie impeccably Windsored. His bald head gleamed as if it was French polished. His face was broad, his brow pronounced, his eyes narrow slits. There was a nasty curve to his mouth not caused by the cigarette wedged between his lips. The hand that plucked it out was large enough to make Sooty wish he had strings.

'And who would you be?' He said in a voice that, like French avant-garde literature and the films of Terrence Malick, was too deep for comfort. His accent was local but had a twang to it.

'You took the words right out of my mouth,' I said, though I'd already guessed who he was. Tank Milligan. Had to be.

'The name's Milligan. Tank Milligan.'

Eat your heart out, Arthur Conan Doyle.

Convention dictated that I reciprocate with my name, but I wasn't in a reciprocating mood. I never am when I'm confronted by men like him. Sometimes I think I've got a death wish.

'You broke in,' I said.

'You don't miss much,' he said.

'You can pick locks?'

'It's a dying art,' he said, which was true. I'd been taught some time ago by an old housebreaker, but didn't know anyone else who could do it, apart from the Sutherland boys. Tank had no doubt waited until old Jack across the way had left for the shop and probably planned to be gone before he returned. I imagined he'd heard me at the door, decided to wait. His eyes found the Yale still in my hand. 'I see you have a key. Who are you?'

'Friend of the family.'

'Oh, aye? So where's Sam Price, friend of the family?'

'Was about to ask you the same thing.'

'If I knew that I wouldn't be here.'

He had me there.

He took another drag from his cigarette, leaned his head back, blew the smoke towards the ceiling. I looked around the room. It was a mess. Either it was the maid's day off or Tank had been searching for something.

I asked, 'Find what you were looking for?'

'No.'

'What were you looking for, if you don't mind me asking?'

'None of your business, friend of the family, if you don't mind me saying.'

I didn't expect him to tell me but thought it was worth a try.

I stared at him.

He stared at me.

It went on for a long time.

If we had some Ennio Morricone trumpet music, we could've staged a spaghetti western.

Finally, he said, 'You know why they call me Tank?'

'Because you retain a lot of water?'

'No…'

'There are pills for that, you know.'

'It's not because…'

'I had an auntie who suffered from water retention. It was so bad her legs opened with the tide. Made her very popular when the fleet was in.'

He stopped me by stubbing his cigarette out. Nothing too

dramatic in that, you might think, but he stubbed it out in the palm of his hand. Now, as a conversation stopper, that has the advantage of being unique, I'd say. Then he stood up. My neck hurt to look up at his face.

'They call me Tank because I can roll over anything or anyone that gets in my way. I'd remember that, if I were you.'

Believe me, it was duly noted. He loomed over me like an overdue tax return, his face neutral, his body relaxed. There was nothing overtly threatening in his manner, but his sheer size and the general feeling that one swat from a hand would send me flying across the room spoke volumes. I considered calling out to Jack across the landing for back-up, but I feared the tension in my body was so tight it'd strangle my voice and I'd end up sounding, well, frankly, a little girly. I gave the space around me another look. The thing about big guys is that they're all strength and no staying power. At least, that's what my Krav Maga instructor told me during my course. When I say course, it was more the Reader's Digest version of the martial art. Just a few moves, enough to get me out of tight spots on occasion. The idea with big guys like Tank was to outlast them without letting them actually lay one on you, because then it would be lights out and goodnight, John-Boy. The flat's living room wasn't so large that I could outrun him for long. He'd roll over me no bother. Rolling is alright when it's over Beethoven, in the clover, in the hay, when you're rocking and if you're Ol' Man River, but it's no fun when it's a Glasgow gangster-cum-behemoth.

Threat duly delivered, Tank spoke again. 'Where is it?'

'Where's what?'

His eyes narrowed even further. 'Don't play the fanny with me, little man. You're a friend of the family, you know what Sam Price was into. I want what's mine. Where is it?'

'Seriously, big man, you're going to have to give me a wee clue here.'

'I want it.'

'Don't we all?'

He stared again. 'So where is it?'

'If I knew what it was you want, I'd maybe help you,' I said. I probably wouldn't, but it doesn't hurt to appear gracious.

He sighed, looked around at his handiwork. 'If it was here, I'd have found it.' I couldn't help but agree, even though I didn't know what the 'it' in question was. His gaze found me again.

'I want it. Sam Price has it. You and his family must know where he is, or where it is. You'd be well advised to hand it over to me before I turn unpleasant. You won't like it if I turn unpleasant.'

'You seem like such a fun guy, too.'

He leaned down to stare directly into my face. A finger as thick as my arm poked me in the chest. For him it was a gentle poke, I presumed, but it would leave a bruise. 'You're funny.'

'Thank you. I'm here all week.'

He straightened again. 'I don't like funny. You know what I do with funny? I twist it until it's not funny any more.'

'You mean like Steve Martin as Inspector Clouseau?'

He breathed out through his nose and I thought I'd made a crack too far. Poking the bear was one thing, but I was tweaking its nose and tickling its armpits. However, Tank exercised self-control. 'I want what's mine, friend of the family. You get it to me.' Another poke, another bruise. 'Otherwise I'll need to take my frustration out on Sam Price's kin.'

He actually said kin. I thought for a minute I was in Arkansas.

He stooped. It looked like he was going to touch his toes but he picked up a dark, snap-brimmed Fedora from a low coffee table, placed it on his head. Swear to God. A snap-brim Fedora, a double-breasted, wide lapelled suit. He was Moose Malloy from *Farewell, My Lovely*. I've seen two actors play him in the movies – Mike Mazurki and Jack O'Halloran. They were big both big men. I couldn't decide if Tank was bigger than both combined. Maybe the 'it' he was looking for was a hard-hearted dame called Velma.

He brushed past me and left the room without another word. When I heard the front door close I realised I didn't know how to contact him should I find whatever the hell it was he was looking for. Tank seemed the type who would find me, though. Although the not-so-veiled threat towards Sam's – ahem – kin did trouble me.

I'd need help with this guy. Help that knew their way around the city's underworld so well they could run bus tours. Help that could take care of themselves when the rough turned to tumble.

Luckily, I had just that sort of help on speed dial.

Chapter Five

I put my mobile on loudspeaker, placed it on the coffee table while I conducted my own search of the flat. It rang a few times before I heard Duncan Sutherland answer. I could hear young people laughing in the background.

'Where are you?' I shouted slightly so he could hear me as I lifted cushions from chairs and felt around upholstery for anything hidden.

'Father Verne's,' said Duncan. Father Verne ran a refuge in the East End for young people who needed to escape drugs, prostitution and abuse. Duncan and Hamish Sutherland helped in ways both public and private. Another burst of merriment rippled in the background.

I asked, 'Hamish isn't doing his mime act again, is he?'

Duncan guffawed. Yes, he guffawed. I've never heard anyone actually guffaw before, was never sure what it would sound like. Now I knew. 'God, no! It wouldn't be laughter you'd be hearing, it'd be a stampede for the door. No, we're showing some of the kids how to be more adventurous in their cooking.'

My first thought was to alert the fire service. My second was to order up some industrial-strength antacids. The Sutherland boys liked to think of themselves as being on the same culinary level as their fellow Geordies, the Hairy Bikers, even though Duncan was hair-free. His brother Hamish made up for it in the hirsute stakes, but their cooking skills were, shall we say, hit and miss. To be fair, their hits were more frequent than their misses with most people, if not with me. I prefer my cooking plain and straightforward, preferably fried. Hey, I'm from Glasgow, cut me some slack.

'We're trying pappardelle with frazzled prosciutto and asparagus,' said Duncan.

'What's papdopullottoaragus?' I asked as I opened the drawers of a wooden cabinet that told me Sam once shopped at MFI. Duncan sighed and repeated it, slowly this time. I'd heard him the first time. I was simply messing with him. Not that I understood what the hell he was saying, of course. I found Sam's passport, so he hadn't fled abroad. I pulled out a wad of old bank and credit card statements, scanned them, looking for any kind of pattern.

'Pasta with ham, broad beans and goat cheese,' explained Duncan.

'Then why didn't you say that in the first place, instead of going all Clemenza on me?'

There was nothing of particular note in the bank statements so I dropped them back again. I turned to a built-in cupboard in the corner just as more laughter erupted. 'What's so funny?'

'Hamish is giving the instructions in an Italian accent.' That made me pause, wishing I could hear it. 'It's more like Dick Van Dyke in *Mary Poppins* A few minutes ago he was like the Indian guy from *The Big Bang Theory*. His accent is so well-travelled he could earn air miles.'

I opened the cupboard, found shelves lined with books.

'What's up, Dom?' Duncan asked.

'You heard of a guy called Tank Milligan?'

Duncan searched what I knew to be an encyclopaedic knowledge of underworld figures on both sides of the border. 'Big fella, likes to wear snazzy suits and hats, like a movie gangster. Talks like Gerard Butler?'

'The very chap.'

'What about him?'

'I've just had a run-in with him.'

Concern coloured Duncan's voice. 'You okay, Dom?'

I was touched by Duncan's reaction. It's nice to have pals. 'I'm fine. We exchanged pleasantries, that's all. Nothing physical.'

Although I could still feel where he'd prodded me twice. 'He made an impression, though.'

'You don't want to get on his wrong side, Dom. In a good mood he's like the Hulk, think what he'd be like if he got angry. What are you working on?'

I filled him in as I studied the titles on display, mostly Tartan Noir, true crime and horror. I recognised some of the authors, others were new to me. The grey spine of one of the true crime titles caught my eye, because I had that one too. It was a history of Glasgow's underworld. I'd met the author a couple of times, back when I was feature writing at the newspaper. He was an idiot.

'I don't think he'll try anything right away. He says Sam Price has something of his.'

'What kind of something?'

'The kind of something that I think he'd hurt people to get.'

'But he didn't say what it was?'

'Just called it "it".'

'*It*? No clues?'

'Nary a one. He's in the Addams Family and looking for his cousin, for all I know. I may need help on this, Duncan,' I said. 'Milligan more or less threatened Sam's family. All he's got is a sister, but she's got a kid and her kid's got kids. And then there's Ginty.'

'Okay.' I knew even before I called him that Duncan and Hamish would be on board, because it's what pals do. They've helped me out more often than I care to count. I owe them my life. I mean that literally.

I'd spotted some photograph albums on the bottom shelf – how very retro – and I carried them over to the table where the phone rested.

'How imminent is this threat?' His voice had become very serious, very Jack Bauer. Any minute now I expected him to rasp, 'Dammit, Chloe!'

'I don't think he'll try anything right away,' I said.

'Good,' his voice dropped then and he must've left the room and closed a door because the noise in the background was suddenly cut off. 'By the way, we think we have a line on Shayleen.'

I'd been flicking through the first photo album, family snaps mostly, but I looked at the phone when he said the name. Shayleen was a young woman I'd met in Father Verne's refuge a few months before. Her brother, Cody, had been pimping her out for the price of heroin. She'd helped us out in a small way when we were trying to protect another young woman, but had subsequently returned to her brother's loving arms. Duncan and Hamish had been sending out feelers ever since to track her down. Now they had. Our paths had crossed only for the briefest of moments, but what can I say? I've got a Galahad complex. Maybe I was Simon Templar after all.

'We're going to get her later tonight, thought you'd want to come along,' said Duncan.

'Bloody right I do.' I'm not a violent man. Okay, that's a lie. Sometimes I can be. But normally I try to avoid the physical stuff because my three classes in Krav Maga only go so far. However, I really wanted to kick the living shit out of Cody. If only because he was called Cody.

Duncan told me that he'd heard he and his pals had based themselves in an abandoned building near Ibrox. I arranged to meet the Sutherland brothers there that night, then turned my attention back to the photo albums. I found a couple of Ginty as a teenager. She wasn't gorgeous, it has to be said. Some people blossom as they age, though. I consoled myself with the hope that some day I may end up looking like George Clooney.

The second album was filled with shots of an older Sam with a sharp-eyed brunette I took to be his ex-wife. They seemed happy enough in them, especially their wedding pictures. They must've thought they had their whole lives in front of them, together, a couple, a unit. That's life, though. You make plans, you scheme, but you're never fully prepared for what's going to happen. I looked at the images of the former Mrs Price. She could most certainly have dyed her hair by now, but I couldn't see the blonde bombshell Jack had seen. The woman in the pictures wasn't unattractive – I like to think we're all attractive in our own way, except for most politicians, of course – but she wasn't the kind to set Jack's pulse racing.

The third album had more family shots, more of the ex-wife, holiday snaps from abroad, the woman in a bikini. She was slim, didn't have the generous attributes Jack had commented upon. She posed in the photographs like she was hoping for a magazine cover. Sam didn't look happy in them, however. His smile looked forced. But it was the ones towards the back of the book that I focussed on. They'd been taken in Scotland, the Highlands. There was a stone cottage and a loch and a mountain. It was sunny. Sam and his wife were there. In one, he stood in front of a gate with a small white sign that read 'Yew Tree Cottage'. He was smiling and it looked natural. He was happy there.

I prised the print from the album and placed it in my pocket. I looked around again, checked the bedroom, the kitchen, even the cistern in the bathroom. I didn't find anything that helped me. I didn't know what Tank was looking for. I didn't know what Sam's involvement was with Tank, but given the big guy's reputation, I could understand why Sam had legged it. I didn't know a hell of a lot, but it was early yet. Plenty of time to get really mystified. I'd hang onto the keys, maybe come back for another look later.

But now, it was time to go to the shop.

Chapter Six

The woman stood against the shop window, face pressed to the glass, hands positioned to shield the glare of the autumn sun. I knew who she was immediately. Old Jack's description had been a tad unkind: she did look like a footballer's wife, but her suicide blonde hair – dyed by her own hand – was on the tasteful side of brassy, and her clothes were expensive. She wore tight black skinny jeans and her legs tapered into a pair of black high heels. She had a white silk shirt on top, under a black bomber jacket with cream collar and cuffs and two pink prancing horses on the breast. I wondered if Jack had said 'keepy-up' or 'giddy-up'. She carried a suede handbag. The jeans, the jacket and the handbag were all designer items, or extremely good knock-offs.

She became aware of my approach, turned, saw the key to the shop already in my hand. She was maybe in her mid-forties. Her make-up was carefully applied but couldn't completely obscure the lines around her eyes and her mouth. She looked as if she was about to say something, thought better of it, began to turn away.

'You're looking for Sam, right?' I said and she stopped, faced me again, squinted against the sun to study me, one hand raised as if in salute.

She asked, 'You know where he is?' Her voice was pleasant, cultured and pitched low as if she was afraid someone would overhear, but pedestrians merely walked by and paid us no attention.

'No, but I'd like to talk to you, if you don't mind,' I said, then held out my hand. 'My name's Dominic Queste.'

She hesitated for a moment, then shook my hand. 'Bree,' she said.

Unusual, I thought, but who am I to talk?

'Is that Bree as in Jane Fonda in *Klute*? Or Brie as in hang on while I fetch the crackers?'

'It's Bree as in the village in *Lord of the Rings*,' she spoke as if she'd had to explain her name all her life. I thought, join the club. She asked, 'Have you read it?'

'I tried once but the talking tree made me worry my ficus was eavesdropping.' It was true. Granted, that was when I was smoking and snorting anything I could get my hands on and paranoia was a way of life. I waited for her to drop a second name, but none was forthcoming and I said, 'Why don't we step inside?'

She hesitated, but nodded and watched while I unlocked the door. We stepped out of the October glare. The shop was, of course, empty. The white tiled walls were spotlessly clean, the glass-covered counter devoid of product. Small posters exhorting customers to buy Scottish beef dotted the walls. A doorway behind the counter was striped with plastic streamers. A magnetic strip beside it was studded with sharp knives and cleavers. Once inside, the traffic noise lessened considerably and I was able to focus fully on Bree.

'Nice jacket,' I said.

'It's a McCartney.'

I looked at the pink horses. 'Didn't know he did Country and Western.'

Her lips pursed. 'Stella McCartney.'

I knew that.

She asked. 'Do you work here?'

'No, I'm a friend of the family,' I said, sticking to the truth. 'When did you last see Sam?'

'Two weeks ago.'

'Where?'

She thought about lying. I saw it in her eyes, but she decided against it. 'In his flat.'

'Uh-huh', I said, nodding wisely. I'll bet I knew what they were doing in his flat. I like jumping to conclusions. It's good exercise. 'And how was his demeanour?'

'His demeanour?' She wasn't repeating the question because she didn't understand the word, she was only giving herself time to think. 'He was…distracted, I suppose you'd say.'

'In what way?'

'In what way?' Thinking again. 'Well, he was quiet,' she said, 'like he had something on his mind.'

'Had you noticed that before?'

'A couple of times. Maybe more than a couple. He'd been kind of funny for a few weeks.'

'And you didn't know why?'

She shook her head.

I asked, 'Did you talk to him about it?'

'Tried to. Asked him what was up, you know? He said it was nothing.'

'Did you think it was nothing?'

'Went on too long. There was something up, I knew that, but he wouldn't tell me.'

'How long have you known him?'

'Sam?' I bit back a smart reply, something like "no, Donald Trump" but recognised once again she was merely saying something to fill the space while her mind worked. 'Over a year now. On and off.'

On and off. Oo-er, missus.

'And you were…what? Friends?'

'Yes.'

'Good friends?'

'Yes.'

'Intimate friends?'

She stared at me through pale brown eyes and I saw something there. Some sort of challenge? Defiance? Whatever it was, I sensed she was wearing it like perfume: something she put on but wasn't really part of her. 'You mean were we shagging?'

31

I smiled. 'I wouldn't've put it so crudely,' I said. The hell I wouldn't.

'Yes, we were "intimate". If you must know, we were "intimate" like bunnies. You want to know our favourite position?'

I still felt she was putting on an act. The tough-talking dame. I didn't know if it was for my benefit or her own. I was tempted to call her bluff but resisted the impulse. I can be professional. It doesn't happen often, but they are moments to savour.

'Okay, so you're friends with benefits,' I said. 'But Sam didn't tell his family about you. Why would that be?'

She looked around her, maybe for a chair. Her feet must've been killing her in those high heels. Seriously, I don't know how women can walk in them. When I was much younger I had a pair of cowboy boots with Cuban heels, and they gave me a nose bleed.

'We didn't tell anyone about our "intimate" friendship,' she said.

I knew what was coming. Oh dear, I thought.

'You're married?'

She nodded.

Oh, dear, dear, I thought.

'Naturally, you didn't want your husband to find out."

She made a face. 'Naturally.'

'Does your hubby know Sam?'

She hesitated again. She did that a lot, but this time it was different. This time there was something else in those cool brown eyes. Not quite fear, but certainly on nodding terms with it. 'He knows of him.'

'What does that mean? He's heard of his prize-winning steak pies? What?'

She gave me a sideways look. 'How well do you know Sam?'

'Never met him. Told you, I'm a friend of the family and they've asked me to find him.'

'Uh-huh,' she said, moved to the counter, peered through the strips in the doorway leading to the rear. 'You think maybe we should go through there?' She jerked her head towards the shop

32

window, where the pedestrians were still doing their thing. 'I feel kind of exposed here.'

There was no reason why not, so we moved around the counter and pushed our way through the strips into a short corridor that led to a rear door. To the right was a heavy metal door which I took to be a walk-in freezer, but we veered into a small office on the left. There was a battered metal desk and a captain's chair behind it with a tartan cushion on the seat. The desk had a phone, an in-tray stacked with paperwork and a small box with paper clips on top. A grey filing cabinet stood to one side like an old soldier on guard and some kind of plant rested on top, its long grey tendrils dangling like dreadlocks. It looked like it needed a good drink and a jolt from a defibrillator to bring it back to life. A large wall planner was pinned to the wall behind it, some of the squares filled with times and addresses.

Bree moved straight to a wooden fold-out chair in the corner, dug a packet of cigarettes from her bag and fired one up. Smoking in the workplace. The health police were missing a bust. And I don't mean the one that caught Jack's eye, the old fox. She was about to put the cigarettes away when she remembered her manners, offered me one wordlessly. I waved a negative. I've never smoked. Well, not tobacco. Done lots of other stuff in my day, though.

I leaned against the doorframe, crossed my arms, watched her take a deep draw then tilt her head back and blow the smoke into the air. 'So,' I said. 'Why does your husband know of Sam Price if it's not his expertise with some rump steak and a slab of pastry?'

She thought about this as she took another nicotine hit. 'Sam's got…eh…business interests other than this shop.'

She sounded as if she knew Sam was into more than just a general air of dodginess. 'Like what?'

'You know what a catcher is?'

I nodded. In baseball he's the guy who crouches in front of the umpire behind the home plate and – wait for it – catches the pitched ball when the hitter misses. It's also a term for a fielder who catches the cricket ball, but I'd never admit to knowing that. However, Bree wasn't talking ball games here. It's not a widely-used term in Glasgow, but a catcher is a person who receives stolen goods. A fence.

'Sam did a bit of that.' Puff. 'Sam did a *lot* of that.'

I thought about Tank and his demand for what was his. That could be a stolen item or the proceeds of its sale. Maybe Sam had ripped off the big fellow and got out of Dodge fast to avoid repercussions.

'And your husband?' I asked, even though I had a suspicion what was coming next. When it did it was almost a whisper.

'My husband's a police officer.'

Oh, dear, dear, dear, I thought.

I could see why discretion was doubly necessary. If Mr Bree found out his wife was playing hide the truncheon with another man, it would be bad. If that other man was on the dodgy side of the Life, that's ten times worse. I wondered who the husband was and how high up Police Scotland he had climbed.

I asked, 'How did you and Sam meet?'

'He supplies meat to me...'

I'll bet he does, I thought.

She saw the smirk on my face and she gave me a look that told me to grow up. 'I have a small restaurant over in Busby. My father left it to me. It's very popular with discerning diners.'

Discerning diners. That'll be the type who don't ask for ketchup.

'Anyway, Sam's quite a charmer when he gets going. He's quiet at first, but then he turns on the patter. My husband...' She thought better of disclosing something about her husband. Drew on the cigarette. Exhaled. 'Well, it just kinda happened. I know you must think I'm some kind of slut.'

'Not at all.' And that was the God's honest. I've been no angel over the years. I've abused my body, I've had impure thoughts. The one thing I firmly believe is that none of us is perfect. Show me someone who says their conscience is without blemish and I'll show you someone whose pants need a good hose down.

'Anyway, we had a good thing going, Sam and me. It wasn't…' She stopped short, stared at the cigarette in her hand. I saw a growing trail of ash at the tip so I tipped the paper clips from the plastic box and handed it to her. She nodded her thanks, gave the end of the cigarette a practised flick to send the ash tumbling like a tiny dark snowfall into the box. 'I don't know why I'm telling you all this.'

I knew. She was worried about Sam and she thought – hoped – I could help. I was also a stranger, which made it easier. Her forthright manner, her "look at me, I'm a blonde bombshell" appearance, the hardness that I knew could creep into her eyes and voice, was a mask. Like the rest of us, she had problems.

'It wasn't a big love affair, you know? Just two people having some fun. Before the passion goes. Before we dry up. Just two friends.'

'With benefits,' I said.

She looked up and I saw the brown eyes were liquid. 'I'm worried about him, Mr Queste. I'm worried he's got himself into something he can't get out of.'

Again I thought of Tank. I also thought of Bree's husband. What kind of cop was he? A good one, a bad one, an ugly one? She'd started to say something about her husband. What was it? Did he play around? Was there no longer anything physical between them? We all need a little tenderness in our lives, a little intimacy. The question was, how would her husband react if he found out Sam was having a bit of habeus with his wife's corpus?

'Like what?' I asked. 'Something to do with his sideline?'

'I don't know, I really don't.' She took another hit of her cigarette, then stubbed it out in the box. She stared at the remains as a dying wisp of smoke snaked upwards, then raised her eyes to me.

'I don't know what it was. All I know is that whatever it is scared the living daylights out of him.'

Chapter Seven

After Bree left I searched the premises. It wasn't a big place, just the shop, which sparkled like a sparkly thing, the office, a small toilet near the back door, a small kitchen and the cold store. I concentrated on the office first. I went through the filing cabinet, found bills, invoices, business bank statements. I scanned them but found nothing to spark my interest, apart from a reference to a storage unit Sam rented in an industrial estate on the South Side. That might prove interesting, and I knew that most storage complexes sold customers padlocks to secure their units. I just about tore that office apart but couldn't find any keys, let alone one that would fit a padlock. I didn't really expect to find it – he probably had it with him, wherever the hell he was. Feeling frustrated, I checked the desk drawers but the only thing of note I found was the certificate that testified that his steak pie had won first prize in the trade competition.

I didn't think there would be anything in the toilet, but I looked anyway, because I am nothing if not thorough. Truth is, I availed myself of the facilities, for I was nothing if not bursting. All I found in the kitchen was a packet of stale digestive biscuits, a nearly empty jar of instant coffee and some teabags. The small fridge was empty and spotlessly clean, all the mugs were stored in a wall-mounted cupboard. The entire place was so pristine it looked as if it had been used for a Dettol commercial.

Then I opened the freezer door and felt the chill hit me like the first kiss of winter.

It wasn't a huge space, though larger than I expected, and Sam had stored what stock he had in here when he had shut up shop. It was, as you would expect, a vegetarian's nightmare. Sides of beef and pork hung from hooks in the ceiling, frozen chickens were stored against the wall, cuts of meat and blocks of sausage were all placed in portable containers. I stepped in, shivered, and ensured there was a device on the inside that would allow me to open the heavy door if I was trapped. I'd seen enough films where people were left inside places like this to die and had no immediate plans to become a Dominicsicle. There was a release button, but I still dragged a box full of what I presumed to be Sam's prize-winning steak pies across the floor to block the door open anyway. I didn't envisage being in there too long, so no harm would be done.

I walked among the dangling carcasses, maybe half a dozen, all frozen rock solid and encased in a thin layer of material. I once had a summer job with a major chain store as a meat porter and I well remember having frozen sides like this hurled at me from the rear of a supplier's lorry. I had to catch them and carry them into the freezer. My chest and arms were bruised for the first month of that job. A slice of steak on a plate is kind of anonymous, but doing that job made me consider becoming a vegetarian. Being this close again to what had obviously once been a living, breathing creature, smelling the flesh and the blood, sparked that guilt once more. I don't scoff dead animals every mealtime (I occasionally have breakfast cereal), but I'm not one to sit down to a plate of greenery either. I resolved to re-assess my diet, see if I could take a more healthy approach to dining. Eat more fish, maybe an egg dish now and then. Maybe – gulp – eat some vegetables. I ignored my Glasgow blood curdling in horror and made a mental note to ask the Sutherland brothers for advice.

I shouldered my way through the dead animals to come to a halt in the centre. I don't know what I expected to find here. I don't know why I was still standing in this freezing cold room with death all around me. It occurred to me that maybe it was another metaphor for my life. There's that streak of Celtic melancholy I told you about.

Then I noticed a rip in the material wrapped around one of the sides of beef and something brown showing. The others were trussed up like corpses in a shroud – my God, I was sliding downhill – but that one had an opening large enough to reach in. So I did. The flesh was hard and, believe it or not, cold, and the sensation of sticking my fingers into what was once alive was far from pleasant. The tips of my fingers felt something pressed hard against the rib cavity and held in place by the wrapping. It was thin and sheathed in plastic and not part of the cow, that was for sure. It was alien, but thankfully not something that was likely to burst out of John Hurt's chest and race into the corner. I managed to snag a corner and draw it clear.

It was a large brown envelope addressed to Sam at home and sealed within a freezer bag. Now, why the hell did he keep this, quite literally, in cold storage? I weighed the envelope in my hand, felt the contents through the cold plastic sheath. Not too heavy. Papers. I shivered and realised it was far too cold in here for further investigation and headed back to the corridor. I pulled the box of steak pies away, hooked one out for myself – I didn't think Sam would mind and I'd already forgotten my vow to cut back on the red meat – and stepped out of the storage room.

In the office I unsealed the bag, slid the envelope free and tipped the contents onto the desktop. It was a pile of newspaper cuttings, some directly from the newsprint – old style – others printed from web editions. I poked them with my forefinger as I studied the headlines. They all pertained to an unsolved murder in the city the year before. A young woman, a music student at the Royal Conservatoire of Scotland, had been found dead in Queen's Park. I picked up the longest cutting – from the *Herald* – and the details of the case came back to me. Paula Rogers was from Edinburgh but shared a flat on the South Side, not far from my own flat. She'd been a brilliant student, her tutors said, was a gifted cellist and had a shining career ahead of her. She had no money worries, Mummy and Daddy were very comfortable, thank you very much. She had a strong circle of friends.

However, she had changed in the weeks preceding her death. Her moods had turned darker. She had become secretive. She missed classes, something she never did.

And then she was found dead in the park, near the bandstand. The killer still hadn't been caught.

I picked up each of the cuttings one by one, wondering why Sam Price had collected and kept them. The echoes of Paula's final few weeks, the changes she'd undergone and whatever was going on in Sam's life were obvious. The change in his demeanour. The secretiveness.

I wasn't getting a good feeling about this at all.

Chapter Eight

She was standing in front of the counter when I pushed my way through the plastic strips. The front door lay open and I realised I hadn't locked it when I let Bree out. When her eyes fell on me there was firstly a flash of recognition, followed by – I like to think – a little bit of delight and, ultimately, a look of suspicion. She was a cop and they always look at me like that. Not the delight bit, but certainly the suspicion.

Detective Constable Theresa Cohan, the pride of Glasgow West Division, red of hair, freckled of face, bundled up in a dark woollen coat.

'What are you doing here?' Her Irish lilt, as always, carried the promise of harps, Guinness and long nights rolling in the peat. The latter certainly not on offer to me, but I'm sure to someone. I was spoken for, after all. And old enough to be her father.

'I might ask you the same, DC Cohan.' I looked behind her at the open door, wondering if DCI Nick Cornwell was not far away. I'd had my gangster and my blonde. He would make the set.

'Routine,' she said. 'Now you.'

'I had a steak pie on order, I came to pick it up.' I emphasised my words by holding up the frozen package. 'They've won awards, you know.' She looked at the pie then dropped her gaze to the freezer bag in my other hand. She made no comment about that, which was just as well as I didn't know what I'd do if she'd asked.

'Shop's shut, Queste,' she said. No Mister, no Dominic, just Queste. She'd been working with Nick too long.

'I had a key. And permission to be here.'

'From who?'

'The butcher's sister.'

'And your connection to her is what, exactly?'

'Friend of the family.' I decided I'd have that printed on a t-shirt. It'd save time in the future.

'Right,' she said. 'Sam Price is missing, did you know that?'

'I did.'

'I'll bet the sister hired you to find him.'

I shrugged. I liked Cohan, but she was still a police officer and my rule of thumb is only tell them what they need to know. She didn't need to know about Ginty's connection just yet. If ever.

'Not on the clock here, DC Cohan. I told you, I'm doing this as a friend of the family.'

'Yeah, right,' she said, and walked round the counter. I didn't like the disbelieving tone. When I'd first met her she was a fresh-faced young detective. Now she didn't believe a word that came out of my mouth. Nick would have told her that too often those words are either lies or wisecracks, or lies that also happen to be wisecracks. It was *his* rule of thumb never to believe me. On balance, I had to agree with him. Sometimes I find it hard to navigate through the web of lies and half-truths I have to tell in my line of work.

She parted the plastic curtain and peered into the office on the left.

I asked, 'What's your interest?'

'He can assist us with our inquiries.'

'And what inquiries would they be?'

She ignored me and moved into the small office, me trailing. She looked around, not touching anything. Then I realised I had permission to be here, she didn't. She wouldn't touch anything, not while I was here.

'Theresa, we both want the same thing here – we both want to find Sam Price. I can help you.'

She made a noise that was halfway between a snort and a derisive laugh that was most unseemly.

41

'I thought we were pals,' I said, and she made that noise again. Seriously, too much time with Nick.

'People like you and people like me can't be pals, Queste,' she said.

Probably true, but it didn't make it less hurtful. I sighed, stepped back and gestured towards the corridor. 'Okay, fair enough. I was just leaving, so unless you have a warrant, I'd like to lock up.' I gave the keys in my hand a little jiggle for added emphasis.

Cohan didn't move. Her eyes drifted towards the filing cabinet and the desk. I wanted to tell her there was nothing in there of any note, but she was the farmer, I was the cowboy, and even though we weren't in Oklahoma where the sun is as high as an elephant's eye, she'd made it clear we couldn't be friends.

'DC Cohan?' I nudged. If I had a watch I'd have looked at it. 'Tempus doesn't half fugit when you're having fun, but I have places to be.'

The first faint rays of a smile in her eyes. 'Latin, Queste? You don't strike me as a scholar.'

'Hey, I've seen *Ben Hur*,' I said.

'They didn't speak Latin in that,' she said. 'You should've said you'd seen *The Passion of the Christ*.'

Dammit! I hate being out-movie-referenced.

A look of resignation took the place of the new-born smile. 'I didn't tell you this, Queste,' she said.

I thrust the keys into my pocket and waited.

'Two months ago there was a break-in at a house up in Hyndland. A bangle was taken that was insured for £750,000.'

'A bangle?'

'A bangle. It was made of Imperial jade from Myanmar – that used to be Burma…'

I gave her a look that told her I knew that. Even though I hadn't.

'Okay, Imperial jade is the most precious kind of jade. It's jadeite.'

I resisted the impulse to make a *Star Wars* joke. I felt I was growing as a person.

'But three-quarters of a million for a bangle?' I said. 'That's a cool quarter million for each member of the group.'

Clearly I wasn't growing as fast as I might. Cohan's face was filled with incomprehension.

'The Bangles?' I said. 'Walk Like an Egyptian? Manic Monday?'

She still didn't get it. So young, so very young. Or maybe she was simply treating me with contempt. I get a lot of that.

'It was owned by the wife of Lord Henry Carswell.'

'The High Court judge?'

'They very same.'

'He lives in Hyndland?'

'Why so surprised?'

'I don't know. I just expected him to have a country pile somewhere. Or at least a flat in Edinburgh.'

'He does – the flat in Edinburgh, anyway. He also has a house in Hyndland.'

I was impressed. 'Wouldn't mind a wee corner of his pay packet.'

'Anyway,' she went on, deciding to move past my nonsense, 'someone managed to get through the house's alarm system – and it was a good one – and break into the safe. The word is the bangle was brought to Sam Price to be moved on.'

I feigned surprise. 'He's a catcher?'

Cohan gave me a hard look she must have learned from Nick Cornwell. I decided Benedict Cumberbatch had nothing to fear from my acting skills. 'Queste, if we're to get anywhere, you need to stop playing the fool. No matter how easily it comes to you.'

I lowered my head, chastened. 'I'm sorry, go on.'

'Now, from what we hear, the guys who stole the thing in the first place have been left with nothing. Price has done a runner with the stolen item or has moved it on and ripped them off. Our informants tell us the thing might've raised up to half a mill on the market.'

Tank Milligan. He didn't strike me as the type to be interested in fancy knick-knacks, but he was interested in cash. All criminals are.

'Who would buy a thing like that?' I asked. 'It could never be seen in public.'

'Collectors. People with so much money they can afford to buy something just to look at it.'

'In Glasgow?'

'The world is getting smaller all the time, Queste. Have you heard of the dark web? It's used by more than just perverts and drug dealers.'

The dark web. That meant the internet. That meant a computer. I'm not computer literate, but I knew that much. Sam wasn't into social media, according to his sister, but that didn't mean he wouldn't have a PC. He'd need one for business, surely. There was no PC in Sam's flat and none in the shop. If he was in the wind, he must've taken it with him.

'Your turn,' she said. 'What do you know?'

I thought about the plastic bag in my hand, but didn't look at it. I thought about the photograph in my pocket of Sam and the Highland cottage. I thought about the storage unit on the South Side. I told Cohan nothing. Yes, I'm a bastard.

'Early days yet, DC Cohan,' I said. 'I've only just started.'

If she was disappointed, she didn't show it. She didn't believe me, though. I didn't blame her. I wouldn't have believed me either.

'I've told you all I know, Queste,' she said. 'I expect you to keep me in the loop.'

She walked past me and swept through the plastic curtain back into the shop. I followed her, fishing the keys from my pocket once more. Cohan stopped at the door, turned back to me. 'Dominic,' she said.

Uh-oh, a police officer was using my Christian name. That's never a good sign.

'Watch your step, okay? From what I hear, the people responsible for this are nasty. If you find anything out, tell me – don't do your slightly tarnished knight thing and go it alone. Let the law

44

deal with it.'

'Theresa!' I said, genuinely impressed. 'Slightly tarnished knight? You made a Raymond Chandler reference!'

She pulled a face. 'I can read. These days it's a prerequisite to joining the force. But listen to what I say. Let the professionals deal with it.'

Good advice. I wasn't being paid for this, after all. If things turned heavy, it would be the right thing to do. Her concern seemed sincere so I promised I would. I hoped my nose didn't grow.

Chapter Nine

The derelict building had once been home to eight families and its stairway, rooms and back yard had once echoed with the sound of talking, laughing, loving, fighting. All the things that come together to make life as we know it, Jim. Now, though, it lay empty. The windows that had once been the eyes to the outside world were blind. The hallways and landings that had once been the veins, pumping the people that were its lifeblood to and fro, no longer flowed. The blackened sandstone building was dead but it didn't know it, because there it was, still standing. If not for long.

There was a time in the city's recent history when a number of these old tenements stood, like memories of a past the city wished to forget – until they were flattened, for Glasgow has regenerated more often than Doctor Who. Across the city, red and blond sandstone buildings have been sand-blasted, windows replaced, roofs re-tiled. But some of those which once defined the more downmarket neighbourhoods, the notorious Gorbals for instance, were flattened to make way for stark, brutalist schemes which made up in ugliness what they lacked in longevity, for many of them have already fallen prey to the wrecking ball and the bulldozer.

This building, standing on its own on a weed-infested square of scrubland on the border of Ibrox and Govan, was due to come down in the months ahead, but for now it was being used by Cody and his rag-tag bunch of compadres as a place to doss. It was what street folk called a skipper and I'd slept in places like it during my wilderness years, when the need for drugs outranked my desire for comfort. It was Father Verne and then the Sutherland brothers who rescued me.

And there we were again, the band back together, snapping on surgical gloves before pushing our way through the strip of corrugated iron that almost, but not quite, covered the rear entrance to the tenement. Cody and the others had nested in one of the first-floor flats, which was in a better shape than the others. According to the information steered to the Sutherland brothers through their vast web of sources, Cody and his bunch of addicts, chancers and general miscreants moved around, from place to place, skipper to skipper, stealing what they could, earning more cash to pay for their habit by selling their bodies. They couldn't deal in drugs – no supplier would trust them, for they knew that their product would be in their veins or up their noses faster than you can say "Just Say No".

Hamish suddenly leaped to the side, the torch in his hand jerking to send the beam darting to and fro. We stopped and stared at him. He gave us a shamefaced look. 'I heard something moving,' he said. 'I thought it was a rat. I hate rats.'

To look at him, you wouldn't think he feared anything. He's a big lad, hair long, but generally tied back in a ponytail, his beard untamed. Duncan once told me that his brother had so much hair on his body he didn't take showers, he went out to be dry-cleaned. I couldn't vouch for that myself, but I could believe it. And here he was, a big strong Geordie who had kicked and punched his way through an army of underworld figures, terrified of a rodent.

'Horrible, creepy little things,' he went on. 'They've got beady little eyes and sharp little teeth. And they carry all sorts of diseases. And they scurry about. I hate anything that scurries about.'

Duncan said, 'It's true. Hamish has never scurried himself. Never been a scurrier. He scampered once, though.'

'Away, man! Never scampered in me life.'

Duncan paused to consider this claim. He couldn't be less like his brother. Where Hamish was big, Duncan was small, but no less powerful. Or dangerous when riled. His head was completely bald, as if he had donated his hair to his sibling.

'You're right,' he said. 'You may have scuttled.'

'Do I look like the kind of man who would scuttle? Dom?'

'Don't bring me into this,' I said. 'Although I'm sure I've seen you gambol on occasion.'

Hamish waved his free hand to dismiss me. 'I've never gamboled, scurried, scuttled, scampered or – before you say it, Duncan – bustled, not once, not ever. I…What the f…' Hamish suddenly moved ahead quickly, his torch darting downwards at the floor again.

'Relax,' said Duncan. 'It wasn't a rat. It was a spider.'

Hamish flicked the torch upwards towards his brother. 'A spider? Whatever it is darting around down there, it's bloody huge, man. That bloody thing could carry luggage, never mind diseases. A spider! Has there been a nuclear detonation here or something? We got mutated spiders running around?'

Duncan laughed softly. 'Calm down, you big girl. Move on.' Hamish reluctantly began moving again, muttering something about rodents and their inherent sneakiness. Duncan grinned at me, let him move ahead, then said, 'But if that wasn't a scurry, I don't know what is.'

Hamish whirled round and was about to continue the banter, but Father Verne had decided enough was enough.

'Gentleman, I suggest we have less scurry, more speed,' he said. 'We wouldn't want to alert young Master Cody to our presence.'

I hadn't been surprised to see the Father there. Normally he left such jobs to the Sutherlands, but not because he lacked the physical wherewithal to deal with the likes of Cody. Father Verne was well in his sixties, but he had done a power of boxing in his day and I know he kept his fist in. The thing was, although he knew it was best to keep his priestly vestments out of anything that might turn unpleasant, he felt personally responsible for Shayleen. She had come to him for help, he had tried to provide it, but in the end she had gone back to her brother. It wasn't Father

Verne's fault – as he once told me, his refuge wasn't a prison. Father Verne had once been tempted to give the young man a severe smite, and I wouldn't have stopped him. Cody was a loathsome little shit for whom a right sore smite was not just necessary, but recommended.

Even so, Father Verne looked out of place beside the brothers and myself. We were not dedicated followers of fashion, tending towards the more serviceable end of sartorial elegance – jeans, working boots, thick cotton shirts, hoodies, heavy jackets or, in Hamish's case, an anorak.

But the Father's black suit was, as ever, impeccable, and it set off his thatch of white hair. He was smaller even than Duncan, but there was muscle there. His skin was tanned and he looked like Spencer Tracy, even in a crumbling Glasgow tenement with something large and unpleasant dashing around our feet. I'd felt it too, and it made my skin crawl, but I was determined not to scurry, scamper, scuttle – or scream.

We'd reached the stairs heading to the first floor and beyond. Light lanced through gaps in the boards blocking the front entrance to the tenement building and I was able to make out more detail than I could in the dim corridor leading from the rear. There had been tiles on the walls of the close at one time, but many of them had been smashed and their debris littered the stone floor. Back in the day that floor would've been scrubbed clean by the people who lived here. Now it was a rubbish heap. The two doors leading to flats on either side had once been sealed with heavy metal plates, but they hung loose. Hamish pulled one aside and shone his torch inside. There was no floor in the hallway. A quick peep through the door of the other flat revealed a similar lack of flooring. Someone had probably come by and taken what they could to be reused elsewhere.

We paused at the foot of the stone stairs and listened for noise from above. We could hear voices and movement as someone clumped on a wooden floor.

I asked, 'What if Shayleen's not there?'

'Then we wait for her,' said Duncan.

'And what if she doesn't want to come with us?'

The brothers each looked at Father Verne, as if the thought had never occurred to them. Father Verne's face was taut as he said, 'She'll come.'

'We can't force her if she doesn't,' I insisted.

'She'll come,' he said. And that, as they say, was that. I knew then the depth of rage and anguish he'd felt when she'd walked away from the refuge. He knew what kind of life she had returned to. We began to climb, taking it softly because we really didn't want to tip them off. We were unsure what we would encounter inside, and surprise was our best weapon.

The flat on the left at the top of the stairs was obviously the one we were looking for because the metal plate was lying wide open and hanging from one bolt, whereas the other doorway remained sealed. When Cody and his mates had chanced upon this flat and decided it was just the job for them, they took the precaution of propping an old wooden door in the frame in order to provide some level of privacy. I stepped forward to push it to the side but Duncan laid a hand on my arm.

'Where's your manners, Dom?' he asked. 'We should knock.'

He nodded to his brother, who took a step back, lashed out with his right leg, sending the door crashing down. He yelled, 'Knock-knock!'

He rushed inside with no hint of a scurry at all. We heard startled cries and anxious movement from the far end of the short hall, but there was no other way out. The floor in the hallway looked firm enough, but that could be deceptive. However, we didn't have time to worry about it – you know, surprise/best weapon etc.

Thankfully the boards were solid, and we reached the room without experiencing a sinking sensation. Hamish barged in ahead of us and half a dozen pale and frightened faces stared at him in something approaching awe. The big fella can be quite an imposing sight. I saw Cody immediately, his sallow, thin face being the first to lose the shock and replace it with a glare. He hadn't improved over the months. His hair reminded me of a toilet brush, or perhaps it was just because I had this yen to hold him face-down into a dirty bowl. It might not have been a bad idea because he looked as if he'd not had a wash in a while. His skin was pitted with angry red welts and the bristles on his chin still struggled to form a proper beard. Poor Cody. He hadn't as much been touched by the ugly stick as battered senseless.

The glare became a sneer. 'Haw, you bastarts,' he said, using the customary Glasgow pronunciation. He was plucky, I'll give him that. We stared at him, expecting something more to be said, but there was obviously nothing further coming. Plucky, but not too bright.

Father Verne ignored everyone and moved directly to the corner, where I saw Shayleen lying on a thin sheet. She looked like she was sleeping. A burly young man stepped out to block his way, but the Father was not to be stymied. He barely broke his stride as he swung a right hook and the young man went down without a sound. Father Verne didn't look in the least contrite as he knelt beside the girl and raised her hand.

'Haw,' said Cody, stepping forward. 'You leave her alone.'

Hamish loomed in front of him, preventing him from getting any closer.

'We're here for the lass,' said Duncan as he treated the room to a hard look to dissuade anyone else from getting in their way. If they had any sense, they'd heed the look. Cody didn't have any sense.

'You leave my sister alone,' he said, trying the nigh-on impossible feat of brushing past Hamish, who casually picked him up and threw him backwards. It wasn't much of a throw, but then there wasn't much of Cody to throw. He flew back like a rag doll, hit the wall and slid to the floor to rest on his backside. He sat there for a few moments, gathering his strength and what might pass for thoughts.

'Don't get up,' warned Hamish, but Cody, having more pluck

than smarts, got up. Actually, he sprang up with a speed which impressed me. This time, though, he wasn't empty-handed. I recognised the weapon he'd fished from a pocket as he idled on the floor, a piece of wood with two razor blades wedged into it. It was a makeshift weapon and he'd wielded one like it before, in the refuge. I'd taken that from him, so this must've been a whole new one he'd made. Woodwork classes in school had obviously not been a waste of time. He threw himself across the room, the weapon swinging. Hamish looked almost bored as he trapped the upward thrust with his left hand and then jabbed his right into Cody's face, bringing him to a sudden halt. Cody rocked back on his heels and Hamish took the opportunity to send his fist darting into the lad's nose again. It burst open, sending droplets of blood flying. That was why we wore the surgical gloves. This was a nest of addicts, and blood will out. Especially when the Sutherlands were involved. Cody slumped to his knees, both hands clasped to his face.

I saw he'd added some tattoos since we'd met last. On the fingers of his left hand were the letters D, O, P and E. The fingers of his right had K, I, N and G. DOPE KING. Jesus, I thought, what a tosser.

'I'm fuckin' bleedin here,' said Cody, his voice strangely nasal.

'Then bleed quietly,' said Hamish. 'And this time, bonny lad, listen to me – don't get up.'

Bonny lad. Hamish loved irony.

Duncan joined Father Verne and hefted the unconscious girl into his arms. She looked pale and emaciated, and she hung like a marionette with its strings cut. She might've been dead for all I knew. Father Verne tenderly brushed a strand of lank hair from her face and then gave Cody a look of such intensity I swear he was contemplating breaking a commandment or two. The rest of Cody's friends watched the show like it was on the telly. The one who Father Verne had dropped was prone on the floor. He wasn't out of it, he just didn't want the priest to notice him again. None of them moved to help. As friends they made a great audience.

Through fingers still wrapped round his bleeding nose, Cody watched Duncan carry Shayleen towards the door, but Hamish still stood over him so he didn't try to rise again.

'She's my sister,' he said, his voice muffled and nasal. I don't know whether he was showing filial concern or was mourning the loss of a revenue stream. I didn't like him, so I plumped for the latter.

'Not any more,' said Father Verne. 'She's out of your life. Don't come after her.'

He gave him a long, l-o-n-g, stare. As stares go, it was pretty meaningful. It said that Father Verne's words should be treated like they came from a burning bush. It said Cody could expect all kinds of tribulations should he fail to heed the word. It said that the seven plagues of Egypt would seem like a mild crotch itch compared to what would be visited on him. Said look and unspoken warning delivered, the Father turned and followed Duncan from the room. Hamish gave the room a final sweep, turned his back on Cody and left. I backed away, keeping my eyes on Cody. I didn't have Hamish's confidence.

Cody watched me, his squinty little eyes oozing hatred the way his nostrils oozed blood. 'Yous cannae dae this,' he said. 'That's my sister yous are kidnapping.'

'Forget her, Cody,' I said. After all, I'd done nothing here. If I didn't leave without a few parting words I'd feel superfluous.

He pulled himself to his feet. He was a bit unsteady, but he managed to fix me with eyes that brimmed with spite. 'This doesn't end here,' he said. 'I'll get yous all back, even that bastartin priest. You'll see. You wait and see.'

I stared back at him. There was enough malevolence in his gaze to remind me that he could be vicious. He was a useless little piece of crap, but a useless little piece of crap can cause a stink.

I left. No point in bandying words, we'd be there all night.

Chapter Ten

I accompanied Father Verne and the Sutherlands to the refuge in the East End. They were in Duncan's black Mercedes while I followed in my battle-scarred Ford. I may have imagined it, but I think Duncan drove even faster than usual to get away from me, as if his pristine vehicle would somehow be infected by the layer of grit and mud that coated mine. Snob, I thought. Undaunted, if not undented, I hung on to his tail, although I do think the Ford's engine protested a little. It needed a service. It needed a wash. It needed caressed with a soft cloth. I knew how it felt.

The Mary Ellis Memorial Refuge, off the Edinburgh Road, was once a hotel, but it had gone bust in the '70s. It lay empty for about twenty years before Father Verne's charity took it over, renamed it after a young addict who died in his arms right in the middle of Mass, and set about trying to save as many of our throwaway society as they could. His work has brought him into conflict with the local authority, the diocese, sometimes the police and, quite often, the dealers, pimps and traffickers who rely on the young people who sought sanctuary here. That was where Duncan and Hamish came in. They discouraged any little ned with mischief in mind from interfering with the refuge's work. They convinced the big men who traded in the rich variety of controlled substances that it would not be in their best interests to get in the way. And when the Sutherlands discouraged or convinced, you best take heed.

Hamish carried Shayleen into the building. Father Verne told me she had awakened only once as they travelled. She was propped up against him and he felt her head rise from his shoulder. She said nothing as she looked at him, then at the Sutherlands in the front.

'She smiled,' he told me, 'and then she fell asleep again. She'll sleep a while longer.'

I looked at the young woman as she hung in Hamish's arms. She looked dead, and I suppose in many ways, she was. Her skin was bloodless, her body limp, her hair lank. It would take a miracle to resurrect her. But then miracles were Father Verne's stock in trade.

I watched Hamish's broad back vanish through the refuge doors. I asked, 'What if she wakes up and wants to go back?'

Father Verne didn't answer at first. His blue eyes were sad. 'Then she has to do what she wants. We've given her the choice, it'll be her decision.'

The people who came to the refuge for help did so of their own free will and they could leave at any time. Shayleen had done that months before. We all feared that her brother was keeping her more or less hostage, which was why we had tracked them down and brought her back. But if we were wrong, she could go. It was her choice, pure and simple. Well, maybe not pure.

I asked, 'And if Cody comes for her again?'

'He'd better not,' said Duncan, and the grim look on his face almost made me feel sorry for the young man. Almost.

Shayleen was placed in a room on the ground floor. One of the other residents volunteered to keep an eye on her, so we retired to the refuge's large kitchen for a cup of coffee and a selection of chocolate biscuits. We sat around the formica table as I filled them in on what I'd gleaned about Sam Price. For Father Verne's's benefit, I went over my encounter with Tank Milligan, meeting Sam's girlfriend Bree, and my chat with DC Cohan. I showed them the cuttings I'd found in the side of beef.

They looked through the sheaf of newsprint. Father Verne said, 'So you think Tank is looking for the bangle?'

'Or the proceeds of the sale thereof,' I said. Yup, I said 'thereof'. Get me.

'Imperial jade is highly prized,' he said.

'Yes,' I said, showing off knowledge I'd gleaned from a quick internet search earlier. 'It's jadeite, the best kind of jade, the experts say.'

'That'd be a jadeite master,' said Hamish, clearly not having the self-control I'd shown earlier.

I tried to come up with a follow-up line, got nothing, so I carried on. 'The other kind is nephrite, which is slightly less valuable. They smuggle the good stuff out of Myanmar. That's what used to be Burma, for those of us geographically challenged.'

Hamish looked up from a press clipping. 'Hey, I watch *Panorama*. I know where it is.'

Father Verne asked, 'So this bangle is worth a pretty penny?'

'And quite a few ugly ones,' I said.

Father Verne held up the *Herald* cutting. 'But what's it all got to do with this poor young woman?'

'Beats me,' I said, truthfully.

Duncan leaned forward over the table. 'Did you speak to his staff and the ex-wife?'

I told him I had, before I'd headed over to Ibrox. His staff comprised of a woman in her fifties and a young man in his early twenties. They didn't tell me much more than Mary had, although one did mention that Sam had shown up with a black eye and bruised jaw the week before. He didn't tell them how he got it. I also visited his ex-wife, and she was just as Mary had described. She kept me standing in the doorway of her Lenzie home and continually looked around as we spoke in case an estate agent saw me and reduced the price of property in the street. She kept one hand on the edge of the door as if she was ready to close it in my face at any time. She had nothing good to say about her former husband. He was useless, aimless, and had no ambition. She was well shot of him, she said. No, she hadn't spoken to him in months. No, she had no idea where he might've gone. No, she really didn't care much. She had a new life, a better life, and Sam Price had no part in it. She closed the door. She didn't say goodbye. I recounted all this and we sat silently for a minute, reflecting on how fleeting love can be. She must've cared for him at one time, but that had died. Or maybe she'd never cared for him, merely thought she did. That happens.

Duncan broke the silence. 'Okay, so let me get this straight in my head. We've got this butcher, Sam Price...'

'*Award*-winning butcher,' Hamish threw in, reminding me of the steak pie still in the back of my car. It'd be defrosted now. I'd better eat it soon.

'This award-winning butcher, who has shut up shop and vanished. But in addition to being a butcher...'

'An *award*-winning butcher,' said Hamish again.

Duncan glared at him. 'Are you going to do that every time I say butcher?'

'*Award*-winning butcher,' Hamish said, with a smile.

Duncan ignored him. 'Anyway, he's also a catcher, and he's taken possession of this Jade bangle...'

'*Imperial* jade bangle,' said Hamish, and received another glare from Duncan in return. Hamish gave him a smile that would've been beatific on anyone else.

'...which has been nicked by Tank Milligan. In the meantime, old Sam has been getting his meat and two veg well and truly cooked by the wife of a police officer. And he's been receiving these cuttings about an unsolved murder in the post.'

I congratulated him on his exposition skills. He scanned a *Daily Record* clipping. 'You know what a cop would make of this, don't you?'

I did. So did everyone else in the room. If a police officer found that package, it would be assumed that Sam Price was taking an unnatural interest in the murder and that would make him a suspect. However, it looked to me as if someone had sent those clippings to Sam. But who? And why?

God, I hate mysteries.

Father Verne asked, 'So what's your next step?'

'I found this photograph in Sam Price's flat.' I slid the snap of Sam in front of Yew Tree Cottage across the table. 'He looks happy there. I'm hoping that if he's running away from something, he'd head wherever he'd been happy.'

Duncan sucked in his breath. 'It's a stretch.'

It was, but it was the only thing I had.

Father Verne looked grim. 'Have you considered that Mr Price is showing the classic signs of depression? Withdrawn. Cutting himself off. Non-responsive to communication from loved ones.'

I had considered that. I've had more than one walk with the black dog myself. I'd inherited it from my mother, who had been so disenchanted with the way her life had gone that she up and vanished one night. She was prone to long periods of introversion. Deep silences peppered with hysterical outbursts over nothing. She's out of my life, but still somewhere in my head.

Father Verne knew all this, and he looked straight at me when he said, 'He may have gone off somewhere to end it all.'

I knew what he was saying and it had also occurred to me. He knew and I knew that some years before, I'd tried to kill myself. It was just after he'd found me in a gutter, cleaned me up, helped me get off the drugs that had put me there in the first place. As I began to think clearly for the first time in a couple of years, I came to realise that I had right royally screwed up my life. I'd lost my job. I'd been a features writer for an evening paper, specialising in crime, and it was my dedication to my job, cultivating contacts, being seen as one of the boys, that had led to me first seeking out as much cocaine as I could get my nostrils around and then, when I couldn't afford it, anything that I could smoke or snort, my fear of needles proving all-powerful. I'd lost my girlfriend because she couldn't stand by and watch me systematically destroy myself. I'd lost most of my friends. I'd lost my dignity, because that's what drugs do to you. It all became too much for me and I tried to finish it by playing find the Smartie with a bottle of pills. One hospital ride, stomach pump and a bedside tongue-lashing from Father Verne later, I was still alive and calling myself a fool and a coward. Well, rather, I was agreeing with the good Father, who

58

was never one to let his compassion get in the way of giving someone a much-needed rollicking.

The black dog still comes sniffing around, but I no longer have any thoughts of self-harm. Unless you count letting my gums flap when I shouldn't.

'I'd thought of that,' I said. 'That's why I'm going up there tomorrow. If he is thinking along those lines, hopefully I get there first.'

'But where exactly is "there", though?' said Duncan, craning forward for a better look.

'I called his sister, asked her. She said that he spent a few summer holidays in a rented cottage up in Perthshire, near Loch Rannoch. I thought I'd head up, have a butcher's…'

'An *award*-winning butcher's,' said Hamish, then ducked as Duncan threw a Kit-Kat at him.

Chapter Eleven

Ginty came over to my flat for something to eat. We had the steak pie and I was no judge, but I could see why it won awards. Afterwards she told me she would come with me to the Highlands. I didn't know what I was going to find up there, and knowing me it wouldn't be anything good, so I tried to dissuade her. I was firm. I was emphatic. Ginty stayed the night and the inevitable happened, so naturally I gave in. Yeah, I'm a rock.

We left early, took the M80 out of Glasgow to join the A9, the rich voice of Hayley Westenra floating from the car's speakers. Ginty was partial to the New Zealand singer and this particular album featured the music of Ennio Morricone with added lyrics, so we had the best of both worlds. I noticed she'd also brought along an Adele album. I could live with that. That's what being in a relationship means.

Ginty quizzed me further on what I'd discovered about her cousin. I tried to be vague, but I felt her fixing me with a sideways look.

'What?' I said.

'What are you not telling me, Erasmus? About Sam?'

I don't know if I've mentioned this, but Ginty has a super power. I've got a spidey sense when something's not right in a situation – okay, it's not that great a super power because like as not, if I'm in a situation, something isn't right – but like a lot of women, she had a sixth sense for bullshit. She could size a person up within minutes of meeting them and she knew when I was lying, which, to be fair, wasn't often when it came to her, but she always knew. I was guilty of a lie by omission here and her antenna had picked it up. Life with her former husband had honed her bullshit-ometer.

Even though I was busted, I tried to stick to my guns. 'Don't know what you're talking about.'

'Uh-huh.'

And there it was. In those two syllables, she expressed complete disbelief. I'm telling you, it's a gift.

I forced a laugh. It sounded as false as a politician's promise. 'Honestly, what could there be?'

'Erasmus, honey, you should never play poker because you've got a tell.'

'Bollocks,' I said, ever the wordsmith, but I was fearful to say more.

'Yes you do. Your voice goes up when you're lying, just a bit, but I notice it.'

I cleared my throat, rasped my next words like the guy on the movie trailers. 'That's so not true.'

She laughed. 'Come on, Erasmus, spill. I can take it. I'm not a delicate flower.'

I knew I was beaten, so I told her about Tank Milligan and the jade. I told her about his affair with the married woman. She was unsurprised. She knew her cousin was dodgy. I didn't mention the newspaper cuttings. She'd said she wasn't that close to Sam, but it wouldn't be pleasant having as much as a vague suspicion that a relative was involved somehow in a murder.

She thought about the new information as the scenery slid by and the lovely Hayley sang her way through the theme to 'Once Upon a Time in the West'. The hauntingly beautiful melody seemed fitting for talking about a man who had apparently left his life behind. Finally Ginty asked, 'So you think Sam's hiding from this fella Tank?'

'Maybe,' I said. 'Maybe it's something else. We won't know until we find him and ask.'

'And you're certain he's at this cottage?'

'Hell no, but it's a start. He was happy here, I saw that in the photos. If he's depressed or just wants to fall off the grid for a while, it's as good a place as any for me to start looking.'

Ginty was silent as Hayley launched into 'Metti, Una Sera a Cena'. I didn't have a clue what the title meant, my Italian stretching only to the phrases I've picked up watching *The Godfather*, but it was another sad little song. I like sad little songs. They speak to that Celtic melancholy.

I thought about Ginty's accusation that I had a tell. Her words worried me. Sometimes I'm forced to lie to the law. I don't like doing it but I have to, to protect myself, to protect the people I'm working for, to protect my friends. Frankly, some of the things we become involved in are on the shady side of legal. If I had a tell, then did the likes of Nick Cornwell and Theresa Cohan also know when I was being somewhat cavalier with the truth? I thought back to my conversation with Cohan the day before. I knew she hadn't believed what I was saying. Had my voice, without my noticing, pulled a Mickey Mouse? Then I realised that Nick never believed a word I said anyway, even when I was telling the God's honest, and Cohan had learned from the master, so perhaps her disbelief was merely a default position.

'Farewell, my lovely,' Ginty announced suddenly.

'You going somewhere?'

She smiled. 'I've been sitting here trying to remember. The jade. Isn't it jade jewellery that goes missing in *Farewell, My Lovely*?'

She was right. Marlowe is hired to help in the return of a supposedly stolen jade necklace. It doesn't mean much to the overall plot in the end, but her words reminded me that that's the book in which Moose Malloy appears – and Tank had reminded me of him. I'd always wanted to be Philip Marlow, but now I wasn't so sure.

For the next few miles we talked about which film version was better, the black and white one with Dick Powell or the colour remake from the '70s with Robert Mitchum. I like them both, but Ginty was fond of the original. I didn't complicate the matter by pointing out there was an older version, part of the Falcon series of B movies with George Sanders. That took us onto movies, TV shows, books and even politics. I found myself forgetting about Sam and Jade and bad guys who wore fedoras. The further we moved from the city, the lighter grew my spirits. I liked being with her. She made me laugh. She made me forget that my life is often less than ideal. She was attractive and she was funny and she was sexy and I was bloody lucky to have her because I'm no George Clooney and my past is as patchy as Tom Sawyer's trousers. I didn't like keeping things from her, but I was doing it for the purest of reasons.

The time sped by. We passed Perth and Dunkeld, where the mist rose like smoke from the wooded hills. After Pitlochry we left the A9 and turned west, crossing a bridge high over the River Garry. Ginty had never been this way before, so the sights were all new. She gasped and told me to stop on the bridge. There was a car behind me so I pulled into a car park on the far side and suggested we stretch our legs. We walked back across the parapet and stared. On one side, trees turning various shades of rust and brown crowded along the valley, framing a high hill rising into the blue October sky. On the other, the valley opened up to reveal the river making its way to the Tay. There was a glimpse of cattle in a sun-kissed field and more hills beyond. I recall camping once, not far from this bridge. It was with Louise, who I eventually planned to marry and would have had I not cheated on her with assorted substances. It rained all night, the integrity of the tent was breached, but in the morning it was bright and sunny, the aroma of fried bacon filled the air and the views were nothing short of spectacular. It all more than made up for having to wear water wings to bed and wringing out my sleeping bag.

Ginty's hand slid into mine and something warmed my chest – and for once it wasn't heartburn. I wasn't sure what it was, because I'd either never felt it before or the drugs had eaten the memory away. I suspected it was happiness. Contentment. Hope for the future, maybe. Whatever it was, it stayed with me as we walked hand-in-hand like teenagers back to the car.

63

A narrow road twisted away from the bridge through a host of mature trees until we found ourselves travelling through an explosion of colour that actually made me stop the car again. Autumn is kind to this part of the country. The hardwood trees turn such a glorious shade of gold and the sunlight diffused through the dying leaves is so breath-taking it would make Michael Bay drop his viewfinder. It's a curiosity of nature that the season of death can be more beautiful than the season of birth. But really, it's only a phase. The leaves wither and die, they fall to the ground, are sucked into the earth to be reborn once the land heats up again. It was the circle of life. I was only a song away from picking up the nearest lion cub and climbing a big rock.

The road to Rannoch had more twists than a Chubby Checker marathon and I took great care in my navigation, the oncoming cars so close I swear they scraped off some of the grime from my bodywork. I'll admit the journey caused buttocks to clench when I saw lorries approaching and I was convinced I'd be run off the road, but thankfully nothing so dramatic occurred. There were more oohs and aahs as we caught a glimpse of Queen's View down the Tummel Valley. I don't know which Queen it was who had taken in the view – Mary, Victoria or four guys singing 'Bohemian Rhapsody' – but it sure was purty.

A few miles away from the village of Kinloch Rannoch, we pulled in beside a phone box to drink in another fabulous vista, this time across a small loch towards the pointed peak of Schiehallion. It's a view I could never tire of. There was a small cottage to the right of us and two young couples were in the garden, wrapped in jackets but enjoying what little heat there was in the sun. Across a field, near a stand of trees, I saw a group of men and heard the sound of gunfire. Every time there was a shot, one or more of the young people looked over, their faces filled with disapproval. If autumn was part of the circle of life, this was the circle of death. The birds were bred to be shot for what could loosely be called sport. They can't fly fast, they can't fly far. I swear a Glasgow ned could bring one down with a well-aimed lager can.

I climbed out of the car, leaned on the gateway. 'Excuse me, I'm looking for Yew Tree Cottage. Would you know where it is?'

One of the young men came over. 'Couldn't say, mate.' He was English. 'There are lots of cottages around here, and we're just up for the week.' He glanced along the road. 'You could ask him, though. He'd know.'

I followed his gaze and saw a Land Rover had pulled up at a gate behind the phone box and two men had climbed out, one with a shotgun in a case over his shoulder, the other with an uncovered rifle. Something told me that wasn't quite legal, but he didn't look as if he cared. He was small and had the face of a man who had sucked too many lemons. There was a tweed cap on his head and he wore camouflage gear; necessary, I presumed, to hide him from the pheasies. After all, if one of the birds saw him I'll bet they could give him a really hurtful glare. The man with him was taller and sported a tweed shooting jacket, his trousers tucked into a pair of gaiters to protect them from any mud. He was a toff, all breeding and no chin. He had a narrow face, eyes that were always distant, and a long nose, ideal to use as a bombsight when looking down on people.

'Excuse me,' my friendliest grin came out, 'I'm looking for Yew Tree Cottage.'

They stopped. The tall one gave me a look that told me he wasn't going to lower himself to speak to me. Camouflage man squinted at me like I was a hunt saboteur. 'You looking for someone?' He was Highland. I was Lowland. We've never been forgiven for Glencoe.

'Well, Yew Tree Cottage.'

'It's rented out, rest of the week.'

'Yes, but can you tell me how to get to it?'

His eyes switched from me to my car. He didn't like what he saw. It was old and it was two-tone – dirt and rust.

'Oh for heaven's sake, Gregor!' The voice came from the woman who had been driving the Land Rover. She climbed out and I saw she was squat and cheerful. Her voice also carried the lilt of the mountains and the glens, but despite bearing the marks of too many cold winters, too much driving rain and too few pentapeptides – whatever the hell they are – her face was open and friendly. 'Don't mind him,' she said to me. 'He's like that with everyone. Gamekeepers – they hand out surliness along with their shotgun shells.'

The man gave her a sour look but said nothing. He turned, walked through the gate being held open by the other man, and they trudged across the field towards the other shooters blasting merry hell out of nature.

'Yew Tree Cottage you want?'

I nodded.

'Keep right on through the village, take the road on the right-hand side of the loch, go past the hotel and you'll find a sign for the cottage. You'll need to park at the side of the road and go up the track to reach it. I wouldn't drive up, not without a four-wheel drive. You can't miss it, it's got a bloody great big yew tree in the front garden.'

That's a coincidence, I thought. I thanked her and stepped back to my car. She followed me a little bit.

'You might have a bit of trouble parking, though, if Mr Price's friend is still there,' she said.

I paused as I began to climb back in. 'Friend?'

She nodded. 'Well, I assume there's a friend there. I saw two cars last evening and again this morning. There's not a lot of space, so you may need to pull in further along the lochside and walk back. There's a viewpoint about 100 yards away.'

'What kind of car was it?'

'Oh, I'm not too good with cars. It was white, that's about all I could tell you.'

'Was it big, small?'

'Smaller than yours. One of those hatchback things.'

I thanked her and climbed into the car. She watched as I pulled out and I waved. She waved back and smiled. That was Highland hospitality. Across the field, there was another eruption of gunfire.

Birds fluttered to the ground, dogs surged forward, men patted one another on the back. Killing for fun. I've known people who have killed. I'm not proud that I've met them, but most of them took no pleasure in it, it was part of their life, perhaps even their occupation. One or two enjoyed it, though.

They were the ones I never wanted to meet again.

Chapter Twelve

We followed the directions, drove through the village to hit the reflective blue expanse of Loch Rannoch at the far end, then passed the Rannoch Hotel on the right. Many of the men braving the dangers of defenceless Scottish fauna back there would no doubt be lodging here. It's certainly not somewhere I could afford.

We slipped through a few places with names but very few houses, and eventually saw the sign pointing to Yew Tree Cottage beyond a wooden gate. There was a rutted lay-by next to it, but only one car, a blue Toyota.

'That's Sam's car,' said Ginty.

'No sign of the hatchback,' I said as I pulled in behind the Toyota. The woman I'd spoken to had been correct, there wasn't a lot of room here and there was no way three cars would've squeezed in. I made sure I was well off the road, for like the one leading from the bridge outside Pitlochry, it was far from wide and I didn't want to lose a wing mirror.

'Maybe it wasn't someone visiting Sam,' said Ginty. 'Maybe someone had just parked here, gone walking, or something.'

I didn't say anything. The woman had said the car had been there overnight and it was unlikely that someone would be walking in the dark. They could be camping out, I suppose, but something told me that the car she had seen was not a good thing. My spidey sense seldom lets me down.

Ginty climbed out and looked across the road to where the loch lapped gently against a small sandy beach. An upturned rowing boat lay on the bank. On the other side of the water another colourful blanket of woodland speckled the hillside. That would be the Black Wood of Rannoch, I presumed, which in its autumn coat did not live up to its name. I'd walked through there once, with my old girlfriend. Happier times. But as I turned back to the track leading to Yew Tree Cottage, I felt something cold breathe against my cheeks.

'Maybe you should stay here,' I said.

'Why?'

What could I say? That I had a bad feeling about this?

'Just till I check it out,' was all I said.

'Erasmus,' she said, giving me her stern school mistress look, 'behave.'

I knew I was beaten. There was nothing I could say that would stop her from coming with me. She pushed the gate open and I followed her. The track led up a fairly steep incline to the cottage and I tried not to pant too much as I climbed. I thought of my unused gym membership and decided that I really should get into some training. Then, just like that, the thought died. There were better ways to get all sweaty and red in the face, and the best one was striding up the hill ahead of me as if there was no gradient at all. Like Rooster Cogburn, she gave the impression she'd freighted iron stoves up harder grades than this. My shame made me think of the gym membership again. Just briefly.

We reached the cottage and I paused to get a feel for the territory. That entailed leaning on the iron gate and catching my breath while I looked around. The air was clean and sweet, but a breeze carried the chill of winter. I looked back down the track to the loch, its surface rippled by the breeze. A few candy-floss clouds hung over the hills and over to the left I saw the sharp point of Schiehallion. It was, as the poet once remarked, a belter of a view. As advertised, the cottage had a bloody great tree in front of it. I presumed it was a yew, but I'm no Alan Titchmarsh. The only tree I know by sight is a Christmas tree, and only then because the lights and tinsel are dead giveaways.

It was a solid stone construction, a typical Victorian-era

Highland cottage with the door set between two windows, two more poking from the slate roof above. A trellis on the exterior wall might've carried flowers in the summer, but they were long gone. The small lawn to the front was well-tended, but as we grew closer we saw that the land behind the cottage was rougher and covered in ferns carrying the advance stages of browning. About thirty or forty feet away they gave way to a stand of pale, slim trees that appeared so very spindly against the mature pines further back. The breeze sighed through the branches and whispered among the dry ferns. Somewhere a buzzard cried out. It was all pretty damned peaceful, even idyllic.

But it was wrong. I knew it.

There was something else in the air. Not a smell. A sensation. A vibration. A chill, as if a dark cloud had passed over the sun.

I pushed the gate open, walked the short pathway to the front door. It was green, but the paint was cracked and flaking, as if it had caught too much sun. I could hear music playing inside. A woman's voice, singing something I couldn't quite identify yet. Ginty was close at my heels.

The door was open, not much, just slightly. Enough to give me the willies, though. Open doors are never good when I'm around. I nudged it further ajar with my knuckles, peeped into the shadowy hallway beyond. I recognised the tune now. Brenda Lee singing 'I'm Sorry', a hit from way back when. It was sad, mournful. It was also, it has to be said, as sinister as all get out.

I held a hand up towards Ginty as she moved forward.

'I really think you should go back to the car,' I said.

There was a flash of irritation as she said, 'We've been over this.'

I made my voice firm. 'I mean it, Ginty. There's something wrong.'

The sighting of the hatchback, the open door, the song playing. None of it suspicious, certainly, but given Sam was running away from something – be it fellow crooks, the law or a cuckolded husband – it all added up to something unpleasant. At least to me. I'd been in situations like this before. I knew they seldom ended well. The thing was, Ginty had no idea what my life was really like. She knew I did odd jobs, like finding her cousin. She knew I had in the past been in harm's way. But she didn't really *know*. She couldn't. Her lips tightened and she pushed past me, walked into the cottage shouting out her cousin's name. I sighed and followed. Nothing good would come of this. You see, I *knew*.

'Sam, it's Ginty,' she shouted. 'We're here to help you.'

We paused just inside the door. The hallway stretched to the rear of the house, where I could see a door opening to a toilet and the foot of a narrow staircase leading to the second floor. I glanced into the door on the right and found a well-appointed and bright kitchen. Breakfast dishes lay on a round wooden table in the corner. A bowl with the vestiges of cereal, a plate bearing toast crumbs, a mug and a juice glass. I moved in, touched the mug. Cold, a drain of coffee on the bottom. I touched the kettle too, but it was also cold. A black box contained empty pasta sauce jars and whisky bottles. I counted six, all single malt.

Ginty had stepped into the sitting room to the left of the front door. By the time I got there she had reached a small CD player that sat on a mahogany sideboard against the far wall and was reaching out to turn off the song.

'Don't touch it,' I said, my voice sharper than I'd intended.

She jumped back as if she'd been stung and gave me a puzzled look. 'Why not?'

I couldn't answer. Not truthfully. 'I don't know,' I said. 'Just don't touch anything.'

She kept her arms at her side and unconsciously put distance between her and any furniture.

'Erasmus,' she said, 'what's wrong?'

I didn't reply as I looked around me. It was a cosy little room, with a settee and two armchairs that didn't match but looked comfortable. The open fire was dead and dark. A beige, hard-wearing carpet was covered in front of it by a dark rug bearing a

71

few scorch marks from where sparks had erupted from the grate. A wicker basket to one side bulged with logs, a discoloured metal bucket to the other half-filled with coal. A low, cheap coffee table in front of the settee carried a half-empty bottle of whisky and a single glass. Sam had been hitting the booze like Rocky going for Apollo Creed, trying to beat his worries into submission. That would've been a waste of time. The booze never hears the man count ten. There was also an open laptop, a black mains flex snaking towards a socket in the corner. The screen was dark. In the corner of the room there was a moderately sized flatscreen TV and a budget DVD player. Brenda was still singing her heart out. They used to call her Little Miss Dynamite and her country and western-tinged tones filled the room and spread through the cottage. It was a song of love. It was a song of loss. It came to an end and then started again. It was a song on repeat. The hairs on my neck started to play the Grand Old Duke of York towards the rear of my skull as I wondered how long it had been playing, over and over, time and again, *I'm sorry, I'm sorry…*

'Sam must be upstairs,' said Ginty, already striding down the hall. I rushed to catch her.

'Ginty, stay here,' I said. She was about to argue. I gave her my no-nonsense face. She gave it back. My patience snapped. 'Listen to me, Ginty, there's something not right here. Believe me when I say it. Now, please, wait outside.'

'For God's sake, stop trying to protect me! I don't need to be shielded. Sam's probably just upstairs sleeping. Or out for a walk…'

'You asked me to find Sam because you knew this is what I do,' I said, cutting her off by grabbing her arms in both hands. 'Listen to me now when I say that I need you to go outside and don't come back into this house unless I tell you to.'

She was going to argue further, I saw it in her eyes, but somehow I must have got my message across. I saw her determination melt as she gazed at the staircase. Perhaps she had felt the underlying coldness that lurked there. I brushed a strand of her blonde hair from her forehead and my tone softened. 'Please, do this for me. Go outside, let me have a look upstairs.'

I could tell she was still torn, but she nodded and without another word walked back down the hall and into the sunlight. Brenda was still singing and it creeped the hell out of me, it really did. I wanted to go out into the crisp, clear air with Ginty. I wanted to get in the car, drive somewhere, have a meal. I wanted to take her across the loch to the Black Wood, where we could walk hand in hand. I wanted to find a nice little hotel and stay the night and we could make love, softly and gently, two of us as one, leave all the unpleasantness that my life seems to consist of outside, just for the night. I wanted to feel that warm feeling again. I wanted to do all that but I knew I couldn't. I had to climb those stairs. I had to find what was waiting above.

I moved up the narrow staircase like I was ninety, each foot placed carefully on the next step. Pausing halfway up, I held my breath and listened intently to the house around me, straining to catch any noise that seemed out of place. I heard nothing, apart from the buzzard outside crying in the wind. Every muscle was taut, as if ready for someone to attack. Even my hair was tense. I reached a small landing with two doors leading off. I took the right one first, pushed the door open slowly. It was a bedroom that would seem compact elsewhere but was large for this small cottage. The room was dull because the curtains were closed, but enough light bled through to see everything clearly.

Unfortunately.

Sam was lying on the bed. He was on his back, the duvet pulled up to his chin. His eyes were closed, and he looked as if he was sleeping. I knew he wasn't, but I said his name anyway. Softly. Almost reverentially. He didn't wake. He didn't move. I didn't think he would.

Downstairs, Brenda was still all apologies.

I tweaked the edge of the duvet with my fingertips. I knew I shouldn't, but I had to know. I eased it back, saw the blood staining the sheet below, through to the mattress. I pulled the cover further back and the blood grew thicker, darker. I kept pulling, I couldn't help myself. The duvet, sheet, mattress were all soaked with blood.

I expected to find a horse's head. I didn't.

What I saw was worse. A lot worse.

I felt the bile rise in my throat and I almost retched, but I knew better. I backed away, bumped into an old wooden dresser, fumbled in my pocket for my mobile. No signal. I felt something lurch in my gut as I stumbled out of that little room and almost fell headlong down the stairs. My system demanded to void itself, to somehow purge the memory of the thing upstairs, but I knew I couldn't – shouldn't – contaminate the scene any further. Anyway, nothing would erase that image from my brain. The blood. The wounds. Everything...

Ginty must have seen something in my expression, or perhaps it was because I stumbled along the hallway towards her. I'm sure I was as pale as a Glasgow summer, and I just needed to get back out into the sunlight, feel something living on my skin. I didn't say anything, I couldn't say anything. I didn't need to. She took a step back, her hand darting to her mouth. I reached out for her but she moved away from me. I tried not to take that personally but didn't quite succeed.

My hand trembled as I took out my phone. Still no signal. That figured. One of us would have to call this in. I knew which one of us it would be.

'I need you to drive back to the village,' I said, aware my voice was hoarse. There was a sour taste in my mouth, my stomach was churning like a machine in a wash cycle and the danger of throwing up remained imminent. 'Find a phone, call the police.'

She drew her mobile from her pocket, checked the screen. We had the same service provider and she saw no bars. She looked from her phone to me and found her voice. 'What happened? Sam...'

She wasn't close to Sam, but they were still family. Even if they hadn't been, we weren't just talking murder here. We were talking something far worse. I tried to think of an easier way to say it, but couldn't. For a man who once made his living with words, I can be woefully inarticulate.

'He's dead, Ginty.'

A slight shake of the head, little more than a tremble. 'How?'

I wasn't getting into that. I was still processing it myself. I've seen violent death before, more than my share, but what I saw up there was butchery. I also knew I had to go back into that cottage, back into that room, and I didn't want Ginty around.

'Never mind now,' I said. 'Go back to the village, find a phone, call the police. Please.'

She wanted to ask something else, perhaps to argue, but she decided against it. She nodded, turned and walked down the track. I watched her disappear from view and stood in the sun for a few moments, letting the weak heat play on my face. I didn't want to go back in there, I didn't want to look at the body that had been ripped open and laid out like a side of beef. I didn't want to smell the blood in the air. I didn't want to think about the man's agony and terror. I wanted to be anywhere but here. But here I was. Here I always was.

I could still hear that buzzard, crying mournfully to the wind and the hills. And Brenda Lee, of course, still singing, still sorry, over and over and over.

Chapter Thirteen

Duncan and Hamish had decided that rather than wait for Tank to make any sort of move on Sam's sister, they would take a more pro-active approach. Patience was never a strong suit with them. You should see them watching a kettle. Duncan has more contacts than Specsavers, and one of them told him that Tank liked to have lunch at a pub called The Crow's Nest on Dumbarton Road. It was an old-fashioned Glasgow pub, but it had paid lip service to the city's gentrification by sweeping up the sawdust and, at least once a week, polishing the old dark wood. Apart from that it was pretty much the way it had been when it had been a favourite of sailors docking on the Clyde. The customer base was predominantly male, middle-aged, old-aged or maybe even dead, given the pasty faces at the bar. The drinks were traditional – beer, lager or spirits. Anyone asking for a white wine spritzer or, heaven forbid, a Prosecco, would get a hard look and told to man up and have a real drink. Even the women. The lunch menu used to be pretty basic. A variety of toasties. Pie and beans. If you wanted to be daring you could have a bridie. If you were sophisticated you could have chips, too. Of late the owner had turned more cosmopolitan with regards to the fayre. He added chicken nuggets and scampi. And rice. My God, the Michelin stars were waiting to shine.

Hamish had ordered the chicken nuggets with chips, Duncan went with a cheese and ham toastie. Hamish had taken a bite of one nugget and pushed his plate away. Duncan devoured his toastie. You can't go too wrong with a toastie.

The bar was doing reasonably well, all regulars. Sky News was on the flat-screen TV above the bar. Duncan watched the door, waiting for Tank to appear. Hamish sat quietly, now and again pushing a nugget with his fork, as if he could bring it back to life.

Duncan gave him a glance. 'Food not to your liking, sir?'

'This chicken is so rubbery it's got a tread on it.'

Duncan laughed. 'We didn't come here for the cuisine.'

'Just as well.' Hamish looked up as the door opened and Tank Milligan walked in, looking like a shit brickhouse wearing a suit. 'Dom said this guy was a big palooka, didn't he? With a hat like a gangster?'

Duncan watched Milligan walk to the bar, place an order, then head to a corner table, back to the wall and a full view of the door. Duncan understood why. He and Hamish were in another corner, a wall behind them and a clear line of sight to all exits. Milligan laid his hat carefully on the chair beside him and unrolled a copy of the *Daily Telegraph*. He looked as out of place as Kermit the Frog at the Rangers end.

Duncan said, 'Did you just call him a palooka?'

'Aye – so?'

Duncan rolled his eyes. 'So I think I need to stop letting you out to play with Dom. He's a bad influence.'

Hamish smiled as they rose from their table. 'What the hell is a palooka, anyway?'

'A big, stupid guy. Comes from a comic strip about a boxer, Joe Palooka.'

This made Hamish pause for a beat. 'How the hell did you know that?'

Duncan smiled. 'I need to stop going out to play with Dom too.'

Tank clocked them before they got within three feet of him. He'd probably spotted them as soon as they stood, maybe even when he'd first walked in. In their business it paid to notice these things, and the Sutherland boys were the kind of guys you'd notice. He didn't move, but watched them over the edge of his

77

newspaper. Even sitting down he looked monstrous. Hamish wondered if it was a specially-strengthened chair.

'Tank Milligan,' said Duncan. It wasn't a question.

Tank lowered the paper, looked at the brothers. 'Help you, guys?'

'We need a word, like.'

The barman brought Tank his lunch of pie, beans and chips. Tank nodded his thanks, folded the newspaper again and placed it beside his hat. 'Kinda busy here. Come see me during office hours.'

Tank unwrapped his knife and fork from the paper napkin – hell, they'll be putting flowers on the table next – and began to slice open his pie. Undaunted, Duncan and Hamish pulled up two chairs and sat down at the table. Tank stared at them as if they had just stolen a chip from his plate.

'Won't take but a minute,' said Duncan. 'We need you to back off from Sam Price.'

Tank hooked a slab of pie the size of a small sheep on his fork and shovelled it into his mouth. He studied the Sutherland boys as he chewed, his gums working like the T. Rex chowing down on the lawyer in *Jurassic Park*. He swallowed and smiled. 'And who might you be?'

The boys introduced themselves and Tank smiled. 'Met a fella the other day. Funny guy, he was. Real laugh riot. Never caught his name, though. You associated with him?'

Duncan said, 'He asked us to keep an eye out for you, yes.'

Tank smiled as he disposed of another forkful. He leaned forward and spoke in a whisper. 'I've heard of you guys, the Sutherland boys. I've heard that you're handy. But you know something? Something tells me you haven't one clue who you're messing with.'

'We know enough, Tank. You're a big lad, like, but we've handled bigger.'

Hamish tried to think of anyone they had ever encountered who was bigger than Tank Milligan. He didn't think there was anyone bigger than Tank Milligan who wasn't one of the Avengers.

Four chips followed the hunk of pie. These were big fat chips, too. They were washed down with a mouthful of Guinness. The pint pot looked like a shot glass in his hand. 'I don't mean me,' Tank said, wiping his mouth with the paper napkin. 'Although I'm not someone you want to get on the wrong side of.'

Yeah, Hamish thought, he'd block out the sun.

'No,' said Tank, 'I mean my partner. He's not the kind of fella you want to piss off, you understand?'

Duncan smiled. 'We're not the kind of fellas you want to piss off, either. Do *you* understand?'

Tank smiled back. He looked at Hamish, who smiled. There was a lot of smiling going on here and damn little to smile about.

'So who is this partner?' Duncan asked.

'Not something you need to know.'

'Shy, is he?'

'He likes to remain *sub rosa*.'

'*Sub rosa*, eh?' Hamish said. 'She the Ukrainian woman that works in the sandwich shop?'

Tank's smile froze as his eyes swivelled from Duncan to Hamish. The tension in the air was so electric it could be a reusable source of energy.

The big man said in a low voice. 'You a funny guy too?'

Duncan decided it was time to ease the atmosphere a touch. 'Not so you'd notice,' he said. 'Unusual accent you've got there.'

'I've been abroad a few years,' said Tank, still staring at Hamish.

Hamish, unfazed by the look, guessed, 'Edinburgh?'

'New York, Chicago, points west.'

Duncan asked, 'Why'd you come back?'

Milligan swivelled his eyes back to Duncan and popped another chip into his mouth. 'I missed the food.'

'Can't get a decent Scotch Pie in the States, then?'

'Hell, no. And you don't get big fat chips like this. Chips you can get your teeth into. It's all French Fries, skinny wee things that make you think the potato's been on a diet.'

Duncan decided they were drifting off topic. 'Sam Price.'

Tank looked at him again. 'Aye, we were getting so chummy there, I forgot. Sam Price. No can do, guys. He owes me some dosh.'

'And your partner.'

'And my partner.'

'For the sale of the Imperial jade?'

Tank's thick eyebrows shot up. If there was anything in the butterfly effect, the movement would've blown a farting cow over in New Zealand. 'See, you know what that tells me? You knowing about that? That tells me you know where it is.'

'We don't,' said Hamish.

'Or you know where Sam is.'

'We don't know that either,' said Duncan. 'But you know our mate is looking for him. When he finds him, we'll get you and your mystery partner sorted for the bangle.'

Tank thought about this while he dipped a chip in his beans. He tossed it into his mouth like a sacrifice to a volcano god. 'And I should trust you why?'

'Because if you know about us, you'll know when our word is given, it's written in stone. Because if you don't trust us, that means we're in conflict. And none of us want that.'

Tank thought about this while another bean-dipped chip was thrown into the cavern. 'A fella, back in the Windy City, he once said we were in conflict. You know what I did? I took a power sander to his testicles. He can't wear trousers to this day, has to walk around in a kaftan.'

If Duncan and Hamish were impressed by Tank's knack for Manscaping with Extreme Prejudice, they didn't show it. They'd faced men like him before. I'm not saying they know no fear, but they know better than to let it be seen. The underworld is all about appearances, and to react might appear weak, though Hamish said later that it took all his strength not to cross his legs.

Duncan's lips thinned. 'Tank, we're just three guys having a chat here. We've asked you nicely to leave Sam Price alone. If you don't, if you approach his sister, his cousin, his paper boy, we'll have to come back and see you. And you'll wish you were back in the Windy City practising DIY with other men's tackle.' He stood, Hamish followed suit. 'Enjoy your lunch, Tank.'

'And stay away from the nuggets,' warned Hamish. 'Those chickens used a zimmer to cross the road.'

They left Tank to his meal, feeling his eyes on them all the way. They stepped into the street and turned to where Duncan had parked his Mercedes.

'What do you think?' asked Hamish.

'I think we'll have trouble with him,' said Duncan. 'And he's no palooka.'

'What about this partner?'

Duncan considered this, then shook his head, the corners of his mouth pulled down. 'We can't worry about something of which we know nothing. The big guy could be conning us.'

'But if there is a partner and he's as tasty as he said, what then?'

'Then we deal with it.'

Hamish silently agreed as they walked, then said, 'Something of which we know nothing, eh?'

'That's what I said.'

'Showing off, were we?'

'I can speak proper, like. You should try it sometime...'

Chapter Fourteen

The first responders to Yew Tree Cottage were two young female officers, and I had the feeling this was their first murder scene. They knew what to do, though. They told Ginty and me to wait outside while they inspected the locus. Those were their exact words, 'inspect the locus'. Straight out of cop-speak for beginners. A few minutes later we saw one of them dash from the stairs into the bathroom and I heard her throwing up. Part of me envied her. I had managed to keep my innards in place, but perhaps I'd've been better to, in the words of the song, let it go.

Ginty watched her mad dash and asked, 'Is it that bad?'

I nodded. I couldn't look at her for fear that if I did she'd ask further questions, and I couldn't handle that. Luckily, the other officer reappeared. She may have been made of sterner stuff than her partner, but there was still a haunted look in her eyes as she stepped outside and breathed deeply. She took brief statements –I was reasonably truthful – then she told us to wait until the full team arrived.

The officers who followed the original pair split Ginty and I up and took us back to Pitlochry. They told me someone would drive my car back later.

I signed a form that declared I was there voluntarily, though I really didn't have much choice in the matter, and they put me into a small room in the police station, a stone building towards the outskirts of the town which I was surprised was still open in these days of cutbacks and call centres. It was good to see. A uniformed sergeant took a longer statement. As before, I was truthful. Mostly. He asked me if I wanted a cup of tea or coffee. I said some water would be nice. He asked me if I was hungry. My mind flashed to Sam's body. I said I wasn't hungry. It would be a while before I'd be hungry again. For the second time in two days I thought I may even turn vegetarian.

I knew I was in for a long wait, because that's what the police do. I'm used to it, so settled myself in as well as I could on the cheap plastic chair – would even a thin slice of padding hurt? – and thought about the story so far.

It was clear Sam Price had fled to that little cottage above Loch Rannoch. He'd told no-one he was going. He'd closed his shop without any warning. He'd shown up with a black eye. His sister and his lover had both noticed the change in his behaviour in the past few weeks. I'd discovered he'd been receiving cuttings about the murder of the student, Paula Rogers. He was also a receiver of stolen goods and was avoiding Tank Milligan over the proceeds of the sale of the jade bangle. The police had him in their sights for that item too. Add to that he was having an affair with the wife of a police officer and what do we have? I'll tell you, a right bloody head-scratcher, that's what.

The method of murder was disturbing on so many levels. Tank might beat him to death, he might stab him, shoot him, strangle him, but I didn't see any Glasgow crook going all Jack the Ripper, even if he had at one time been an apprentice butcher. On the other hand, I didn't know much about him. Duncan had said he wasn't the sort I wanted to cross and he didn't make such comments lightly. Tank wanted his money or he wanted his bangle. I was certain he would do anything to get what he felt he was due, but evisceration?

Unless, of course, he was looking for the key to the storage unit. Maybe he thought Sam had swallowed it. I considered this. The bangle was worth a small fortune and a man like Tank might butcher the butcher to get to it. These days, though, would it be a key card rather than a padlock key to get into the unit?

83

Maybe both. Would Sam' swallow something like a keycard? It was more likely he would keep them close by, especially if he had a fortune stashed away in there. Back in the cottage I'd plucked a man-size tissue from a box by the bed to hold over my hand while I had a look around. I hoped aloe vera balm didn't leave some sort of forensic fingerprint. There were no padlock keys on Sam's keyring. There was no key card in his wallet. I even went through his clothes and his travelling bag. I found his car key and ran back down the track to search the Toyota parked at the roadside. I knew I was on the clock and I kept a wary eye out for approaching blue lights, so couldn't exactly tear the vehicle apart. Back in the cottage I poked at his laptop, the tissue still tented over my fingertips, but it was password protected so that was me stymied. I found nothing. Nada. The big zipperoo.

The cuckolded husband was another thought. I didn't know who he was but had the feeling he was a ranking officer. Bree wasn't the type to mess around with a mere constable, her dalliance with a dodgy butcher from Partick notwithstanding. I needed to find out more about her and her husband.

That left the cuttings and the other murder. What was that all about? Did Sam know something about it? Why would someone send him cuttings about an unsolved killing? He'd hidden them away in the shop because he obviously hadn't wanted to bring them with him and he didn't want them in his flat. He'd put them in cold storage, as if the freezing conditions would somehow protect him from them. He then put distance between him and them. And whoever sent them.

Seriously, my head was nipping as I thought about it all. It was something of a relief when a slim woman with high cheekbones as sharp as her eyes entered. She was wearing a smart dark suit and her black hair was cut short but was threaded with grey. She had black sensible shoes and a crisp white shirt and she carried a large thermos in one hand and a computer tablet in the other. She was tall and had the sturdy look of someone who worked out. She smiled at me, a nice friendly grin which showed off white, even teeth, then sat down across the small table from me and laid the flask and the tablet between us.

'I'm DI Valerie Roach,' she said, holding out a hand. Her voice was rich and strong. Her grip was firm. Yup, she went to a gym all right. 'I'm from the Murder Investigation Team in Perth. Sorry to keep you waiting.'

'That's alright,' I said, 'gave me a chance to count my legs.'

She smiled again. That was nice of her. 'Would you like a cup of coffee? It's French roast.'

I said I did, even though I couldn't tell French roast from a French letter, and she twisted the first cup from the flask, lifted another from within and began to pour. 'I brew it myself because I know from experience that the stuff around here is so vile the local farmers use it as sheep dip. Never go anywhere without my flask.' She pushed a cup towards me, reached into one pocket of her jacket and produced a handful of brown sugar sachets and a small stirring strip. From the other pocket came four plastic containers of long-life milk. 'Sorry – no cream,' she said as I tipped the contents of two of the sugar sachets into the cup. She took hers straight and sipped it as she watched me pour in some milk and stir. I took a sip. I tried not to grimace. I don't understand all this fuss over this coffee or that, French roast, Colombian, Brazilian. I'm a Nescafé man myself.

'So,' she said, settling back. 'Dominic Queste.'

'Present,' I said.

Another smile. She liked to smile. 'I've heard a lot about you in the past couple of hours.'

'All good, I hope.'

Smile. 'Nothing wrong with hoping. I spoke to a Detective Chief Inspector Nicholas Cornwell in Glasgow.'

Uh-oh, that's never good.

'Ah, dear old Nick,' I said. 'He's like a father to me.'

'He said if I had the chance I should throw the book at you. Failing that, hit you with it.'

'He doesn't believe in sparing the rod. He can be a bit Dickensian at times. Although he can't grow mutton-chop whiskers. Funny, that.'

She ran a finger over the tablet and it flickered to life. I could see what looked like an official report on the screen. If there had been a bookie handy I'd have laid a bet it was about me. 'He keeps your name flagged on the system, so if anyone logs it, he's contacted. Any time, day or night. Did you know that?'

As it happens, I did know that. 'He worries.'

'So when I routinely put your name into the system, he phoned me. I told him what it was all about, given we're all Police Scotland. One big happy family, after all.' She stretched her fingers on the screen to magnify the image then read a few lines. 'Seems you lead a colourful life, Mr Queste.' She looked up. 'Or may I call you Dominic? Or do you prefer Dom?'

'Call me what you like. I also answer to "Hey, you".'

A smile again. I was beginning to think I'd found the most smiley police officer on the force. It didn't seem forced, either. I took another sip of the coffee. Her smiles didn't make it taste any better.

Her finger was still roaming over the screen. 'A *very* colourful life, Dom. It appears this isn't the first dead body you've found. Why is that?'

I shrugged. 'It's a gift, Val.' We were being chummy here, so I felt I could get away with calling her by her first name. She didn't react at all.

'DCI Cornwell tells me you've found so many that there's a firm of undertakers who keep you on retainer.'

That Nicky, such a wag.

She flicked the file on me away and opened up another folder. Photographs, bright and colourful. I couldn't see them clearly from where I sat but I recognised the room. And the blood immortalised by flash photography. Val's smile was gone now. I couldn't blame her. 'And now there's this new one. Nasty.'

I couldn't help but agree.

She didn't look at me when she asked, 'Why were you there again?'

I'd already told the officer at the scene and the sergeant at the station. But she wanted me to go over it again. Along with keeping you waiting, it's what the police do. 'I was asked by the dead man's cousin to find him. He'd turned strange and gone missing.'

'His cousin being Mrs Reilly?'

'That's right.' I don't normally bandy the name of clients about in police interview rooms – there is a code, you know, and I live by it – but I surmised Ginty would have told them. 'Where is she, by the way?'

'She's waiting outside for you.'

That told me they weren't going to keep me. I must admit, I relaxed. I'd found the body, I led a colourful life and police can sometimes put two and two together to come up with a very long time in the slammer.

I said, 'The family were very worried about him, especially the way he'd cut them off and seemed to have sealed up his life. I'm sure I don't need to tell you, Val, that none of that is a healthy sign.'

Her eyes flared slightly in agreement.

'I was worried that he may be contemplating self-harm. So when I discovered pictures of him from a previous visit to that cottage, I took a flyer, came up here and there he was.'

She looked at the photographs again. 'There he was indeed.' She laid the tablet down and a finger gestured vaguely in its direction. 'And this isn't self-harm.'

I deliberately didn't look at the screen. 'No,' I said, 'it's not.'

Her eyes lingered for a moment on the image before she closed it down with a flick of a finger. She placed her elbows on the table, laced her fingers in front of her face and leaned forward. 'So what are you?' She asked. 'A private detective?'

'Not as such. I'm an odd-job man, of a kind.'

'Really?' There was the hint of a smile. 'You any good with plumbing? Because my ballcock needs attention.'

I wanted to respond with a Sid James leer but felt it was

87

unseemly. I gave her a weak smile. I knew I was letting the side down but, even though the pictures of Sam Price's gutted corpse were no longer on the screen lying between us, their memory was a real mood killer.

'Dom,' she said, 'I need you to help me out here. DCI Cornwell tells me you've a habit of keeping information from the police.'

She waited for me to deny it. I didn't. Maybe that was keeping information from the police.

'If there's something you're not telling me, then I need you to do the right thing.'

Other Spike Lee films are available, I thought.

'This is a brutal piece of business,' she continued. 'Mr Price wasn't just killed, he was defiled.'

Good word, I thought. All murder is brutish, disgusting, but this one was different to anything I'd ever encountered. There was a degradation to it. This wasn't murder, it was desecration.

Her eyes were serious now. There was no smile. We weren't horsing around. 'Is there something you're not telling me? About Sam Price?'

A little voice, a smart little voice, whispered *tell her about the bangle and Tank Milligan*. I told that smart little voice she probably already knows about that – it would be in the system. *Tell her anyway*, it whispered back.

'Nothing springs to mind,' I said.

'Are you sure?'

Tell her about Bree, said the voice. I don't want to, I thought back, not unless I have to. *You have to*. No, I decided, it's part of the code: don't ruin anyone's life unless absolutely necessary. I knew that if I mentioned her, Val would be duty-bound to question her. And the police are not noted for their discretion, especially in regard to officers who are not part of their immediate sphere. Police Scotland may be one big family now, but families can be dysfunctional.

Val looked at me as if she could hear my internal dialogue. 'I think there is something, Dom.'

The cuttings, the smart little voice screamed, *tell her about the cuttings.* But I don't know what that's all about, I decided. *For God's sake, Queste, you're not even getting paid for this! Why the hell are you digging a hole for yourself?* I shut the voice down because it was making far too much sense for comfort. However, I had to give Val something. After all, she was being so friendly, giving me her French roast coffee and all. And smiling, too. Police officers don't usually do that, not with me. And I liked her.

'There was a white hatchback parked overnight at the bottom of the track leading to the cottage.'

She found this interesting. 'How do you know?'

'I asked directions and a woman said she'd seen the car there last night and again this morning.'

'Who was this woman?'

'I don't know. She drove a Land Rover.'

She grimaced. 'That should narrow it down to a couple of thousand, give or take.'

True, the Land Rover can be pretty ubiquitous in rural areas, but I had more. 'She was dropping off a gamekeeper called Gregor at a pheasie shoot on the other side of the village.'

Val's face brightened. 'That'll help. Anything else?'

I listened for a final appeal from the smart little voice but he was off somewhere in a sulk. 'No, nothing.'

She sat back, stared at me for a long time. Nick Cornwell would've been threatening me right about now. Or calling me a liar. Or thinking sincerely about tearing my head off. Or all three. Val merely nodded. 'Okay, thanks for the help, Dom.'

'I can go?' I couldn't keep the disbelief from my voice. I'd only been here four hours. Back in Glasgow they'd have kept me as long as they could without charging me with something, grievous talking without thinking maybe, just to keep me off the streets.

'Yes, you've been very helpful.' I couldn't tell if she was being ironic. Or sarcastic. I can never tell those two apart. She slid a white card and my car keys to me. 'You'll find my mobile on there. Anything you want to tell me, don't hesitate. Your car's outside in the public car park.'

Val stood, even opened the door for me. I thanked her, stepped through, and was just about to head down the corridor when she said, 'Oh – just one more thing…'

I couldn't believe she had Columbo'd me. I should've seen it coming, but with all the smiling and French roasting, she'd sucker punched me. I stopped, turned, waited.

There was that smile again. 'Did you find what you were looking for?'

I adopted a puzzled frown, wondering if some technician had worked some alchemy and found the aloe vera. 'Come again?'

'In the cottage. You sent Mrs Reilly off to call us…'

'Neither of us had a signal.'

She waved that away, like a bothersome fly. '…leaving you free to have a nose around. I've read your file, I've spoken to DCI Cornwell. I think I know you. You stayed behind for a reason. You've a habit of snooping where you shouldn't. Did you find anything?'

I knew she didn't expect me to tell her, she just wanted me to know that she knew. She now knew that I knew that she knew. She was no fool, this Highland Detective Inspector. I'd need to watch her.

'Not a damn thing,' I said, feeling it was okay to be honest with her. 'But I can still go, right?'

She flicked a hand to the hallway beyond the open door. 'Of course. After all, DCI Cornwell has given me a tip should I ever need to speak to you again.'

'What's that?'

'Find the nearest dead body.'

Her smile was still friendly, but I saw something working in her eyes that told me I'd have to keep my wits about me with her. Still, I liked her. She had me at ballcock.

Chapter Fifteen

Ginty gave me a hug as soon as she saw me. It was so close I might've needed hosed down if it had gone on much longer. She put her mouth to my ear and whispered she was sorry.

'What for?' I whispered back as I caught the officer behind the counter watching us. Get your own blonde, I thought.

'For being such an arse back at the cottage.'

Then she kissed me, right there in the public area of Pitlochry Police Station. My God, she was brazen. Still, I wasn't complaining.

When we disengaged, I led her outside to where my car was parked. 'What's going on, Dom? Who would kill Sam?' she asked.

'I don't know,' I said, truthfully.

The journey back to Glasgow was relatively quiet. I listened to BBC Radio Scotland news, but there was nothing as yet about Sam's death. That wouldn't last. Something would get out, something always does, no matter how hard the police try to keep a lid on things. The more people they speak to, the greater the chance that someone will let the media know. I warned Ginty not to talk to the press if they tracked her down. I hoped they didn't. I didn't want Tank getting wind of her connection to Sam.

We were at Stirling when she suddenly spoke. 'You shouldn't worry too much about me, you know.' Christ, was she really telepathic? 'I'm not a delicate flower. I've seen things. Been through things.'

'You didn't need to see that back there, is all,' I said.

'I know. But don't hide things from me, Erasmus. Don't keep secrets. I don't like secrets.'

I dropped her off at her East End flat between London Road and the Gallowgate. She gave me another long kiss. I liked it. I was getting used to this kind of thing. I wanted to go with her into her flat so we could work off the tensions of the day, but it was dark and I was tired. I think I would've been a major disappointment to her, and that was something I didn't ever want to be.

I called the Sutherland boys before I set off for home. They told me about their encounter with Tank.

I asked, 'So who do you think this silent partner is?'

'Could be anyone,' said Duncan, 'but whoever it is, Tank felt he was someone we should be worried about. And he doesn't seem the type to be worried about anyone.'

I thought about this. 'Should we be worried?'

'Worrying doesn't get you anywhere, Dom.'

This was true, but it didn't prevent a few niggles.

Duncan invited me over to the flat he shared with Hamish on Alexandra Parade for something to eat. They were having grilled octopus. I declined. I generally don't eat anything that can give me the finger. As I drove from Ginty's flat to the South Side, I slid some John Barry into the CD player. The soundtrack to *Somewhere in Time*. Who needs tranquillisers when you have his music? It soothed me, it always does.

Sometimes my street is so crammed with cars that I have to park some distance from my flat, but there was a space open right outside the entrance to my building – a blessing, because I was seriously beat and didn't think I could walk very far. I got into my flat, realised I was so hungry I could almost be tempted to try the Sutherland's signature octopus. I popped some bread into the toaster, clicked the kettle on and walked into the living room to fire up the TV. Something mindless to fall asleep to was needed, but not reality TV. There's mindless and there's brain dead, and my brain was mushy enough, thanks.

But all thought of food and telly and falling asleep after one and in front of the other was banished when I saw the mobile phone sitting on the small coffee table in the middle of the room.

It wasn't in itself threatening – it looked like a cheap Pay As You Go – but the fact that it wasn't mine sent cold fingers dancing down my back. I normally enjoy that sort of thing, depending on whose hands the fingers belong to, but these belonged to Stephen King.

I looked around the room as if whoever had left the phone was lurking in a corner. It's not a big room and remarkably free of lurking spots. I listened to the noises in the tenements and the street outside. I stared at the phone for a few moments.

Then I picked it up.

And that was when it beeped to tell me there was a text. Something told me it was for me.

Hello, Mr Queste

I'd barely noted the formality when it beeped again.

You have been selected

I thought about switching it off right then to prevent anything further, because I knew whatever was coming next was going to make more than one orifice pucker.

It beeped. I opened it. I couldn't help myself.

FOR DEATH

This was no prank. This was real. This was connected to Sam Price. This was something to do with those cuttings he'd been receiving.

This was not good.

Not good at all.

And then the phone rang.

I literally jumped. If I was a cat, I'd've been hanging from the ceiling. I held the cheap little phone in my hand, stared at the read-out. Number withheld. That figured. I contemplated not answering and refusing to play whatever game this guy was engineering. But like that figurative cat on the ceiling, I was curious. I just hoped it wouldn't kill me.

I pressed RECEIVE.

The first thing I heard was breathing: harsh, asthmatic, metallic. Darth Vader in serious need of a suck at an inhaler. I waited, remained silent, listening to the laboured breath. Then there was a chuckle.

'I know you're there, Dominic.'

The voice was high-pitched, almost robotic, Stephen Hawking on helium.

'Who are you?'

That chuckle again. It'd be throaty in its raw state, but the voice manipulation made it sound like a witch's cackle. Hubble, bubble, toil and trouble.

Something wicked this way comes.

'You know I won't answer that, so why ask?'

'God loves a trier,' I said.

'You don't strike me as being devout, despite your association with that priest.'

That made me hold my breath. He knew about Father Verne. What else did this guy know about me? If it *was* a guy because really, there was no way to tell.

'What do you want?'

'You got my texts.'

'Yes.'

'Then you know what I want.'

It occurred to me that he had to know I was home in order to send the texts and make the call. That meant he must have been watching. I moved to the window, prised open the blinds and peered out. All I saw was parked cars. 'So if you're going to kill me, why not come ahead?'

Another chuckle. 'All in good time, all in good time, my friend.' The voice paused, treated me to some heavy breathing, as if this was some obscene call. Then, 'I like to play with things a while – before annihilation.'

A movie quote. The creep was hitting me with a line from a movie. The opening to *Flash Gordon*. Max von Sydow as Ming to Peter Wyngarde. I continued to scan the street outside.

'You still driving that white hatchback?'

If he was surprised I knew about his car, I couldn't tell. The voice remained conversational. 'No, that's gone. So don't bother looking for it.'

Was he watching me at that moment? Was he in a car out there, maybe fixing binoculars on me, enjoying this? I zeroed in on a white van parked on the opposite side of the street, about 100 yards down, in the shadow midway between two lampposts. No light shone into the front so I couldn't see if anyone was sitting there. I tried to recall if I'd ever seen it before.

'Is this what you did with Sam Price? Sent him cuttings, torment him with a phone?'

'Ah, you found my cuttings? I thought you might. When I didn't find them in his flat or his shop, I thought of you.' So he'd searched both places too. Must've been when I was up north. 'But in answer to your question, no, not the phone. This is especially for you. I thought you'd enjoy the dialogue. I thought it'd be a scream.'

I let the blinds drop back into place and turned away, began to pace the living room. 'You're a pretty sick puppy, aren't you?'

That chuckle again, then the breathing. 'Oh, Dominic, you don't know the half of it. But you will, my friend, you will before this is all over. But first, some rules…'

'You don't set any rules, you–'

'Don't interrupt,' the voice sharpened, 'it's rude, or didn't your mother tell you that?'

'Well, pardon me all to hell.'

The good humour returned. 'I'll take that as an apology. Now – the rules. There are only two. Rule number one is you don't talk about this. Rule number two is you really do not talk about this. To no-one. Tell no-one about our little relationship here. Not the police, not your friends, not your priest, not the neighbour's dog. If you do, I can't be responsible for my actions.'

'What's that supposed to mean?'

'Think about it, you'll get there.'

My mind whirled. 'You're saying that if I tell anyone, you'll kill someone, right?'

The chuckle again, but there wasn't anything remotely funny.

'Give the boy a cigar! It could be anyone, just whoever takes my fancy. A salesperson, hairdresser, doctor, dentist, lawyer, tinker, tailor, soldier, spy. Should you breathe a word of what passes between us then I will take someone's life and it will all be down to you and the fact that you couldn't keep your mouth shut. Loose lips sink ships, Dom, remember that. Look what I did to poor Sam. Do you want that happening to someone else? Think of the guilt, Dominic, think of the shame that you were the cause of someone's death just because you couldn't follow one simple rule.'

There was no hysteria in the voice. It was calm. It was measured. It creeped the shit out of me. 'Why are you doing this?'

'Because there's nothing on the telly. Because sport no longer fascinates me. Because I've lost interest in politics. Because it's something to do. My motives are unimportant. What is important is that I can, so I will. Believe me when I say this, you cannot escape this. Where you gonna go? Where you gonna run? Where you gonna hide?'

I knew those words but couldn't place them. My brain scrambled to pin them down but came up with nothing. But I knew them, *I knew them*.

'I'll be watching you. Maybe not all the time, but you'll never know when. And sometime soon, just to show you that I'm not bluffing – although you saw poor Sam, so why would you? – I'll send you a little message that will sharpen your focus.'

'What sort of message?'

'You'll know it when you hear about it. But it will tell you that we have a future together, you and I. How far that future will stretch depends on your discretion and my interest. Keep this phone powered up – you'll find the charger in the box on the mantelpiece.' I automatically checked, saw the box. 'And don't lose it. Wouldn't want to lose contact, would we?'

The line was disconnected before I had the chance to say anything further. I didn't know what I was going to say, right enough. Something witty and brave would've been nice, but witty and brave just weren't playing right then. The image of Sam Price lying gutted and dead in that bed flashed before me. Whoever this guy was, he wasn't bluffing. I knew that. Whatever his message was, it was unnecessary. But I knew he'd send it anyway.

And that scared the hell out of me.

Then something else happened that made my grasp of bodily functions somewhat tenuous.

The doorbell rang.

There's a baseball bat I keep lying around, not because you never know when someone's going to challenge you to a game of rounders, but because my life can, like Michael Keaton's Batman, be complex. It was only a few months before that I came out of the shower to find a London drug dealer waiting for me with a gun, nothing on but a towel, and nothing to defend myself with but some dodgy one-liners and a loofah. Hence the presence of the Louisville Slugger.

I edged down the hallway to the front door, the bat held at shoulder height. I wasn't expecting visitors and was mindful of the message promised by the person I had already dubbed the Nightcaller – I'm an ex-journalist and we need a label. Perhaps this was the message. If it was, I was ready to come out swinging. I don't have a peephole because, to be honest, I'd seen too many movies where someone puts a bullet or something sharp into an eye. I pressed my head against the wood and listened. I don't know what I expected to hear. Breathing, maybe.

My voice was, I admit, a bit thin and as unsteady as an ostrich in high heels when I called out, 'Who is it?'

There was a pause. Maybe the person had amnesia.

Then…

'Erasmus?'

Ginty's voice. The muscles in my neck and shoulders, which had stretched and tightened with the tension, wilted with relief. I opened the door and she gave me her patented look of amusement.

She asked, 'When did you start asking people to announce themselves?' Then she saw the slugger in my hand. 'And what are you doing with that?'

I couldn't think of a reasonable explanation. 'I'm polishing it.'

She stepped past me. 'You're polishing your bat? I hope that's not a euphemism.' I closed the door as she walked up the hallway. 'Because that's my job,' she threw over her shoulder.

I followed her into the living room, laid the bat against the wall beside the door. She took her coat off, threw it onto the settee. 'What's up?' I asked.

'This,' she said, and stepped into my arms, placed both hands on my face and kissed me. It was one of those kisses that people write songs about. It was long but at the same time too short, soft but firm when it needed to be, filled with longing and promise and, it has to be said, tongues. In *The Princess Bride*, it's stated that there are only five kisses in history that rated highly in terms of passion and purity. This one didn't make the five because there was very little purity about it. After all, this was no fairy story. Ginty's kiss made me forget about the Nightcaller, Sam Price, Imperial jade and, frankly, my own name. I like to think I gave as good as I got, but somehow doubt it. She had all the advantages.

When we broke apart I took a moment to breathe before I said, 'And what was that for?'

'Because my cousin is dead and we're alive,' she said. 'Because we should celebrate life every chance we get. Because I'm scared and I want to be with you tonight.'

All valid reasons, I thought, especially the last one because I didn't much fancy being alone either. My mind turned to the Nightcaller. If he was watching the flat he would've seen her come in, but something told me he'd know about her already. He knew about Father Verne. I was doubly glad she was here. I could protect her. I was her man. I would die before I'd let anything happen to her.

Okay, maybe that's a bit overly dramatic.

She kissed me again. If anything, it topped the first one, which was quite a feat. This time there was touching and unzipping and unhitching. One thing led to another. To hell with purity. It's over-rated anyhow.

Samuel Pepys got it right.

And so to bed.

Chapter Sixteen

The dark figure loomed out of the darkness at the rear of my building.

It was tall, it was lean, it was hooded.

It hovered.

It opened my front door like it had a key, floated inside, allowed the door to swing shut behind it. The figure didn't touch the floor, had no other movement other than forward motion, no face visible within the shadow of the hood. It slid through the darkness of the flat with ease, came into the bedroom and hung above me. I was asleep, yet I watched.

A hand reached out – no, not a hand, a claw, something scaly and sharp. Pointed at me.

Then the hand was something else.

A knife.

And it swung down...

I'd been sleeping fitfully, but the dream shocked me awake. My first thought was for Ginty, lying beside me. She was asleep and snoring softly – what can I say? She's not perfect. I lay still for a full minute, letting my breathing and heart rate stabilise, then eased out of bed without waking her and padded down the hallway to ensure the front door was secure. It was. Not that it mattered – the bastard had already picked my lock once and could do it again. There was a security chain, but a sturdy set of bolt cutters could take care of that. I stood in the darkness, nude, my ears straining for alien sounds. The world inside and outside the flat was silent. I tiptoed back to the bedroom, unhooked my ratty old dressing gown from behind the door, pulled it over my nakedness. I watched Ginty sleep for a few moments, envying her, for I knew the dream would rob me of rest for the remainder of the night.

I didn't click on the lamp in the living room. There was sufficient illumination slanting through the blinds from the streetlights outside. I poured myself a Jim Beam, drank it straight. I normally added soda water, but I needed the manly hit. A single malt would've been preferable, but my budget these days didn't stretch to that. I poured another, sipped it this time as I paced around the room. The Sundance Kid aimed better when he moved, I think better when I pace.

I replayed what I could recall of the phone conversation with the Nightcaller.

I'd never identify the voice: whatever electronic distortion it had gone through made it unrecognisable. Such devices are readily available and it's easy to change pitch and timbre until no-one could say with certainty whether a caller was male or female. So instead I concentrated on the content.

I've had some strange conversations in my time, but there was something about this one that kept ringing bells. And that final line – 'where you gonna go?' – was really bugging me. I'd heard it before, somewhere, delivered in a dull monotone, just as the Nightcaller had done.

I had another taste of Kentucky fire water and wandered over to my bookshelf, studied the spines of the array of pulp thrillers, then to the cheap wooden shelves that carried my DVD collection. I idly scanned the titles, had another hit of booze, tried to remember where I'd heard the words. The Nightcaller had used them for a reason. It wasn't random. He was making a point, as if he was goading me. It was something I should know, but it was tantalisingly out of reach. I saw the DVD of *Flash Gordon*, which the Nightcaller had quoted. Maybe he was a fan. I let my gaze move along the spines, came to my box set of the first three

Scream movies. The voice echoed in my mind.

I thought you'd enjoy the dialogue.

Thought it'd be a scream.

A scream...

I almost slapped my forehead like a cartoon character. Of course! Movie references. He'd threaded the conversation with nods to films. I let my gaze roam along the DVD spines, taking in the titles. They were all up here on my shelves. Phone calls played a vital part in the *Scream* movies. His rules were straight out of *Fight Club*. He'd mentioned *Tinker, Tailor, Soldier, Spy*. I had both the BBC series and the film version because I'm nothing if not a completist. The whole breathing thing could well be *Star Wars*, but I sensed that was too obvious for my boy. He would want to be cleverer than that. I looked down two shelves, found my copy of the 1962 Blake Edwards thriller *Experiment in Terror*. I pulled it out, stared at Glenn Ford on the cover. Ross Martin was the bad guy in that, terrorising Lee Remick with an asthmatic voice from the darkness. Could even be *Halloween*, because Michael Myers' breathing through the old white-painted William Shatner mask played its part. But the Nightcaller didn't stop there. He wanted to get really obscure. The pitch of the voice itself. I saw Doris Day, I saw Rex Harrison. I searched the shelves, looking for a particular title. *Midnight Lace*, a curious little thriller with Doris being stalked by a high-pitched voice in the fog – and on the phone.

And then there was *I'll be watching you. Maybe not all the time, but you'll never know when.* That was from *Dirty Harry*, one of my favourites.

Dear God, maybe the Nightcaller was a film geek, just like me. Or perhaps he'd studied my collection when he was in the flat then found the quotes he needed on the internet. It was so easy even I could do it.

That just left 'where you gonna run?'

But I was onto him now. I knew what it was. There have been four versions of *Invasion of the Bodysnatchers* and I had them all.

In 1993 the title was shortened to *Bodysnatchers* and Gabrielle Anwar starred alongside Forest Whitaker. Neither of them said the line. It was Meg Tilly, after she'd been replaced by an alien.

The bastard had tailored the whole conversation towards my predilection for films. He knew I'd pick up on the references. I smiled, but there wasn't much humour in it. I knew something about him now. I turned away from the DVDs and moved to the window, opened the blinds. The sky was beginning to lighten. A new day. The white van was gone, but if he was out there watching, he'd have seen me tip my glass towards him.

The game had begun.

The only thing was, I didn't know the rules.

Chapter Seventeen

I asked Ginty to stay with me the next day. She laughed, told me she had to work. She had appointments all day. I said she could cancel them. She laughed again. Then she stopped, gave me a sideways look and suddenly I was sixteen again and being studied by a woman in the off-licence as I tried to buy booze for a party. I'm older now, more adept at evasion. I lasted all of five seconds before I looked away.

She asked, 'What's this about, Erasmus?'

'Nothing,' I said, piercing the last of my fried potato scone with my fork. I'd cooked up a full Scottish. I was being stalked by a mad person, so cholesterol was the least of my worries. Anyway, I'd been awake half the night and I was hungry.

'Uh-huh,' she said, still giving me that look. 'You remember what I said yesterday? About secrets?'

'Of course.'

'So what are you not telling me?

There's no easy way to say that some psychotic killer was sending me creepy messages, so I kept my face as open as I could. I even managed a laugh. Of sorts. 'Nothing! Just thought you might like to hang around today.'

I decided to say nothing more lest my tell betray me further. I chewed the final mouthful of breakfast. I needed to know she was safe. Normally, I'd've brought in the Sutherlands, who were both very fond of Ginty and recognised that she was good for me, but that would entail telling them about the Nightcaller and I hadn't decided what to do about that yet. His warning about telling no-one was still fresh. It could be a bluff. It could be bluster. Did I want to take the risk?

Finally, she shook her head, said again that she couldn't and that was that. To push it would confirm there was something else on my mind and I didn't want to worry her. I'd promised never to keep secrets, but this was different. She'd be in her salon all day. She'd be surrounded by customers and staff. She'd be fine.

I hoped.

* * *

I paid another visit to Sam's shop to check his records for the address of Sylvia's restaurant. She'd said it was in Busby and on the wall planner I found an entry for deliveries to an eatery called Acapella. I wondered if that meant the serving staff dressed up as barber shop quartets and treated customers to a verse or two of 'By the Light of the Silvery Moon'. I hoped not.

While I was in Partick I also called on Mary. I knew the police would have informed her of her brother's death by now and I wanted to say how sorry I was. I said that I wished it had worked out differently. I said I wished I'd got there in time. I said I would do everything I could to find out who murdered him. She was polite, she was downcast, and it may have been the grief, but I felt a coldness between us, as if she blamed me for her brother's death. I asked one question – had he ever mentioned the name Paula Rogers? He hadn't, I hadn't expected him to, and Mary didn't ask why I wanted to know. She had other things on her mind, but I felt she was relieved when I left. How to make friends and influence people.

The sun was shining as I drove from the west of the city to the south, with one eye on the rear view. The Nightcaller had said he'd be watching me, but I don't know what I was looking for. The van from my street the night before, maybe. However, I saw no suspicious vehicles, vans or otherwise. No-one appeared to be keeping tabs on me from a discreet distance, I saw no-one turn when I turned. All the same, I made a series of rights and lefts at various intervals, just in case, but I still couldn't scratch the itch in the back of my mind that someone was watching me. As the saying goes, I was paranoid – but that didn't mean they weren't out to get me.

Acapella was situated along a side street in Busby, once a village in its own right. But cities like to stretch, and even though it's not officially within the Glasgow boundary, it's seen as a well-to-do suburb to the south. Normally it wouldn't have taken me long to get there from my flat in Battlefield, but my various detours added fifteen minutes to my travel time. It's a leafy area mixing high-priced villas with modern apartment blocks, none of which I'd ever be able to afford. My flat is rented and, thanks to my doomed love affair with controlled substances, my credit score is so low I'm about to be relegated.

The restaurant sat on a road that ran parallel to what locals called a river but was really a stream with delusions of grandeur. Mature trees lined the edges of the water and hung over the road, mounds of fallen leaves (a dirtier brown than their distant relations up north) piled at the side while some strays formed part of a slippery carpet of mush on the street surface. The building was on one level and sat on its own amid a line of villas, a little island of commercialism surrounded by suburban domesticity. It was discreet, though; no big sign, no blatant attention-grabbing. Bree had said it catered to the discerning diner and it looked it. The small car park in front was empty save a pale blue little sporty number I took to be Bree's. It was too late for breakfast, if they served it, and too early for the lunchtime rush, if there was one at a place like this. I pulled in, checked the menu before I entered. As I thought, I'd need a letter from my bank manager to order a starter. No matter, I had a lunch date later anyway.

I pushed the door open, stepped inside. It was gloomy, particularly as I was coming in from the morning sunlight, but I wasn't there to inspect the place. I lingered for a few moments in the reception area to let my eyes adjust. A dark-haired young man with the kind of tanned complexion you don't get by sunning yourself on Glasgow Green in October appeared from behind a large green plant. I don't know if he'd been lurking there, or if he'd just been passing as I entered. He may have been inspecting it for greenfly, for all I knew. He was a good-looking bugger with the kind of well-honed physique that made clothes sit well and women take notice, so I disliked him on principal. Nevertheless, I sucked in my gut and straightened my shoulders.

He gave me a look that made me think he was wondering where the broom was and asked, 'Can I help?' There was an accent there, and it wasn't Govan. He hailed from a place where they cooked with garlic and deep-frying a Mars Bar was cruelty to chocolate.

'Looking for Bree,' I said and received a frown in return.

'We have no Bree here,' he said.

There couldn't have been two Acapellas in Busby so I pressed my case. 'She owns the place.'

He shook his head. 'No, no Bree owns Acapella.' His accent made the name of the restaurant sound musical. Which, of course, it was.

'So who does own it?'

He took a step back, gave me another look up and down, fully taking in my brown leather jacket, jeans and lightweight hiking boots. Again, I saw the notion of sweeping me out of the door occur to him. 'Who is it who asks?'

'The name's Queste, Dominic Queste.' I don't know why I said it like Bond, James Bond. It's just the way it came out.

'And what is your business?'

I smiled the smile I smile when dealing with those who tell me that Donald Trump is misunderstood. 'Well, that's between me and – what did you say the owner's name was?'

He thought about this. He knew he hadn't said a name. I knew he hadn't said a name. He knew I knew he hadn't said a name. There was a lot of knowledge between us. However, he sighed as he decided there was no harm in telling me. 'Sylvia.'

'Can you tell her Dominic Queste would like to see her?'

'Dominic Queest?' At least, that's how his accent made my surname sound.

'Queste. Like best, only better.'

He paused to take this in and I thought I saw the beginnings of a smile, which may have meant he was warming to me, but it was dark and could well have been a touch of wind. He told me to wait where I was then gave me a withering stare that also told me not to touch anything. Maybe he'd just polished everything and he didn't want to have to fumigate it too. I waited until he'd walked through the restaurant proper and then through a small door beside the tiny bar before I gave the broad leaves of the plant a thorough stroking. I'm such a bad boy.

Sylvia appeared a few minutes later, the young man at her heels. And yes, Sylvia was Bree, although she was dressed more formally than before. She'd gone from a footballer's wife to the team manageress, all tailored black jacket and matching trousers, blue blouse, high heels. Still designer, though. The only thing she'd take off the peg was her washing. She did not look pleased to see me. I'm used to that.

'Thank you, Julio,' she said and he nodded. But he also gave me a strange look that I couldn't quite decode. Then, with a lingering look at his boss, he left us through another door hidden behind the plant. Julio. Perhaps that was the way to Paul Simon and the schoolyard. But I'd caught something in that final glance at Bree, or Sylvia, or whatever she was calling herself today. He was infatuated with her. And that look he'd given me was a warning not to step out of line. He didn't know who I was or why I was there, but he was already jealous.

'What the hell are you doing here?' Her voice came out like a hiss.

'Nice to see you too, Sylvia. Or is it Bree?'

'It's both, if you must know. Bree is my middle name and I prefer it, but Sylvia better suits the business.'

Made sense, I suppose. Someone could call her name and a waiter might think they were ordering another course. At one time I would've said that out loud. Not today. I lowered my own voice. 'Can we talk?'

Her eyes strayed to the restaurant entrance. 'My husband is due any minute.'

'It's okay, I won't make a pass at you. I've got news.'

Her face was rippled with indecision, but finally she nodded and jerked her head to indicate I was to follow her. We retraced Julio's steps through the tables to the door, which opened into a small office. A window looked out to the rear of the restaurant, where she had a fine view of a small area paved with concrete slabs and a collection of large wheelie bins. Oh, the glamour of the restaurant trade.

She plucked a cigarette that was burning in a small ashtray and whirled round to face me like Bette Davis in *All About Eve*. I buckled up for a bumpy ride.

'So what do you have to say?' she demanded, then took a drag from the cigarette. I didn't think it was legal to smoke inside, but I let it pass. I had the feeling her nerves needed the nicotine hit. And what I had to tell her wouldn't help much.

It was my turn to hesitate now. Although I spend much of my time around death – too much time if you ask me, but I don't seem to have a choice in the matter – I'm not comfortable delivering bad news. I've had to do it a few times, never get it right, so now I tend to jump in with both feet, get it over with, like ripping a plaster off.

'I'm sorry, but Sam's dead,' I said.

She blinked.

She sucked on her cigarette again.

She blinked again.

She blew the smoke out.

She crossed her arms.

She blinked. Again. And again.

And then the tears began to well. She fought them, but they were determined little bastards.

'I'm sorry,' I said. It never hurts to say it again. And I really was.

Another blink and a droplet of moisture broke from the corner of one eye. 'What happened?'

I swallowed. I couldn't tell her everything but couldn't lie to her either. 'Someone killed him.'

Her fluid eyes widened and a few more tears made the trip south. 'Who?'

'I don't know.'

'But you're trying to find out?'

'Yes.' It's what Simon Templar would've said and it seemed to satisfy her. She lowered herself into the chair behind her desk, stared at the smoke drifting upwards from the cigarette in her hand. I heard movement in the restaurant, the clink of cutlery, someone whistling. Julio, preparing tables for lunch. I couldn't identify the tune. Something from his homeland, maybe. Something that spoke of sun and laughter and love in a warm climate and not death in a cold one.

Bree's voice was dull and flat when she spoke again. 'Where was he found?'

'A cottage in Perthshire. I was the one who found him.'

A frown. 'Why was he in Perthshire? Why didn't he tell me he was going?'

Judging by Julio's whistling, he was right outside the door. I wondered if he was trying to eavesdrop. My back was to the door and I stepped further from it. It wasn't easy and I may have violated Bree's personal space but I didn't think the staff should know about the boss's private life. I sidestepped her questions, asked one of my own.

'Did he mention anything about a self-storage unit on the South Side?'

She shook her head. I believed her.

'Did he ever mention a Paula Rogers to you?'

I saw something register in her eyes, behind the tears. 'No, why should he?'

This time I didn't believe her. She'd heard the name. 'Are you sure?'

'Of course I'm sure. Why would Sam mention her? What would he have to do with a murdered girl?'

'So you do know who she is?'

'Of course I do. My husband is in charge of the case.'

Okay, I'll admit, I didn't see that coming. I searched my memory for the investigating officer's name in the reports, came up with DCI Gregory Hambling. So that made her Bree Hambling. Or Syvlia Hambling. Or Snookums Hambling.

'Could your husband know anything about you and Sam?'

Right on cue, I heard the office door opening and something like a shadow darkened her face. It was fleeting and quickly bottled up again, but I recognised it. This time it was genuine fear.

I turned to find a tall man with the look and build of a rugby player draped in the kind of suit that Kojak could only dream of. DCI Hambling, I presumed. He had a broad face with a broken nose, iron-grey hair and eyes that didn't miss much. He didn't look like the kind of husband to call his wife Snookums. He looked like the kind of man for whom sex was a flying tackle and a communal bath.

He stared at me in silence, his eyes immediately suspicious, and then turned to his wife, waiting for an introduction. Bree gave her cheeks a quick swipe with both hands and attempted a smile.

'Darling, I'll be finished here in a moment.'

He couldn't have missed the tell-tale signs of the tears streaking her make-up or the catch in her voice, not if he was any kind of detective, but he didn't comment. His gaze returned to me but I kept my eyes on Bree. I'd seen that shadow again. Something about him scared her. I wondered if he'd spotted it too. I wondered if knowledge of his wife's fear pleased him.

When I turned my attention to him I found him studying me again. He was sizing me up, wondering why I was here, wondering what business I had with his wife, wondering why we were alone in a room together.

'And you are?'

'Just leaving,' I said, but he was blocking the door and didn't seem inclined to move.

'I didn't catch your name.' His voice sounded as if it had been scratched out of a gravel pit.

'It's pretty nippy on its feet. But it's Queste.'

He filed it away for future reference. 'What's your business with my wife, Mr Queste?'

I sensed Bree was about to say something but I broke in ahead of her. 'I'm here about one of her suppliers. Sam Price?' I watched his face closely for any sign of recognition. If he knew the name, he was good at hiding it. 'He supplies fresh meat to the restaurant,' I added, still studying him, still nothing.

He asked, 'What about him?'

'He's been murdered,' I said. This guy was a cop, he'd be able to check it out easily. He'd also see my name attached, hence my uncharacteristic attack of candour.

'And what's that got to do with my wife?'

'Nothing. He disappeared and I was asked to find him. I did, but it was too late. He was one of Mrs Hambling's suppliers, so I thought I'd ask her if she'd noticed any change in him over the past few weeks.'

'You a private detective?' He made it sound like something that should be flushed away.

'Not as such. Friend of the family.'

His lips pursed as if he was sucking a lemon. 'A friend of the family who appears to be interfering in police business.' Always a cop, I realised. I bet he and Nick Cornwell were like blood brothers.

'Just asking a few questions, that's all,' I said. 'Is there a law against it?'

He declined to answer that. 'My wife has nothing to say.'

We both looked at Bree. She still appeared dangerously close to breaking down. I'd really only come to tell her Sam Price was dead, but learning the cop in charge of the Paula Rogers case was her husband was interesting. A coincidence? I hated coincidences. They're so random.

111

Hambling stepped aside. 'I think you're done here – Queste, was it?'

'That's right.'

'How are you spelling that?'

'Very easily, I've had years of practice.'

I swear I heard a grunt, then a hand landed on my chest. It was a big hand, not as big as Tank Milligan's, but big enough to stop me in my tracks.

'I don't think you'll have any need to bother my wife in the future, will you?'

I looked at the hand on my chest, then back at him. I waited until he had removed it before I answered.

'I hope not.'

He gave me his best stare, the kind they used to hand out at police college on graduation day along with the suspicious look, the sarcastic comment and the ability to make a bruise on any part of the body look like the person walked into a door. He'd taken an instant dislike to me, and my personality is usually so winning.

'Don't hope,' he said. 'Pray.'

We exchanged hard looks for a few seconds then, with a final nod to Bree, I walked through the restaurant. Julio was standing at the small bar with two other members of staff. They were talking, laughing, but he wasn't. His eyes followed me all the way out.

Chapter Eighteen

Father Verne was a good man; a caring man, a compassionate man.

But he had his limits.

He believed in tough love and sometimes not the love part. The Bible might say turn the other cheek, but to him, that only left you with two sore cheeks. He had decked that young addict in the skipper when he tried to come between him and Shayleen. I'd seen him face down dealers in the street. I'd seen him verbally lacerate politicians who got in his way. I'd seen him grab a procurer of young flesh by the scruff of the neck and throw him bodily out of the refuge when he came to retrieve one of his young boys. In short, Father Verne could handle himself.

But he couldn't handle bullets.

And that's what Cody brought.

Father Verne was in Shayleen's room on the ground floor of the refuge when Cody arrived. The young girl was sleeping again. She'd had a restless night and Father Verne had been there with her. She had been severely doped up when we found her but was now coming off the stuff, so there was a lot of forcible ejection of bodily fluids. And pain. A doctor friend gave her a shot of something to help – the first of many, I'd imagine, not to mention Methadone – but it wasn't enough. She writhed, she sweated, she vomited, she screamed and raged and vomited and cursed and promised and threatened. And then she vomited some more. And all the while Father Verne was there, easing her through it, his voice gentle, his touch soothing, his patience infinite.

He heard the screams and yells coming from the corridor and then Cody's voice shouting, 'Where is she? Where's my sister?'

Shayleen didn't hear. She slept but still shivered and murmured as her demons whispered to her through her dreams. They were little bastards, those demons, and they would hiss and spit and slide through her thoughts until she believed the only thing that would silence them is another hit. The trick in beating addiction is to understand that the only thing that will silence them is not to take a hit. But that's a hard road and a long road, and Shayleen was only taking her first step.

Cody was almost at the door to her room when Father Verne opened it. The young man took a step backwards, raised his hand. The hand with the gun. Along the hallway, towards the front entrance to the building, some of the other residents clustered together, terror clear in their eyes. One of the eldest, a young man who had been clean for two months, began to edge towards them, but Father Verne shook his head, telling him to keep his distance.

Father Verne stood very still. 'Cody,' he said, his voice level. Cody might've been pointing a feather duster at him. 'This is not the way.'

Cody ignored him. He was shaking, Father Verne couldn't tell whether from rage, fear or need of a fix. He guessed all three, but he knew that meant the young man was in a very dangerous state.

'I want my sister,' Cody said, his words sounding like they were being forced through a wet towel.

'This is not the way,' said Father Verne again and took a step forward. Cody jerked back, the arm with the gun stiffened, the barrel wavered alarmingly. If that trigger was delicate, this could get very messy very quickly. 'Easy, son…'

'Don't you "son" me – just don't! You're not my dad, you're not nothing.'

'Put the gun away, Cody. We'll talk…'

'No! No talking! Just give me my sister, nobody gets hurt.'

'She's ill, Cody. You can't move her…'

'She'll be fine. She's my sister. She should be with me.'

'She can't come with you, not right now. She needs to rest. She needs treatment.'

'*No!*' The word came out in a scream. Cody was in pain. His body convulsed, his grey flesh sheened with sweat. He wasn't in control. Whatever creatures forced him to find solace in heroin were in control. And they wanted to be fed. They needed to be fed. They would do anything to be fed. They were shrieking inside his brain and crawling around under his skin. They wouldn't be denied. He shook his head as if he was trying to clear it, backed away another step, came up against the wall. He leaned against it, his body beginning to sag, and his voice that of a little boy.

'I need her… I need her…'

The hand with the gun lowered slightly, the barrel pointed at the floor, as if he didn't have the strength to aim it any longer. His knees buckled but the wall held him upright. He wiped his forehead with his free hand, then smeared the hard tears away with the back of the same hand. Father Verne saw the young man was almost done and moved forward slowly.

But Cody's creatures, those demons that raged within both him and his sister, were awake and alert and dangerous. Cody saw the movement and was instantly erect. The gun whipped up. He shouted, 'Don't!'

And he jerked the trigger.

The report cracked up and down the hallway and somewhere a young woman screamed.

Father Verne felt the bullet sing past his head, where it burrowed into the wall behind him. It was a substantial building, the walls on the ground floor solid brick, so it did no harm. He realised he'd closed his eyes, expecting the slug to hit him. When he opened them again Cody was staring at the gun as if he'd just realised it was there. He seemed surprised. Rage began to build inside the priest. This little shit had come into his refuge with a loaded weapon. He'd threatened the young people. He'd discharged the gun. His patience only went so far. He clenched

115

his fists and darted forward, ready to knock the gun flying and then tackle the man – the boy – behind it.

Cody snapped the gun directly into Father Verne's face.

Father Verne froze. He so wanted to slap the weapon away. He so wanted to slap the boy away.

'No,' said Cody. Just one word. His voice steady. Even.

There was a different look in Cody's eye now. A more determined look. It was as if firing the gun that first time had given him confidence: it had shown what he was capable of, had made him realise the power he had in his hand. Father Verne realised at that moment that it hadn't been shock he'd seen in the young man before, it was an awakening. The convulsions had stilled, even the sweating had stopped. Cody was a new man now. And he was ready to do what was necessary to get his sister back, as well as payback for all the slights, all the disappointments, all the shit that had rained down on him from the day he was born. The priest before him was the embodiment of all that was bad in his life and perhaps if he could do this one thing, this one very small thing, simple really, just squeeze the trigger, send a round the two feet between them and into his head, then perhaps it would make up for it all. A little bit. Just a little bit…

His finger tightened on the trigger.

Father Verne knew there was nothing he could do but wait.

'Cody, don't…' The voice was soft and weak. It was filled with agony and dread. It was at once a plea and an order. It was Shayleen.

She stood in the doorway to her room, her t-shirt and track suit bottoms soaked with sweat and clinging to her bones. She hung against the frame, a wisp, a wraith, a shadow, so pale and transparent she seemed between this world and the next. And yet she had the strength to climb out of bed, to come to the hallway, to stare now at her brother, her face set, her eyes locked on his.

'Enough, Cody. Please.'

Her voice was not as strong as her will. It was hoarse and thin.

116

'You're coming with me, sis,' said Cody, the gun not moving a fraction.

She shook her head, slowly, gently, as if any sudden movement would send it tumbling from her shoulders and bouncing down the hallway. 'No,' she said.

Cody risked a quick look at her. 'You don't belong here, sis.'

She shook her head again. Her strength was failing. She couldn't stand up much longer.

'You belong with me, sis,' said Cody, his tone rising. 'We need to be together.'

'I can't, Cody. Not again. Not now. Not ever.'

Tears dammed again. 'You're my sister!'

'And you'll kill me. And you'll kill yourself.' She'd managed to pack some power into her words and they hit home. Cody stiffened, but the gun still didn't lower. 'We're dead, Cody, as good as, if we go on like this. If *you* go on like this. Dead. I don't want that. I don't want to be dead. I want to be alive.'

'Their life? His life?' Cody waggled the barrel a little in the Father's face.

'My life,' said Shayleen. 'I want my life. And I can't have it with you.'

Cody searched for the words. He hadn't expected this. She'd said something like this before, but she'd always come back. This time something stood firm behind the words. This time she meant it.

Father Verne spoke softly. 'Listen to Shayleen, Cody. You don't want this to get any worse.'

Only Cody's eyes moved, flitting back and forth between the priest and his sister.

'Give it up, Cody,' said Father Verne.

Slowly, so very slowly, he raised his hand until it hung beneath the gun. If Cody saw the movement, he didn't acknowledge it. His eyes had settled on Shayleen. The tears were flowing now. His voice was once again that of a little boy. 'Please, sis…'

Shayleen shook her head once more, then turned away, disappeared with faltering steps into her room.

'Sis!'

He watched the open door, hoping she'd reappear, but she didn't. He knew then. She'd never return to him again.

'Cody,' said Father Verne, gently, and he waited until the youth's gaze eased his way. 'Let me have the gun.'

Cody stared at him and then he focussed on the weapon hanging between them. He didn't move as Father Verne raised his hand and gently wrapped his fingers around the muzzle. He didn't resist as the priest forced the weapon down until the muzzle was pointed at the floor between them. He didn't protest as the gun was eased from his grasp.

Father Verne inhaled deeply, feeling the tension that had gripped him slough as he exhaled. He slid the magazine out and ensured the chamber was empty, then tucked the automatic under his jacket. He reached out for Cody's shoulder, but he jerked away. 'Leave me alone,' he mumbled.

'Cody – son – you need help.'

Something like his old defiance returned and Cody straightened his shoulders. 'Not from you. Never from you.'

Then he turned and walked back down the hallway, the onlookers scattering in his path. At the exit he turned back. 'I won't forget this, ya bastart,' he said. 'You've split up my family. You've stole my sister. I won't forget this. I won't forget either of you.'

And then he pushed himself through the double glass doors and was gone.

Chapter Nineteen

If I hadn't been keeping an eye on my rear view, I might've missed it. It wasn't a white hatchback and it wasn't a white van, it was a blue Vauxhall and it was following me. I knew it. Yup, spidey sense. It picked me up as soon as I left Acapella. It was parked along the road and when I pulled from the small car park, I saw it nose out. As we headed city-wards on the East Kilbride Road, it hung at least two cars behind me. I repeated the process from my journey to the restaurant, made some turns, watched it make the same turns, still keeping its distance but clearly on my tail. I couldn't see how many people were inside, but there was certainly more than one.

I turned into a small side street, watched it follow. It was one of those narrow, very quiet suburban streets with cars parked nose-to-tail on either side of the road, leaving a navigation space in the middle so narrow you felt as if you should breathe in sharply. I slowed, for there was always the danger of a child or a pet darting out suddenly, and checked my mirror. Yup, they slowed.

I'd had enough of this. I was certain they'd been on me all the way to Busby but I hadn't seen them. Now they'd made their presence known. Well, as the wise man once said, bugger this for a game of soldiers.

I slammed on the brakes and jerked the gear into reverse. Many people aren't comfortable with going backwards but it doesn't bother me. In fact, I'm quite good at it. Even so, just for a moment I wondered what the hell I was doing. They, hopefully, thought the same. The Vauxhall came to a halt and the driver tried to reverse but the car's tail wavered slightly and was in danger of slamming into one of the parked cars so he gave up, came to a halt. I brought my Ford right up to the Vauxhall's nose and climbed out, being careful not to dunt the car parked closest to me with my door. The Vauxhall sat at a slight angle and I could see there were three men inside. As I approached, a few well-chosen curse words ready to spring to my lips, the passenger door opened and Tank Milligan unfolded himself through the door, as if the car was giving birth. It was quite a feat in the cramped space available. I almost handed out cigars. He placed his hat squarely on his head, swung the door shut and moved in my direction.

'Dominic Queste,' he said, unnecessarily, I felt, as I know my own name.

'Tank Milligan,' I said, as we were being formal.

'Someone wants a word.'

'And what word would that be, exactly?'

Tank held out a mobile phone and I put it to my ear, heard a voice saying, 'The word would be keep your fuckin nose out of my business.'

It was considerably more than one word, but that didn't matter. I knew the voice.

Fast Freddie Fraser.

'Get over here, Queste. And I mean now. Just you, don't phone they Sutherland bastards, otherwise I'll be hyper un-fuckin-chuffed.'

The line went dead. I knew if I didn't do as I was told, the phone wouldn't be the only thing in that condition. After all, he'd asked so nicely. However, me being me, I wasn't about to go meekly.

'Tell Freddie I've got an appointment,' I said, and turned. Something big and powerful grabbed me by the back of my leather jacket. The leather was already distressed, but the muscle behind the grip caused it considerable anxiety.

'Don't screw around, Queste,' Tank said. 'The man says he wants to see you, so that means the man will see you.'

I like to think I squirmed out of his hand somehow, but I think in actual fact he simply let me go. I turned to face him. His face was impassive. He knew I was coming along with him. I knew I was going along with him. However, I wasn't done being an idiot just yet.

'Fine,' I said. 'I'll follow you over there.'

He smiled. Well, his face creased, at least. 'No can do, wee man. Something tells me you'll go on your merry way and we'd need to find you again, not that it'd be a problem. Or you'd phone your pals and get them to meet you, which doesn't make any difference to me, but Freddie wants you and only you. I don't want to disappoint Freddie. He's really looking forward to seeing you.' Tank squinted over my shoulder, bobbed his head. 'There's a space up ahead. You can leave your heap there and we'll drive you back when Freddie's finished with you.'

Thoughts of taking issue over his dismissal of my car were banished when he gave me what was for him a gentle shove. I staggered back a good four feet and he followed me. He gestured to whoever was driving the Vauxhall to follow us. It was obvious he had no intention of letting me get in the car alone. I decided to acquiesce. After all, I'd made an effort to protest, so my manly pride was salved. Tank crammed his bulk into the passenger seat and stared straight ahead as I settled behind the wheel.

'You know, I don't need a co-pilot,' I said. 'I can park all by myself now. I can even do a three-point-turn.'

'Yeah, right,' he said. 'Pull in up there.'

I sighed and did as I was told. He was right not to trust me. I didn't want to see Fast Freddie. The diminutive little gangster didn't like me much. He didn't like many people, to be fair, but he had a special lack of affection for former customers who have crossed him once too often. Whatever I was heading for, I wasn't going to like it.

Chapter Twenty

Fast Freddie earned his nickname as a youth, when he was so fleet of foot no-one could catch him. He would've been quite the athlete had his tendency to steal everything that wasn't nailed down, glued tight or just too heavy to heft not proved more powerful. I suppose it wasn't his fault: it was in his genes. His father was a thief, his grandfather was a thief, his mother was so sticky-fingered they could sell her hands as flypaper. Someone somewhere took a leak in his gene pool and he was destined to be what he was. Which was a right little bastard.

Now, though, he was one of the city's big men: an ironic statement if ever there was, for he could model for garden gnomes. He sold drugs, he extorted, he used to back armed robbery, but that's gone out of style now. Now he bankrolls identity theft schemes and online scams. In fact, if there's anything crooked going on in the West of Scotland, Fast Freddie's in there giving it yet another twist. He was in his sixties now, his face tanned through regular visits to his villa on the Costa del Crime and his running days behind him. He sat at a desk so huge it always made me wonder if he's over-compensating for something. According to filthy rumour, he was both short in stature and manhood. He was married but that didn't stop him from coupling with any female who was overawed by his criminal – and violent – reputation. One loose-lipped former consort once confided in a drunken moment to Hamish that she'd seen larger cocktail sausages. As for his performance, she'd experienced longer and more satisfying sneezes.

Tank followed me into the office overlooking the vast discount carpet warehouse Freddie used as his base. The building had once been a cinema, but it had closed in the '60s, when the industry was in decline. Freddie had established his office in what had been the projection booth and fitted a large picture window so he could watch his salespeople making him more money. Not that he needed the income, because his criminal enterprises were the real cash cows. It was said he was a multi-millionaire. I don't know if it's true, but knowing the vast and varied array of underhand activities in which he was involved, I could believe it.

He didn't ask me to sit, so I didn't. Tank stood behind me like a threat waiting to be uttered. Beyond him, at the only door out of the room, another two bruisers played at statues, both big men but reduced to hobbits in comparison with Tank. They watched us with bored expressions. I wondered if they'd still look as bored if Freddie set them on me. They probably would. After all, it was business, not pleasure, and I was nothing to them.

Freddie sat back in his big leather chair, looking like Ronnie Corbett without the laughs.

'You could've called me, Freddie,' I said. 'Issued an invitation. There was no need to send the heavy mob.'

'I wanted to make sure you came. On your tod.'

In other words, no Duncan and Hamish. Freddie didn't play well with others at the best of times, but he really didn't like dealing with the boys. He didn't much like traitors, and that was how he saw them since they had crossed the floor to the side of the angels. Well, sort of. In truth, the Sutherlands were positioned somewhere between devils dancing and angels singing. Freddie looked at me with the distaste of a Brexit supporter for a Continental breakfast. I was an ex-junkie and he didn't like ex-junkies. Junkies lined his pockets, ex-junkies didn't. Tank's presence bothered me, but Freddie didn't normally station men at the door. The inference was that I may not be leaving without assistance. And said departure was perhaps via a window.

Putting on my brave face and trying not to think of forcible defenestration, I said, 'Okay, so how about we get to the point?'

He got right to the point. 'Where's my gear, Queste?'

'What gear would that be, Freddie?'

His little face creased with irritation. It does that a lot, especially around me. I have that effect on a lot of people. 'Don't mess me around, bawbag. The jewellery Tank here gave to that bastard Price to shift.'

'What's that to you, Freddie?' I'd already guessed that he was Tank's silent partner, but I like to piss him off. Probably not the wisest course of action, given the collective muscle I sensed flexing and extending behind me, but no-one ever said I was wise. Freddie would have provided the necessary seed money to get the job done. Theresa Cohan had said it was a professional job. A house in Hyndland, owned by his Lordship the judge, with a top-of-the-range alarm system and a safe considerably more secure than a jewellery box on the sideboard. I didn't see Tank having the dexterity or know-how to pull it off, so specialists would be needed and specialists like to be paid. Sometimes it's a cut of the proceeds, sometimes it's a flat fee. I was guessing this was a flat fee deal. I also began to wonder where Tank heard about the jade in the first place. He wasn't exactly the sort to rub shoulders with those who rubbed shoulders with judges.

'What it is or isn't to me is neither here nor there,' he said, then paused, presumably to give me time to figure that one out. 'I want the gear or I want my cash, simple as.'

'I haven't got either,' I said, then added, 'simple as.'

He studied me. 'I could have Tank here go to work on you – you know that, don't you? One word from me and he'll tear off your right arm and use it to beat the living shit out of you. You want that?'

I threw Tank a look over my shoulder. He smiled back, letting me know it would be his pleasure. I really didn't want my right arm torn off. It's one of my two favourite arms. But I gambled Freddie wouldn't do that because it would bring the Sutherlands into it. He didn't like them, but he had a healthy respect for them. Unlike me, Freddie was pretty wise. At least, I hoped he was.

I decided to tell him something. 'Sam Price is dead, Freddie, did you know?'

I could tell from his expression that he didn't. 'What happened?'

'He was murdered.' I looked back at Tank again. 'Where were you the night before last, Tank?'

He smiled. 'You think I offed him?'

'It's a possibility.'

'Why would I do that? I needed him alive to move the take.'

Move the take. Under different circumstances, Tank and I could've been buddies. Or perhaps not.

'Maybe he already had moved the take,' I said, thinking on my feet. 'Maybe you killed him and then pocketed the proceeds.' I gave Freddie a pointed look. 'All of the proceeds.'

I saw Freddie's beady little eyes slither away from me and onto Tank. The big guy was aware of it too, because his little smile was gone. 'Bullshit,' he said.

'I dunno,' I said, warming to this idea. 'That Imperial jade? It's worth a fair bit. For all I know you could've decided to trouser the whole kit and caboodle.' I wondered briefly what a caboodle was and why it needed a kit, my thoughts being easily distracted, but I forced them back to the matter in hand. 'Someone gave him a going over a couple of weeks ago. That could've been you, Tank. Maybe that same someone scared him enough to make him leave town fast. But that someone tracked him down – you were in his flat, you could've seen the same photographs I did, come to the same conclusion. I saw the body. It wasn't pretty. The kind of work a butcher might do. Know anyone who used to be a butcher, Tank?'

Tank's good humour had evaporated by the end of my little speech and he stepped forward, a hand raised in my direction. I stepped back, realising I'd gone too far, and prepared to make some show of defending myself. But I knew I was in for a world of pain.

Freddie's voice stopped him. 'Relax, Tank, he's just trying to get your goat.'

I was, but that didn't mean I'd scored the big man off my suspect list. He could easily have headed up to Perthshire after our chat in Sam's flat and then be back in time to run into the Sutherlands in the pub, not to mention pick the lock on my front door and leave me the phone. Sure, the whole disembowelment thing was heavy-handed for a Glasgow crook, but Tank had been in the land of the free and home of the serial killer for some years. Who knew what bad habits he'd picked up?

He stopped, but his angry eyes remained locked on my face. He wanted to hurt me very badly.

'Tank,' said Freddie. He didn't need to say it loudly. He may have been knee-high to an ewok, but he wasn't someone you wanted to cross.

Tank took a breath, let his muscles relax and fixed his smile back on. 'I never double-crossed a partner in my life,' he said.

I shrugged as if it remained to be seen. I'd planted a seed in Freddie's head. I'd also pissed off Tank, which was perhaps not a good idea. But hey, one more person pissed off at me didn't matter, in the grand scheme of things.

Freddie pinned me with those beady little eyes of his. 'Right, Queste, here's the deal. You find my gear. You bring me back my gear. Or the money. One or the other, makes no difference to me.'

'And if I can't find it?'

'Then Tank here does what he does best.'

Tank grinned. I was less than enthused.

I kept my voice nonchalant. 'And what's in it for me?'

'You mean apart from keeping all your limbs?'

I admit that sounded like a good enough reason, but I wasn't going to let him bully me. Well, not easily.

'Freddie, I've been threatened before. In fact, if I'm not threatened at least once a day, life gets a little dull. And you know and I know that if anything happens to me, my pals will come right for you and man mountain here. He's a big lad, sure, but that only makes him an easier target. So, you want me to find the jade or the proceeds thereof? I want to know what I get in return.'

He sighed. 'Jesus, Queste, can you no take a warning like a normal person?'

'This is business, Freddie. You want the gear, you want me to find it, you pay me.'

Tank butted in, 'How do we know he won't take it right to the cops if he finds it?'

'That's exactly what I'll do if we don't reach an agreement now.'

Tank made a sound that was a cross between a laugh and cough. 'You're a funny guy, Queste, I said that before. I didn't know you were a tough monkey too. I like tough monkeys. I like the sound they make when they snap in two.' The way he said 'tough monkey' made me think of Ernest Borgnine as Fatso Jutson in *From Here to Eternity*. That made me Frank Sinatra as Maggio. I kind of liked that. But Fatso killed Maggio. I didn't like that. Tank made his intentions clearer.

'Let me work on him, Freddie. I'll not hurt him much. Just a little.'

Freddie seemed to be considering this, and I feared I'd pushed it too far. I didn't want to be hurt, not even a little. I'm allergic to pain, especially my own. Thankfully, Freddie shook his head.

'No,' he said. 'He's just at it, so he is. He likes to think he's a tough monkey, but really he's just a scared little chimp. He'll do what I want because not doing what I want will piss me off. And he doesn't want to piss me off.'

He was talking to Tank, but he was looking at me. I knew there was no offer of money coming. I wasn't surprised: Freddie's so tight, if he was diagnosed with too much sugar in his urine he'd pee on his cornflakes. He was right, though – I really was just trying to piss them both off. It's a bad habit I should break myself of, before someone broke me. And Tank was up to the job.

'So we finished now?' I asked.

He sat back in his chair, narrowed his eyes. 'Aye, you can bugger off now, Cheeta.'

Cheeta – a Tarzan reference, the loincloth's chimp pal. I was impressed. I didn't know Freddie knew anything but how to screw people in order to make money. It occurred to me there was a primate theme to the room – I was both a tough monkey and a chimp, while there were two gorillas at the door who would unzip me like a banana if Freddie gave the word. I moved to the door, circumnavigating Tank like a roundabout. I almost indicated.

A thought struck me. 'By the way, Tank – does the name Paula Rogers mean anything to you?'

His face crinkled. 'Never heard of her. Who is she?'

'Forget it,' I said. I got to the door, nodded to the two gorillas, still looking bored, before Freddie spoke again.

'And Queste?' I turned back. 'Pray you don't piss me off.'

That was two pieces of advice on seeking divine guidance in the space of an hour, from two different people. Maybe it was a sign. Or maybe Father Verne had been outsourcing.

* * *

True to his word, Tank accompanied me to where I'd left my car. I sat in the back with him while one of the gorillas drove. I sensed Tank was displeased with me. I think it was the forceful push as I climbed in that tipped me off. On the way over he'd been silent but relaxed, now I sensed tension. I had the impression we weren't BFFs any more. We drove in sullen silence for about ten minutes before he spoke.

'You were out of order back there, Queste,' he said. His voice was a low rumble. I swear I could feel it vibrating the car. It was like holding a conversation in Sensurround.

'Sorry I hurt your feelings,' I said.

His head swivelled to face me and his eyes were deep, cold pools. 'You think you're something, don't you? You think because you've got those Sutherland boys at your back you're invincible.' He leaned in closer and his voice dropped. 'You're not invincible, and neither are they. You get in my way? You piss me off any further? I'll roll over them and I'll roll over you, no problem.'

I was about to make a smart retort when he suddenly lashed

out. I've been hit before, but never like this. I jerked sideways, banged my head against the car window. I think I may even have passed out for a brief moment, although I'm not sure. I remember the pain, I remember the flashing colours, I remember contact with the glass. Then the next thing I remember is Tank hauling me upright by the shoulder and getting in my face again.

'You deserved that, you son of a bitch,' he said, his anger bringing his years in the US out. 'You try any of that shit again, I'll tear your goddamn head off.'

I tried to say something but my mouth just wasn't working. My brain seemed to have downed tools too. I hoped my bodily functions wouldn't come out in sympathy.

I don't know how long I lolled in the back seat with the pain burning its way through my face, certain I could actually feel my jaw swelling. Tank didn't say anything further, not even goodbye when the car stopped beside mine and I all but tumbled out. I stood beside my car, fumbling in my jacket pocket for my keys, as the Vauxhall took off. The rollercoaster in my head was coming to a halt, but the pain remained, and I felt a little sick. I managed to get inside and slumped behind the wheel, my head against the seat rest. I eventually eased forward and studied my face in the rear view. It wasn't pretty. Of course, George Clooney has nothing to fear at the best of times, but my encounter with Tank's fist had made things worse. There was already a dark smudge growing on my cheekbone in the centre of a livid patch. I feared I may end up with a black eye. That was my chance of getting on the front cover of Vogue out the window for the foreseeable future. I might've made Facelift Monthly, though.

After a few minutes I felt the candyfloss in my brain fully evaporate and I set off for the city centre.

Chapter Twenty-One

'You're late.'

There was no irritation in the voice, it was simply a statement of fact. After all, I really was late.

'Ten minutes,' I said.

'Late's late,' said Alicia, seizing her handbag from the back of the chair and throwing it over her shoulder. 'Come on, I need a smoke.'

She gave the owner of the bar a wave and pointed outside. He nodded, knowing her habits. Alicia couldn't go fifteen minutes without a smoke, so he'd keep the small table in the corner of the bar open. Her high heels rattled a brisk tattoo as we headed out, her long brown hair swinging like a pendulum ahead of me. I was wearing sensible shoes, but I still had to put a spurt on to keep up. Alicia was small and ever so slightly overweight, but she moved like the Bionic Woman on laxatives. She walked fast, she spoke fast and she thought fast.

We stepped outside, where four other customers had already fired up. Nicotine was never one of my problems, thank God. However, in my day I'd had enough trouble with other substances not to condemn anyone who did. Of course, that was then and this is now, and I'm a different man. As Mae West said, I'm as pure as the driven slush.

It was fairly gloomy inside the bar and once in daylight, she paused from groping around in her handbag to peer at my recent disfigurement. She wore glasses when she was writing, but refused to wear them in what she called 'real life'.

'Should you not be ringing a bell somewhere and saving Esmerelda?' She asked.

She's all heart, is Alicia.

'Bit literary for a tabloid hack,' I said.

She shrugged, went back to rooting inside her bag. 'Saw the film,' she said. 'Who knew Victor Hugo created singing gargoyles?'

Alicia surprised me by producing an e-cigarette from her bag and sticking it in her mouth. She saw me looking at it.

'Doctor's orders,' she said. 'Got to cut down on red meat, get more exercise and give up smoking, so I thought I'd give one of these bloody things a go.'

'How's it working out for you?'

'Like smoking Doctor Who's sonic screwdriver.'

For as long as I'd known her, and that was a long time, Alicia Wickes had been enveloped in a cloud of smoke. Sometimes talking to her was like being in a scene from *Backdraft*. She was one of the canniest reporters on the newspaper, a smart operator with the sharpest nose for a story I've ever encountered. And her tongue could slice bread when she needed it to. She's one of the few former colleagues who would still talk to me, for when I fell from grace, I disappointed a lot of people. I hurt a few. Even stole from a couple. Addiction is hard on friendships.

She studied my cheek again. 'So what happened?'

'My face threw itself at a guy's fist.'

'Stupid face.'

It's been said before, I thought.

The e-cigarette bubbled as she took a draw, then blew out the smoke. Or whatever it was. 'So,' she said, 'Paula Rogers. What's the interest?'

'You mean, what's in it for you?'

She smiled. 'I was being nice.'

We were pals, but that only goes so far. Alicia hadn't kept her position as Queen Bee of the city's crime reporting clan without taking care of business. She'd seen free sheets come and go, she'd seen the rise of the young, sober techno kids, she'd seen accountants have too much say in the running of news desks. She'd been threatened by crooks, cops and corporate lackeys. And she was still standing.

'I promise you'll have first crack at the whole thing, once I know what it is.'

'And you don't know what it is right now?'

'I don't even know what day it is right now, Alicia.' That was true. I was still a bit punchy. 'But I'll get there.'

'You always do.'

This time I wasn't so sure, but I kept that to myself. 'So what can you tell me?'

She didn't take out a notebook or a tablet, or even an old fag packet covered in scribbles, as one veteran reporter of my acquaintance was wont to do. Alicia had an incredible memory, hence her nickname, Wickesepedia.

'Paula Rogers, age 22, originally from Edinburgh, over here to study at the music college…'

'The Royal Conservatoire of Scotland,' I corrected.

She grimaced. 'Aye, always make me think of posh jam or a fancy garden shed, that name. Anyway, she played the cello – was bloody good, from what I heard, and would've gone on to be a leading light in some orchestra somewhere, boring the arse off people who raise their pinkie when they slug their wine.'

I smiled. It hurt, but I did it. Alicia was a strict rock-and-roll chick for whom culture was something that grew in petri dishes.

'Right, so she's this really bright, really outgoing lassie – pretty, too – who's apparently all the fun of the fair but then, all of a sudden, she changes, turns introverted, uncommunicative, misses classes. She even stops playing her cello.'

All this I knew, but I also knew better than to interrupt Alicia when she was in full flow. That way can lie a split lip. She took another drag, then jerked her head over her shoulder at two other customers who had joined the happy band of smokers and were now puffing on similar devices.

'It's getting like Planet of the Vapes out here,' she said. 'So, right. Where was I?' She paused to gather her thoughts again. 'Aye, she goes off the rails. Really downhill. Her pals try to get her to talk about whatever the hell was bothering her, but she snubbed them. Told them it was nothing. But there was something. Her flatmate knew it but he couldn't get it out of her.'

She was taking another mouthful of fake smoke so I risked a question. 'Flatmate or boyfriend?'

'Strictly flatmate. He's gay, another music student. Wants to write Broadway musicals. Christ, he's a walking cliché, but he's a nice lad.'

'Has he got a name?'

She shook her head. 'Nah, he likes to be known as a symbol, like Prince used to.' She gave me a stern look. 'Of course he's got a name. Les – for Leslie – Lancaster. Les Lancaster. It's like something out of a superhero comic, isn't it? Anyway, he says there was something really bothering her. He thought at first she was upset because she'd broken up with her boyfriend.'

'And the boyfriend? How'd he take the break up?'

'He didn't seem to care much that he'd been dumped, by all accounts. Seems he was less serious about the relationship than she was. Men, eh?'

I remained silent. I am one, after all, and it wasn't my place.

'Les says there was something else, something that made her dump the bastard down south. But he didn't know what.'

I had a suspicion that Paula did it to protect her boyfriend, but I kept it to myself.

'And then she was found in Queen's Park. A dog walker found her body up near the flagpole. I don't know what we'd do without these dog walkers finding bodies up and down the country. Poor lassie had been dead for hours by that time.'

'How did she die?'

'Police have never released that information.' Alicia sucked her e-cig again, then put it away in her bag.

'But you know, don't you?'

She gave me a look. 'Does it matter? The girl's dead and some bastard killer her.'

'It matters,' I said, experiencing an unwanted flashback to Sam Price's corpse. I shuddered. Alicia clocked it.

'You cold, wee lamb? Come on, let's get you inside where it's warm. Don't want you catching a chill.'

We bustled back inside, where a glass of whisky and water awaited Alicia's return. She was old school, all right. We settled back at the table and a waitress came over and asked me if I wanted something to drink. Alicia's eyebrows raised when I ordered some water. I said to make it sparkling. I like to live dangerously.

'Water?' She said as the waitress left.

'I'm driving,' I said.

'Sucker,' she said, looking at the menu.

'So,' I leaned forward, 'how did Paula die?'

Alicia turned the menu over, studied the specials. 'She was beaten and she was strangled.'

I sat back, took this in. I expected her to be stabbed. A different MO from Sam's death. 'Did she put up a fight?'

Alicia nodded. 'She scratched him. They found skin and blood under her fingernails. But there's no DNA match.'

That meant her killer had never been arrested before. He was nameless, faceless.

A shadow in a cowl...

Pushing the image out of my mind, I said, 'You got the address of her flatmate?' She was way ahead of me. She slid a yellow post-it slip across the table.

'Remember, darling, anything you get, you come to me.'

'Always,' I said.

She smiled. It was meant to be pleasant, but it reminded me of a shark. 'Good,' she said, then returned to the menu. 'I think I'll have the double bacon burger and chips.'

'I thought you were on a health kick?'

She gave me an innocent look. 'It'll have lettuce and tomato on it!'

We ordered – I had a plain burger and chips, if you're interested

– and then I asked, 'What about the cop in charge of the case?'

'DCI Hambling? What about him?'

'What's he like? A good cop? A bad one? Efficient? What?'

She sipped her whisky. 'Ambitious, good clear-up rate, the Paula Rogers case apart, of course. He's got the reputation for being a bit of a bastard, though. Can be a bit on the fiery side. There have been a couple of claims he's been a bit too fast with his fists, but nothing's ever stuck. He is not someone you want to piss off, Dom.'

'As if I would.'

'Just saying. From what I hear, he's not above taking you up a back alley and kicking seven shades out of you.'

I thought about the look he'd given me in the restaurant. 'Anger issues?'

'And then some.' She caught something in my expression, because she stopped short. 'Dom, you haven't got in his face already, have you?'

'Maybe just a little bit.'

'He give you that?' A finger raised towards my cheek and I instinctively recoiled.

'No, that was someone else.'

'Been making friends and influencing them to batter lumps out of you again, then?'

'It's a gift.'

'Same old Dom. Well, if you irritate Hambling I've only got one question – you like red or green grapes by your hospital bed?'

I thanked her for her concern. If I told her I'd also annoyed Fast Freddie and Tank Milligan she might've upgraded it to some magazines too.

Chapter Twenty-Two

I spent another two hours with Alicia – she'd explain her lengthy lunch to the desk by saying she was talking to a source, which was the truth – and then swung by Ginty's salon in the East End. I knew I shouldn't do it – I wasn't in the habit of popping in – but couldn't help myself. The Nightcaller had me rattled and I needed to make sure she was okay.

She was fine, she had another two stylists with her and they each had customers. She looked at the welt, frowned, but said nothing. That wouldn't last.

The address Alicia gave me was on Allison Street, near Queen's Park, and on my way home, so I called in. It was a third-floor flat in a tenement block made of sandstone stained almost black by generations of dirt and smoke. I knocked at the door, pressed the bell and knocked the door again, but no-one answered. Scribbled a note with my phone number and dropped it through the letterbox. I hoped I'd catch the would-be Sondheim sometime soon.

As I drove to Battlefield, I passed the gates to Queen's Park at the top of Victoria Road and considered wandering up to the flagpole where Paula's body was found, but decided against it. It wouldn't help me and, anyway, it was a steep hill. To be honest, that was the clincher. Give me a break, I hadn't slept well the night before, a big palooka had just used my face as a punchbag and I was tired.

It was dark by the time I reached my street. There was no convenient parking space near the opening to my building and I had to walk back from the corner. It had been sunny and dry all day, not warm but not exactly chilly. Now that sun was gone there was a noticeable nip in the air, and I hunched into my leather jacket.

I didn't see them waiting for me in the parked car, but I heard the window being wound down and an instantly recognisable voice reached out as if it was feeling my collar.

'Queste.'

I leaned down and saw Nick Cornwell's big boxer face staring out at me. He wasn't smiling. He seldom does. Well, not at me. At home he could smile like a politician on the stump, for all I knew.

'Get in,' he said, before I could greet him with one of my usual witticisms. Truth be told, I was so tired and sore, I was tapped out. Still, a please would've been nice.

The back door swung open and I saw Theresa Cohan waiting for me. I gave her a smile. She gave me one back. She took in the lump on my face as I ducked in but didn't say anything. Then as I settled, I saw there was another person in the car grinning at me over the passenger seat.

'Val,' I said, genuinely pleased, 'good to see you again.'

'And you, Dom,' said DCI Roach, toasting me with the cup from her Thermos. So she really did travel with her coffee. I liked her consistency.

Cornwell grunted. He had a variety of different grunts to suit each occasion. This one was a disapproving grunt because I was so informal with a visiting police officer – and she was equally informal in return. I ignored him. Hell, had I not been a proper Glaswegian, I'd have leaned over and air-kissed her.

'So what brings you to the big city?' I asked.

'Oh, you know, I like to come down every now and then to gaze in awe at the big buildings and the paved streets.'

'We've got electric lighting too.'

'So I see! We live in a wondrous age.'

I laughed. She laughed. Theresa stifled a laugh. Nick Cornwell grunted.

Val noticed the bruising. 'What happened to your face?'

'Slipped on a bar of soap,' I said.

Nick turned round and had a look for himself. I swear there

137

might even have been the faint glimmer of a smile. 'Lucky that fist was there to break your fall.'

'Might've hurt myself, otherwise.'

He grunted, no doubt wishing it had been his fist, but he didn't press the matter.

'DCI Roach has come down from Perth on inquiries, Queste,' he said. 'It turns out we have mutual interests in Mr Samuel Price.'

'Deceased of this parish,' I said. I can't help it. Nick just brings out the worst in me.

'I spoke to Mr Price's sister,' explained Val.

'Nice lady,' I observed.

'Very nice lady,' she agreed.

'Too nice to have a scumbag in her life,' said Cornwell. 'But he's out of it now.'

'Now, now, Nick – mustn't speak ill of the dead. It's unbecoming.'

He twisted round. 'I wasn't talking about her brother. I was talking about you.'

'Nick, sticks and stones may break my bones, but words can lead to therapy.'

'Stick a sock in it, Queste. I'm here to tell you to cease and desist whatever the hell you're doing. Whatever you're into, it stops now. These are big boy's games we're playing here. Murder most foul.'

'Thank you, Margaret Rutherford,' I said.

Nick gave Val a sort of "what did I tell you?" look and turned away again.

'Dom,' said Val, ever the gentle touch, 'we need to know everything you know. You saw what happened to Sam Price. Whoever did that must be caught.'

I'll bet a reporter somewhere was dusting that final quote off for use in a story.

'We found nothing in the cottage that helps,' Val continued.

'And someone had turned over Price's flat here in Glasgow,' Cornwell threw in. 'I wonder who that could've been?'

'Wasn't me,' I said, which was almost the truth. 'What about Sam's computer?'

'Password protected,' said Val. 'But it was no match for our techno geeks. They're the real deal – they have *Star Wars* toys on their desks. They got in, but there was nothing of interest on his hard disc or in his email account. So just at this moment, you're all we've got. We need to know what you know.'

'Val, what I told you was the truth. I was asked to find Sam, I found him. Naturally, I would prefer that I'd found him hale and hearty, but that wasn't to be.'

'We think it's connected to the jade, Mr Queste,' said Theresa, the formality for Nick's benefit, no doubt. 'If you have anything to tell us about that, it could help.'

I jerked my head imperceptibly towards Nick. 'It's okay,' Theresa added, 'I told DCI Cornwell about our little chat.'

I'll bet that went down well, I thought. He wouldn't like me knowing the time, let alone details of an ongoing criminal investigation.

'I don't know anything about that,' I said. 'If I did, I'd tell you.' I hoped my poker face was holding. The numbness from my cheek helped. I offered a silent prayer that my voice wasn't doing a Michael Jackson.

'First time for everything,' Nick muttered.

'Dom,' said Val, 'you need to listen to us. You need to pass anything on that might help us catch this killer and then you need to stay out of this.'

It was tempting, it really was, but it wouldn't help me with the Nightcaller. They didn't expect me to back away, they were just going through the motions. I saw Val glance at Nick Cornwell and he gave her a nod. She took a sip of her coffee and then said, 'You told me about a white hatchback parked outside Yew Tree Cottage. We made routine checks of filling stations, just to see if any vehicles answering that description were recorded on their forecourt videos.'

'Needles and haystacks come to my mind,' I said. There must be a load of white hatchbacks on the roads.

'Yes, but we are very thorough out there in the wilderness. And we got a break. A white hatchback pulled into a small petrol station in the early hours of the morning, heading back to Glasgow. The filling station owner doesn't have CCTV, but he does make a habit of recording the registration numbers, makes and models of all vehicles who pull in. He's been stung by people filling up and driving away. We got a hit, someone known to the police, as they say.'

She paused, sipped her coffee. I think it was for dramatic effect. It worked. 'Well?'

'The car is registered to William Milligan, an address in Knightswood. Do you know a gentleman called William Milligan?'

My cheek burned at the mention of the name. 'I've heard of a Tank Milligan.'

Nick's grunt had a 'Why am I not surprised?' feel to it. I ignored him. Val gave him another glance and received another barely imperceptible incline of the head. 'We wondered if you might know where he is? We've called at his home address, but he's not there.'

Another surge of pain at my cheek. 'Not a clue,' I said.

DCI Roach stared at me. She had the same look in her eyes that Ginty had when she knew I was lying. It's most unsettling. I glanced at Theresa beside me. She had it too. I wondered if it was a female thing, but then I saw Nick had twisted round again. Nope, the look knew no gender barriers.

'Do yourself a favour, Queste,' said Nick, 'if you know where Milligan is, tell us.'

'I don't know where he is,' I insisted, which was true. What I wasn't telling them is that earlier in the day I'd been up close and painful with him.

Nick made a noise that was part sigh, part clearing of the throat and all exasperation before he turned away again. 'You can go now,' he said.

I was dismissed. I almost saluted before I climbed out of the car. No-one said goodbye. And I thought we'd been getting on so well.

Chapter Twenty-Three

The first thing I noticed when I entered my building was that the lights on the ground floor were out. Some brightness from the street lamps probed the long corridor leading to the two flats on the ground floor, while the lights on the half landing above were still working, but the passageway leading down a short flight of stairs to the rear exit was a pool of black. It took me back instantly to my childhood in Springburn when we used to avoid the 'Dunny', the lower floor leading to the back courts. As kids, we never ventured down there after dark, for an old man who lived there scared the bejesus out of us. I'm sure he was a perfectly nice senior citizen, but we thought he was a vampire. If the lights in the passages of our close weren't working it could only mean, in our childish imaginations, that he had extinguished them and was waiting for us to venture into the darkness. He'd grab us, take us away to his flat in the basement and it'd be fangs for the memory. I didn't give the lights in my building being out now much thought, however. I'm older and I'd put away childish things. Bulbs, after all, can fail. Anyway, I was tired and I was sore. I wanted a drink, a bath and another drink. I wanted to sleep and not think about murder and psycho killers and gangsters who might be psycho killers.

I dragged myself up the stairs to my first-floor flat. Each step was laboured because, frankly, I'm getting too old for all this stress. I might not've wanted to think about Tank Milligan and Sam Price, but I did. So the hatchback may have been Tank's.

But if he was the killer, he would've known what he was going to do when he headed up to Perthshire, so why use his own car? He was an experienced criminal, he would know there was always the chance it would be traced.

It was as I reached the half landing that I heard it.

Breathing.

Worse.

Asthmatic breathing.

I stopped, listened, felt my nerves tingle as I tried to pinpoint the direction. I blocked out all other sounds, focussed on that one.

Downstairs. In the well created by the stairs and the rear door. The Dunny, said a child's voice so very like my own, where the monsters live. Down there. In the dark.

I froze, listened to the laboured breath. I leaned over the bannister, stared into the black hollow. I saw – thought I saw – something move, something solid, something large.

And then...

'Hello, Dominic.'

The distorted voice was mocking, goading even, and it spurred me into movement.

I took the stairs two at a time – I don't know where I found the energy, but fury and adrenaline is a powerful combination – and reached the ground floor just as I heard the back door bang against the wall as someone (*something*) wrenched it open. I threw myself through it and out into the night air. The back yards were hemmed in on all sides by the tall tenements. Squares of light dappled the dark walls of the buildings, but very little reached the rear courts themselves. I paused, my heavy breathing frosting slightly, my eyes straining through the darkness, but I saw no-one running away, heard no footfalls echoing in the night. My eyes accustomed themselves to the gloom and I began to make out the dark shapes of the bin shelters and the metal railings which separated each tenement's back yard from its neighbour. I cocked my head, listening for breathing, and heard nothing but a faint breeze ruffling the patchy grass and weeds.

'I know you're out there,' I said, keeping my voice low. There was no need to disturb the neighbours. 'Come on, why not finish this now, show yourself?'

I stepped gingerly forward, heading towards the low level brick construct that housed my building's wheelie bins. He could be hiding behind there, inside there. He could've leaped over the fences and made it out of the back courts, for all I knew. If I'd seen him fleeing I reckon I could've cleared the railings too, given the right motivation and a decent run-up, but I didn't seen any dark figures doing the two-minute hurdle so I didn't try. Still, it didn't do any harm to talk. I took careful steps forward, my eyes doing their best to pierce the shadows around me.

'So what is it, then? You frightened of me? Eh? That what it is?' I suddenly lunged round the corner of the shelter, but there was no-one there. I froze again, listened. No breathing. No sinister chuckling. No voice from the darkness saying my name. I waited. Stopped breathing. Kept listening.

Nothing.

Then: something moving, from behind the bins. I leaped back. I may have given a girlie scream of which I'm not proud and was very glad Hamish hadn't witnessed. Something slipped away in the darkness; something low down, on all fours. A cat. Or a very big rat. Or that guy's head that sprouted legs in *The Thing*. I let my heart settle down and peered again into the darkness, ears straining to pick up harsh, laboured breathing. Other than my own.

But nothing else moved in the gloom, nothing asthmatic wheezed, no hooded figures skulked. There was just the breeze and, faintly, the sound of a TV being played too loud. And, eventually, blood pounding inside my head.

Even so, as I made my way back to the rear of the building, I was certain I could feel unseen eyes burning into me. Something unreal but itchy crawled up my back and nestled on my neck and I whirled round, expecting to find a figure made of darkness watching me from a safe distance. But there was nothing.

Telling myself to behave, I headed to my flat.

* * *

I knew he'd been in the flat again. Maybe it was the strains of 'I'm Sorry' floating from the living room that tipped me off. I stood in the doorway for a moment, letting Brenda's feisty but melancholy voice wash over me. I gave the lock on the door a look that would've made it cringe in shame had it been human. I knew the flat was empty, but I picked up the baseball bat all the same. It comforted me. I held it two-handed and shoulder high as I moved carefully into the living room. The logical part of my brain told me there would be no-one there but the illogical part vowed to swing like Joaquin Phoenix in *Signs* if there was. I stepped through the door, my eyes automatically flicking to my mini cd player, where I could see a disc spinning through the plastic cover. I clicked Brenda off mid-apology and looked around. Nothing seemed out of place. He'd left no new gifts, as far as I could see. So what the hell was he playing at?

And then the phone in my pocket beeped.

His phone.

I took it out, saw another text.

Turn on TV. Press PLAY on DVD.

Dread building, I fired up the screen and followed the instruction. I felt something lurch deep inside when I saw Ginty inside her salon. He'd obviously filmed her from across the road; the only sound was that of traffic and, faintly, harsh breathing. The zoom was unsteady and slipped in and out of focus as she moved. She was smiling and laughing with customers, unaware that a bloody maniac was watching her. The image tightened further, into her face, became fuzzy and then sharpened again. My fingers squeezed the remote as I thought of him being so close to her. There was a time code in the corner. Today. While I was with

Alicia. While I was scoffing a burger, this maniac was scoping out my lover.

I wasn't surprised when the phone rang. I knew he'd call.

'You bastard,' I said, and was greeted by a wheezy chuckle.

'Just a reminder, my friend. I can get to her anytime I want. *Any time* I want.'

'You bastard,' I said again. I'm sorry, but my rage was such that my command of language escaped me.

'You've been nosing around, haven't you? After I told you not to.'

'No, you didn't,' I said. 'You told me not to tell anyone about our little chats.'

Another chuckle. 'Well, that was my bad, wasn't it? Then let me add another little rule. Keep out of this, Dom. Your friends will be all the better for it. I promised you a warning, you've had it. Soon, I'll send you a message that is…shall we say, more pointed?'

I was fed up with his games. 'Let's get this over with, eh? What the hell are you waiting for? Let's end it.'

He laughed. It sounded tinny through the distortion. '*Mano a mano*, eh? How very macho of you.'

'No. I've simply had enough of your shit. Let's stop the game playing, eh? How about it?'

'No, no, no! I'm still having fun. Are you having fun?'

And then he hung up. I recognised his final words. Another movie reference, this time *Fallen*. The words were uttered by a demonic killer to Denzel Washington. Jesus, he was either a real movie nut or he'd done his homework.

And what the hell did he mean by a message that was more pointed?

Chapter Twenty-Four

The figure glided across the back court. The door opened as if by magic. Up the stairs to my front door, which swung open as if in welcome. Down the hallway, into the bedroom just like before. I watched it from the bed but was unable to move. I still couldn't see its face but I could hear its breathing. Strangled. Laboured. It was painful to listen to, but it didn't impede its almost graceful movement as it floated to the side of the bed and leaned over to study Ginty, sleeping by my side. It gently caressed her hair, a slow movement, loving even. She didn't stir.

There was a sound I couldn't identify.

Something monotonous. Something insistent.

The figure's head turned to me, saw I was awake. But I couldn't move. I heard a chuckle, something deep and forbidding that rose from the depths of the throat. The face was in permanent shadow, but I knew it was smiling at my impotence. It stepped aside and showed me what lay behind. Three bodies: Duncan, Hamish and Father Verne, their throats raw and oozing.

And the sound, still there. In the distance. Faint.

The claw moved suddenly,, grasped Ginty by the hair, dragged her upright, exposing her naked body, making her scream and struggle but it wouldn't do any good and she called out my name and reached out to me but I couldn't move, I tried but I couldn't, and I couldn't make a sound, I tried but I couldn't, and I couldn't save her, I tried but I couldn't.

All I could do was watch as the figure held Ginty firmly with one claw and then with the other slice a bloody furrow across her throat…

146

And the sound stopped.

I sat up in bed, a cry strangled in my throat. I looked at the space beside me. Empty, of course. Ginty hadn't come over the night before. After I'd watched the DVD, I'd asked her to, but she said no. I said I'd go over there, but again no. She had early appointments in the morning, needed a decent night's sleep, and she knew that wouldn't happen if we were together. I knew that too.

I told myself she was perfectly safe. The Nightcaller needed her as a pressure point. That was fun for him. But all the same, I urged her to ensure her door and windows were locked. I know she found that strange, but I didn't care.

'Erasmus,' she said, 'what the hell is going on?'

She had questions that I wasn't ready to answer. At that point, I just had to be certain she was safe.

I put a smile into my voice. 'Can't a fellow be concerned for you?'

There was a silence, and I knew she wasn't buying it. 'Secrets, Dom,' she said, her voice sharp. Like a claw. And then she hung up.

I lay in bed, the echoes of the sound from my dream still with me, but now I was awake I knew what it had been. My phone had been ringing, but the nightmare had such a hold that I couldn't wake. I heaved myself out of bed, still weary, and felt the tightness on my cheek. I wondered if it was simply bruised or if Tank had broken my cheekbone. I checked the mirror on the sideboard as I passed. My jaw was swollen and blackened, but I could still work it. I could still crack wise when the notion came upon me. I was pleased, even if the rest of the world wouldn't be.

As I padded into the hallway I glanced at the front door. It was locked and bolted. I knew it would be, yet I needed the reassurance. The nightmare had given my heebie-geebies the willies. In the living room I picked up the phone and dialled 1571. Two messages, the first from Les Lancaster, Paula's roommate, telling me he'd be available for a chat between ten and eleven that morning.

The second was from Father Verne. There was a tension in his voice I'd never heard before.

'Dom, you need to get over here. Something's happened.'

I glanced at the clock. It was eight. I had time to get over to the refuge in the East End and then back to Allison Street before eleven.

* * *

The blood covered the flattened grass in a long streak. It was thick and dark and glistened with the remains of early morning dew. Mist hung around the small copse of trees behind the refuge, muffling the sound of traffic on Edinburgh Road. We were standing a fair bit way away from the blood stain, but we could still see it clearly. A couple of stony-faced uniforms made sure we kept our distance. The trees were taped off and I could see plainclothes officers and some technicians doing whatever the hell it is they do. Me? I was having a flashback to my dream.

A hand like a claw, holding Ginty...

'Young Jason found it,' said Father Verne. 'He'd had a bad night and he came out here at first light for some air. He likes to walk through this little wood; it seems to help.'

I didn't know young Jason, but knew what he was going through. Sometimes you had to get out and hope the cold air will cool your fevered mind.

I asked, 'But no-one saw anyone hanging around last night?'

Father Verne shook his head. 'There's no exterior lighting. Someone could stand here for hours and not be seen.'

'Probably turn out to be pig's blood,' Hamish said. 'Some idiot dealer or pimp's idea of scare tactics.'

It wasn't unusual for the low-lives to try to warn Father Verne off. Hamish, of course, could have been right. Only I knew he wasn't. I knew who did this.

A throat, gaping...

Blinking away the image, I watched as one of the crime scene technicians knelt, tweezed some items from the grass and placed them in an evidence bag.

'What's that?' Hamish asked, squinting to see.

'Fag ends,' said Duncan, his eyes always keener.

'Whoever smoked them stood for a while,' I said. 'His back to the tree, probably watching the refuge. Someone came up behind him, sliced his throat.'

Hamish asked, 'How the hell can you tell that, Sherlock?'

'The size and direction of the spray – the killer cut the artery. It would've gushed like a bastard. The victim would've bled out in minutes. None on the tree.'

They were unimpressed by my deductive powers. Hamish snorted. 'Dom's been watching *CSI* again.'

I didn't answer him. I didn't have anything to say, I had no quips. No one-liners. No snappy comebacks. Just the image of a hooded figure, made from darkness.

Pushing it from my mind, I turned to Father Verne. 'Everyone accounted for?'

He nodded. 'Everyone's safe, no-one missing. Thank God.'

'Still think it'll be pig's blood' Hamish said, but there was doubt there and we all fell silent as we watched the investigators doing their thing. Then I realised that Duncan was staring at me. They'd all noted my bruised face when I arrived and I saw no reason to avoid telling them how I got it. I knew that next time they met, Tank would be chastised, and I for one was not about to do anything to stop it. But that wasn't the reason for Duncan's stare. It wasn't pig's blood, but it was a warning.

I saw a claw, holding Ginty. Another claw, arcing upwards, opening her throat…

This was the Nightcaller's pointed way of telling me to back off. But I knew he had me in his sights and he wouldn't stop until he'd done what he set out to. The question was, did I involve the brothers and place them in harm's way?

I returned Duncan's gaze as innocently as I could, but he knew I was hiding something.

Chapter Twenty-Five

Les Lancaster wasn't what I expected. He was a student – arts – and I'd been prepared for someone carefully scruffy, maybe with a beard and longish hair. What I got was a man in his twenties with a smart haircut and a suit. He had a beard, though – one of those hipster things that look as if it's been cultivated like a garden. The suit was grey pinstripe, with a blue silk handkerchief carefully flowering from the top pocket. He wore a blue tie on a white shirt with a grey strip so understated it was almost an hallucination. I wondered if it was a pose, or perhaps some kind of artistic statement. Do you still get young fogeys? I don't know. For my part, I was like a charity shop on legs in my customary distressed leather jacket, jeans, brown boots. No tie. I only have one tie, a black one, which I keep rolled up in my glove compartment in case of funeral emergencies.

The flat in Allison Street wasn't what I expected. It wasn't in the least rundown or untidy. It was neat, it was tastefully if inexpensively and minimally furnished, and it was painted uniformly white. There was no clutter, no rock or protest posters on the walls either. It was so spick and span I thought I'd wandered into an episode of a TV design show. After a diet of *The Young Ones* on TV, this young man was blowing a whole host of preconceived notions on student life out of the water.

Lancaster gestured to me to take a seat on the two-seater couch against the wall and said, 'I'm still getting ready for college, Mister Queste, so can we chat while I do so?'

He was English, very well spoken. I wondered why he came

north for his education, then recalled that the Conservatoire has an international reputation and attracted students from around the globe. Even Dundee. I took in his suit, crisp shirt and carefully knotted tie. Still getting ready? He looked more than ready to me. Did he sleep in that suit?

But all I said was, 'No problem.' I can curb the smart-arseness when I need to, and anyway, my mind was still filled with the blood streak at the refuge and my quandary over telling Duncan and Hamish about the Nightcaller. I noted that in my mind it wasn't an *if* any more, it was a *when*.

The young man stood over me for a beat, taking in the bruise on my face. 'That looks nasty,' he said. 'How'd that happen?'

My hand automatically twitched towards my cheek, then dropped back again. 'Wasn't looking where I was going. Walked into something.'

He didn't need to know that something was a fist. He nodded, having no reason not to accept my clumsiness, and turned to the door. 'I'll be just in here – sing out what you need to know.'

He vanished into the small hallway and I saw him turn right into what I'd noticed was a box-like bathroom. I had the impression he was eager to talk. Perhaps this was the most exciting thing that had ever happened to him. Perhaps he really wanted to help. The police investigation seemed to be getting nowhere and it was possible he wanted someone, even a stranger, to tell him that Paula's killer would be caught. Even so, I didn't want to launch straight into it. Better to ease my way in. Get him talking about himself to break the ice.

'So, you're a student at the Conservatoire?'

'Yes,' his voice slightly echoing in the bathroom, 'studying composition.'

I already knew the answer to my next question, but I asked anyway. 'What would you like to write? Classical music?'

A cabinet door opened and closed. 'Good grief, no! I want to write musicals – Broadway, you know?'

'Sounds good.'

'You like musicals?'

'I've been known to whistle a happy tune, now and then. Matter of fact, I've always thought there should be a follow-up to *Oliver* using songs from the '60s,' I said. 'It could be called *Let's Twist Again*.'

Okay, I was tired and worried, but I wasn't dead yet. There was a pause. That often happens when I crack a joke. It doesn't bother me. I know they're laughing on the inside. He let the line go unremarked and next thing I heard was the sound of something being slapped onto his face, aftershave or cologne, maybe. Something tasteful, I'd bet. Maybe it would cover the stink of my joke. I suspected this guy was all about the skincare too. And who's to say he's wrong? I'd had a shower, brushed my teeth, shaved with an electric razor, squirted some deodorant on, and that was the extent of my toilette. I knew I could benefit from a touch of the metrosexual. Let's just say I was under some stress and the interrupted sleep patterns were taking their toll. The bags under my eyes were so heavy I'd soon need a porter to carry them, and my skin was badly in need of some kind of reviving unguent. However, I'm a middle-aged Glasgow male and we don't do that sort of thing. Next thing you know we'd be hugging.

Time, though, to get to the point. I began with the easy one. 'So, what can you tell me about Paula?'

'She was a lovely girl,' his voice floated through the open door. I heard the cabinet close again. 'Bright, outgoing, beautiful. She filled a room like sweet music.'

That seemed an overly florid way of describing her, but he was arty. He wanted to write musicals. Maybe he was composing a song about her.

'But she changed, right?'

'Yes,' he called back. 'It was very noticeable. She became... Shadowy is the only way I can put it.' He came back into the room carrying a dental floss container. I hoped he wasn't going to use it in front of me. There's something about watching someone slipping a piece of thread between their teeth that I find discomfiting. Thankfully, he didn't.

'Shadowy?'

He nodded. 'Before she was like…'

'Sweet music?'

'Bird song,' he said, just to spite me. 'But then she became carrion call. All low register, sinister. Like a sudden shadow across the sun.'

Good grief.

'And any idea of the cause?'

He shook his head, stepped away again. I knew he was flossing because I could hear the change in his voice, it became a touch strangled, less distinct, as he threaded. 'She wouldn't talk to me. Just stayed in her room, didn't go out much, missed classes. It really wasn't like her. It was like she had a worry so deep that it was permeating her every thought, eating at her like a cancer.'

I thought of the Nightcaller. I thought of the video of Ginty. I thought of my dream. I thought of the blood trail at the refuge. I pushed them all away. I can do that easily. I've had lots of practice.

'I take it her belongings have been taken away?'

'Her parents took most of it, the police took some. The rest is still here, in her room.'

That surprised me. 'You've not taken another flatmate?'

There was silence for a moment and when he stepped back in his eyes were dipped towards the floor. 'No. I felt it was somehow…disrespectful.'

'You don't need help with the rent?'

'No, I'm blessed in that regard.' His eyes raised again and I saw they were bright with tears. 'Would you like to see her room?'

I did. He led me across the hallway and opened the door to a remarkably large bedroom with windows that looked down onto Allison Street. It was obviously a woman's room. It was bright and clean. The curtains were full and flowing. The bed was large and covered with soft cushions. The duvet was floral. A framed print of something colourful and continental hung on the wall

153

opposite the bed. A cello – a big, bloated violin – sat in the corner of the room on a stand like a memorial.

I asked, 'Is that Paula's?'

Les looked wistful. 'Yes. Her people couldn't bear to take it. It spoke too much of her, I suppose. She was very talented, a new Jaqueline Du Pré. Are you familiar with the classics?'

'A little.'

He leaned back on his heels, studied me. 'Tchaikovsky, right?'

He had me pegged. If old Pyotr Ilyich was alive today, he'd be writing film scores. 'Mostly.'

He stepped to the cello, reached out and caressed it. There was something tender in the movement, something loving. 'She was perfecting the Elgar Concerto when she…' He let the thought hang there. 'She could move you to tears with a single sweep of the bow.'

He fell silent as he stared at the instrument and stroked its polished wood. He rocked to and fro, as if he could hear his friend once again playing something soft and mournful.

I left him to his thoughts for a moment, then asked, 'Did Paula receive any strange mail?'

There was another silence while he gave me a curious look. 'You're the first person to ask that. The police didn't.'

They didn't know what I know, I thought. 'Did she?'

'I can't say for certain, but I did notice she seemed to dread the postman. That didn't stop her from getting to the mail first when it came.'

'Did you notice any large envelopes addressed to her?'

He sat down on the corner of the bed, smoothed out some wrinkles on the duvet cover with the same tender movement as before, and faced me. He sat very upright, legs together, and folded his hands on his lap.

'Mister Queste, why are you asking these questions? What exactly is your interest in Paula's death?'

I'd been surprised he hadn't asked that before. All I'd said in my note was that I was looking into it. 'It may have a bearing on another matter,' I said.

He studied me, thinking this over. 'Do the police know you're asking these questions?'

'They're aware of me,' I answered, carefully.

'Aware of you,' he repeated, and for the first time I sensed real suspicion.

Time for some truth. 'Les – can I call you Les?' He nodded. 'Listen to me. Paula was murdered. Your flatmate. Your friend, right?' He nodded again, but I could see he was beginning to wonder if talking to me was a good idea. 'The police aren't getting anywhere, you know that. Now something else has happened that relates to Paula's death. I can't tell you what it is because, believe me, you're better off not knowing.'

'There's been another murder, hasn't there?'

I didn't say anything. I didn't need to, he could see it on my face. He stood up again, walked around the room, a sudden nervous energy galvanising him. I thought for a minute he might burst into song.

'I knew it. I knew it would happen again. I knew it…'

'Why?'

'Paula. She changed, you know that. Something made her change. It wasn't natural, whatever it was, it was…'

He looked for a word. I ventured, 'Unnatural?'

He stared at me, probably gauging whether I was mocking him. I wasn't. It sometimes just comes out that way. 'Whatever it was, Mr Queste, it was vicious, nasty.' He paused, I thought for dramatic effect. 'Something evil.'

Normally I'd have smiled. Normally, I'd have made a smart comment. I didn't. Because – and I pause here for dramatic effect too – what had forced Paula to change was, in fact, evil.

Les returned to the corner of the bed, sat down, smoothed the duvet again, arranged his legs just so, adjusted the crease in his trousers so they hung correctly, clasped his hands, rested them on his lap. Then he took a breath. 'Yes, Mr Queste, I saw one large brown envelope, but she snatched it away from me. She wouldn't say what was in it, just took it into her room, closed the door. But

I heard her through the door. She was weeping, Mr Queste. I'd never heard her weep before. She was usually like...' He paused to think of another description.

'Bird song?'

'The first rays of the sun on a summer day...'

Dammit!

'But whatever was in that envelope made her weep.' He paused, reassessed his words. 'No, more than that,' he said, 'whatever was in that envelope made her *keen*. Do you understand?'

I nodded. A keen is an Irish funeral song. When used as a verb it means to wail. Paula had done more than simply cry as she sat alone in her room, no doubt staring at the contents of that envelope, whatever they were. She had grieved. She had lamented. And as I stood in that bright, airy room, I thought I heard the faint echoes of her sobs still.

'And you told the police about that?'

He nodded. 'They didn't ask straight out like you, but I told them about it, as an example of how she'd changed. She was always very open about her life, prior to that. It was if she didn't care what people knew of her, of her life. She'd leave bank statements lying around, didn't care that I knew about her finances. I didn't pry, but I'll admit I saw them. She didn't have any money worries, in case you were going to ask.'

Alicia had already told me there were none, but it never hurt to check, so that was one question scored off my mental list.

'She was a free spirit, Mr Queste, free and open and delightful. And beautiful, a truly beautiful person.' Tears began to brim as he thought about her. 'I loved her, Mr Queste. Not in a sexual way, for my tastes lie other ways, but in a truly romantic way. I begged her to talk to me, to confide in me and the old Paula would have. But that Paula? The shadowy Paula?' He shook his head, one hand dabbing at the moisture seeping from the corners of his eyes. He rose sharply, moved to a box of Kleenex on a small bedside table. He plucked two out and sopped up the tears properly. I wondered why he didn't use the hankie that bloomed from his jacket and guessed that was just for show.

'And you never found out what was in the envelope?'

'No.' He took a breath. 'But I did wonder if it was something to do with a man called James Mortimer.'

'Who's James Mortimer?'

'I borrowed her laptop once, I saw it there. She'd forgotten to close her internet search and the file was still open. A newspaper report on this man Mortimer. He'd been murdered a few months before.' He looked straight at me. 'It remains unsolved.'

A cold breath tickled the hairs on the back of my neck. A cold, asthmatic breath.

'Did you tell the police about this?'

'Yes, but they didn't seem to think it was important.'

'And she never talked to you about it?'

'No. As I said, I tried to get her to talk, but she wouldn't. She shut me out completely.'

'Is there anyone she would've discussed it with? Her boyfriend?'

Lancaster gave a small laugh, but there wasn't much humour to it. 'Him? No. He was just something pretty who liked to have something just as pretty on his arm. Totally self-obsessed. She wasn't so much a girlfriend to him as an accessory. He wasn't the sort of person you could have an intimate conversation with, unless it was all about him. Paula was besotted with him, but she was aware enough to know that he wasn't the person to turn to. Unfortunately, neither was I, as far as Paula was concerned.'

'And there was no-one else? Her parents, maybe?'

A slight shake of the head, then a thought. 'There was Julio, but he told me she cut herself off from him too. That affected him deeply, because he always had a secret longing for her.'

I thought, *Julio?* Then I said, 'Julio? He doesn't work in a restaurant in Busby, does he?'

He nodded. 'Acappella, yes. Julio worshipped Paula, and not from afar. He was like a little puppy at her heels. She was kind to him, liked him well enough, but not in that way. I do know she confided in him.'

So Julio had a connection to Paula Rogers. And he worked in a restaurant owned by the wife of the cop in charge of the case. And he had a crush on Paula – and, from what I'd seen, one on his boss. Interesting.

I carried on, 'But not her parents? He shook his head. 'Any siblings?'

'Only child.'

'So there's no-one she would talk out problems with?'

'Her uncle, but he passed away.'

'Could that be why she turned from bird song to carrion call?'

A shake of the head. 'No, the accident happened after she changed.'

'What kind of accident?'

'He was hit by a car,' he said. 'Hit and run. They never got the driver…'

Chapter Twenty-Six

I had decided to have another look around Sam's shop, hopefully uninterrupted this time. When I found the envelope I more or less gave up – and then DC Cohan had arrived. The job was half done. I should've checked the other sides of meat for the keys to the storage unit. As I drove from the South Side to the West and Partick Cross, I thought about the new developments.

Sam Price was being tormented by whoever had killed Paula Rogers. Paula was being tormented by whoever had killed this James Mortimer. There was no link I could see between Paula and Sam, apart from the fact he was giving Bree, the wife of the detective in charge of the case, some choice cuts. I thought about that. Something wasn't quite right. Bree really didn't strike me as the type to fall for a butcher. Sam was born in Partick, he lived in Partick, he worked in Partick – hardly the ghetto, but certainly not the land of milk and money. He was rolls and sausage and brown sauce, she was ciabatta and some up-market meat I've never tasted. And no sauces out of a squeezy bottle. I know love can be blind, but those two just didn't scan. Then again, I'd sensed something about her husband. I'd seen fear in her eyes. She'd hidden it well, but it was there. And he came across as (not to put too fine a point on it) a bit of a bastard. They say all coppers are, but I know that not to be true. Sure, Nick Cornwell could be tough, but he was (generally) fair. Was there something going on in the Hambling home that had Bree seeking solace elsewhere?

And then there's Julio. Paula's confidante. Bree's employee.

159

Coincidence? They happen, but if this was fiction, no-one would believe it.

A line of traffic held me up at lights on Eglinton Street, and I seized the chance to dial Alicia's mobile. It went straight on to voicemail so I left a quick message asking her if she knew anything about James Mortimer's murder and to give me a call back. She'd know something, I was certain. The cars began to edge forward and I turned left to head for the Kingston Bridge and across the river.

Dark clouds were forming over the city. Our period of sunshine was at an end. That's Scotland for you. If you can see the sun, it means there's rain coming. If you can't see the sun, it's raining already. I was halfway over the bridge, high above the grey waters of the Clyde, when my mobile rang. As usual, I glanced around to make sure there were no police cars before I answered. This is not recommended – don't try this at home, kiddies. Or rather, in the car. But I saw it was Alicia's number and I needed to talk to her. I managed to hit the button to put it on loudspeaker.

'What are you into, Dom?'

Despite the gloom that was making serious inroads on my normally sunny disposition, I smiled. 'And hello to you too, Alicia.'

'Bugger the small talk, Queste. What's your interest in this James Mortimer?'

'Still can't tell you, Alicia.'

There was a sigh and I heard the bubble of her e-cig. I could hear traffic and some muted voices behind her, and I visualised her standing outside the office having one of her many fag breaks. When I worked with her, sometimes there was so much smoke around her desk she was like Kong Island sitting in the middle of the fog bank, but that was then and this was now, and innocent lungs have rights.

'I don't see why I should be your personal clippings service,' she said. 'Why can't you use the internet like everyone else?'

'Because it would cut down on my search time for Jennifer Aniston naked,' I said.

160

She snorted. 'Yeah, I'll bet you're that sad. Not to mention desperate.'

I couldn't decide if that was a slight on me or the divine Ms Aniston, but I let it pass. 'So what've you got, Alicia?'

Another sigh, another hiss of vapour. 'James Mortimer was middle-aged, unmarried, no lasting relationships, not even a budgie, worked as a claims adjustor, found dead in his home, no sign of forced entry.'

'How did he die?'

'Strychnine. On a pizza.'

James was poisoned, Paula strangled, Sam gutted. Three different murders, three different MOs. One killer?

'Did the police have any leads?'

'He kept himself to himself, mostly. He was gay, but not openly. The feeling was that he picked the wrong man up.'

'And the guy just happened to have deadly poison on him to add to the pizza topping?'

'I know, no-one really buys it, but they hit a dead end.'

Dead end. I didn't like that kind of finality.

'What about Mortimer himself? Any personal details at all?'

'Apart from him having no family, no private life as such, no pets and no friends?'

'Everyone has a private life, Alicia, you know that. Did he read? Go to the movies? Watch a lot of telly? Make models with matchsticks?'

'The only thing he seemed to like was music.'

I had steered off the bridge and was heading west on the Clyde-side Expressway. 'What kind of music?'

'Classical. He went to every concert he could, apparently.'

'Classical music,' I said, but Alicia was way ahead of me.

'Paula Rogers was a classical musician.'

I didn't say anything, but my hands gripped the steering wheel tightly. I passed under the covered walkway that led to the SECC and the Hydro concert venue. I'd faced down a killer in that plastic tunnel once and he'd scared the living shit out of

161

me. That was nothing to the effect Nightcaller was having.

'Dom, do you think there's a link between James Mortimer and Paula Rogers' deaths?'

'Yes,' I said. There was no point in lying.

'You have to let me run with this,' she said, her voice excited.

'Not yet, Alicia.'

'Dom…'

'Listen to me. If I'm right, this is a bigger story than you know and you'll get it, I promise. Hell, you may even get a book deal out of it. But you need to give me time.'

'How much time?'

'As much as I need.' In my mind's eye, I saw her about to argue. 'No-one else will get this, Alicia, I promise you. The police haven't even made the link.'

If there was one. I was tired, stressed and my off-kilter eating habits meant someone was barbecuing in my gut. Maybe this whole thing taking shape in my mind was all shadows and fog.

The turn-off to Partick was just ahead. 'I have to go, Alicia – but promise me you'll keep this to yourself for now.'

There was a pause and I wondered if she'd hung up and was heading back to her desk, an intro already forming in her mind. Then I heard the sound of a lorry passing on her end of the line and knew she was thinking. 'Okay,' she said, but there was a sulky tone there, like a child who'd been told she wasn't getting her way. 'But you screw me with this, Dom, and I'll personally have your balls for earrings, you get me?'

'Have I ever screwed you before?'

'Only in your wildest dreams, darling,' she said, and then she was gone.

Chapter Twenty-Seven

When the door to Sam's shop closed behind me I stood still for a moment, taking in the peace and quiet. Okay, the traffic snarled up on Partick Cross still roared, but I was able to tune that out and bask in the relative silence. It had been a busy few days, and to be truthful, I'm not in the first flush of youth. I'm not old enough yet to need someone else to chew my food, but I do avoid crunching hard sweeties. My body ached. Tension will get you like that. Stress tightens muscles you didn't even know you had until they're hard enough to bounce pennies off. Whoever was barbecuing inside my gut had set fire to the surrounding brush. I couldn't keep this kind of pace up, I knew it.

I willed my body to relax, tried to force the tension from my neck and shoulders, down my arms to my fingertips, where it could burst free. It didn't work. The bastard sat where it was and stuck its tongue out at me. Ginty was always trying to get me to meditate, but I told her I did that on the potty like everyone else. Maybe there was something in it, though. Maybe I should take some time to burn some incense candles, stick some sitar music on, squat on my hunkers and get my 'ummms' out.

I flexed my shoulders, cricked my neck one way, then the other, felt those muscles protest like angry fanboys over the very idea of female Ghostbusters. I fished around in my pocket for a stray antacid, found an old extra strong mint, which was soft and chewy but would have to do. I stepped around the counter to the back rooms. I'd pretty well looked everywhere in the office, toilet and kitchen so I opened the walk-in freezer door, feeling the icy air rush against my face. I propped the door open with a plastic box filled with solid cuts of meat and, shivering, stepped in.

The sides of beef and pork still dangled from the two metal rails in the ceiling. I examined the one in which I'd found the envelope first, but didn't expect to find anything more. And I didn't. I systematically frisked the rest of the hanging meat, ignoring the cloying smell and unpleasant feeling of the hard, cold flesh under my hands, but there was nothing further hidden away under the thin coating of gauze. Standing in the doorway, I watched the dead animals swaying slightly on their hooks. I'd convinced myself that Sam would've stashed the storage container keys here. They weren't in his home, they weren't in his office, I was certain. He hadn't taken them to Perthshire, or if he had, he'd hidden them very well. He hadn't given them to his sister. Bree said she didn't know anything about them. His ex-wife knew nothing. There was always the possibility that the Nightcaller had taken them from the cottage, but what interest did they have for him? Unless I was looking at this all wrong. Believe me, that was possible.

I heard the shop door open and close. A customer was my first thought, looking for a prize-winning steak pie, so I left the cold room and pushed my way through the plastic streamers.

Tank Milligan glared at me over the counter. He wasn't a customer, but he was out for blood. His eyes burned like the acid in my stomach. His fists were bunched. They looked like anvils in a cartoon. I had the impression he was somewhat irked.

'You son of a bitch,' he said. His voice was soft, but there was enough venom to confirm his irkedness. That's not a word, but I didn't really care.

'Shop's closed, Tank – you'll need to get your raw meat else-where,' I said. I was going for breezy and I think I hit something to do with wind.

'Been looking for you, you goddamn piece of shit,' he said, suggesting that he really wasn't happy with me. I tried to think what I'd done recently to piss him off but came up with nothing since he'd brought extra colour to my cheek.

'And you've found me. You want a prize?'

He didn't answer my question. 'You called the cops on me,' he said. That raised another question.

'What?' Okay, as a question it wouldn't cause Jeremy Paxman to consider putting his microphone in a drawer, but it did the trick.

'The cops,' Tank said, moving closer. I moved back into the corridor. 'They came to my apartment, looking for me. You dropped a dime on me, you son of a bitch.'

Fine. I'd got the message that he was none too impressed with my immediate ancestry – hell, there was part of me that agreed with him.

'Nothing to do with me,' I said, injecting what I hoped was a hard edge into my voice. 'They got to you all on their lonesome.'

He stepped forward again. I stepped back again. 'Oh, yeah?'

I thought for a minute he was going to advise me to go tell the marines, but he didn't. I felt I had to fill the conversational void.

'Yeah,' I said. Were you expecting something witty?

He moved then, snatching one of the big knives from the magnetic strip on the wall. He was fast for such a big man, and if I hadn't been on full alert he might've caught me unawares. As he blundered through the streamers, I leaped back and dodged away from his outstretched hands. I knew my rudimentary Krav Maga was no match for him. I knew I couldn't trade blows with him, for he'd knock me clear through to next Wednesday with one punch. Anyway, the knife in his hand told me he wasn't planning on a boxing match. My only hope was to keep out of his reach until he tired. Big men tire easily.

I threw myself into the freezer before I knew what I was doing. Instantly I realised I might've made a mistake, for all he needed to do was kick the box away and close the door. Sure, I could open it from the inside, but he could wait until I came out, frozen, and then snap me in two. But he didn't kick the box away. His blood was up and he wanted instant gratification. He followed me inside and I backed away.

I weaved between the rows of hanging meat. 'Tank, listen to me, I didn't put the police onto you.'

'Says you.'

I knew I'd said it, I'd recognised my voice, but this was not the time for banter, no matter how weak. 'They traced your car in Perthshire.'

That brought him up short. His brow furrowed. You could've planted crops in it. 'My car?'

'You got a white hatchback?'

His eyes narrowed and he cocked his head slightly. 'It was stolen.'

'Really?' I said. 'Is that the best you can come up with? It was stolen?'

'You don't believe me? I'm hurt.'

I kept at least two sides of beef between us. 'Well, it's kind of convenient, don't you think? The car that was spotted outside the cottage in which Sam Price was murdered – a man you had reason to feel somewhat peeved about – was also sighted at a petrol station in Perthshire, and it's registered to you. Now you say it was stolen. Come on, Tank – wouldn't you say it's all about too pat?'

He thought about it. I rested both hands on the beef nearest to me. It was still swinging slightly after I'd searched it. I kept the motion going.

'I don't give a shit how it sounds, Queste,' Tank said, his lip curling. 'I didn't kill Sam Price.'

'Fine,' I said. 'All you need to do is tell that to the police and they'll thank you for clearing it up and send you on your way. They'll maybe even make you a cup of tea and give you an Empire Biscuit.'

He shook his head. 'No,' he said, 'bullshit. No way my car was up there, no goddamn way.'

And then he lunged again. I put my shoulder to the side of beef and swung it towards him. The twin momentum of his leap and the swaying beef met with a thud. A lesser man would have been

166

sent reeling, but not Tank. The beef bounced off him like a rubber ball, and he kept coming. I swerved away from him. If I could get to the door I might have a chance. Or maybe not.

We danced around the freezer, me ducking behind the carcasses, pushing them in his direction in the hope that I would hurt him somehow, him taking it like they were made of papier-mâché and swinging that bloody huge knife, the blade singing off the solid meat. I didn't know about Tank, but I was getting weary. I looked for signs of fatigue in his face and saw none. So much for big men tiring easily.

'Tank,' I said, finally, hoping some dialogue might give me the chance to catch my breath. 'Think about it – why would I tell the police about you? We're partners.'

That made him laugh. 'We're not partners.'

'Fast Freddie wants me to find the jade.'

'I'll find it, don't you worry. Freddie'll be happy.'

I edged towards the door, putting half a pig between him and me. 'One question – how'd you find out about the bangle in the first place?'

That threw him. He stopped, a look of incredulity thrown at me as he held out the knife. 'You're asking me that now? Here? When I'm fixing to cut you belly from brisket?'

The idea of me becoming a prime cut didn't appeal, but I managed a nonchalant shrug. 'It passes the time. Who told you about it? Freddie?'

He smiled. 'Screw you, Queste. This isn't no interview here.'

'Come on, Tank, what've you got to lose?'

I was about four feet away from the door by now. If I moved quickly I could make it. Tank shook his head. 'Uh-uh. Break's over and the music's playing. Let's dance.'

I didn't wait for him to lunge again. I leaped backwards, spun, making for the corridor. I didn't know what I would do out there – maybe get into the shop, grab another knife, even things up a bit – but I felt it was the only option open to me, short of him being struck by lightning, and I didn't think that was going to happen anytime soon. I moved fast but he was faster. What the hell – was he on castors?

He grabbed me by the hair just as I reached the door. Now, if there's one thing that makes me go all Hulk-like, it's my hair being pulled. Ever since I was a kid, it has sent me into an uncontrollable rage and in that respect I've not matured. I'm not sure I've matured in any respect, but certainly not that. That little bit inside me that comes to the fore very seldom was awakened and immediately took over. I bellowed, yes, actually bellowed, and lashed back with my elbow, not really feeling the sharp pain that resulted. I was lucky because I jammed it right into Tank's eye and he yelped – yup, yelped – and let go. He stumbled backwards, his free hand rubbing at his injured eye. I knew my lucky strike had presented me with an advantage, albeit temporary, and I had to capitalise on it. I didn't much fancy the bone-jarring agony of punching him, so I did what any self-respecting, red-blooded male would do – I delivered what I hoped was a devastating boot directly to little Tank. A throttled groan escaped from his throat and his face turned purple, then pale, as both hands clamped over his injured manhood. He wilted but still wouldn't go down. And he still held that knife.

I knew I had to capitalise on this immediately, because he might recover in the time it took me to get to the front shop. I needed a weapon. I needed an equaliser. My eyes rested on the box at my feet. I flipped it open, reached in, snatched a plastic bag filled with cuts of meat frozen into solid blocks. It was heavy. It was sturdy. It would do. I swung it with force into his face. Tank rocked back. I swung it back again, this time crashing against his temple. He swayed, went down on one knee but, sickeningly, still retained his grip of the knife. Had he superglued the damn thing to his hand? I held the bag in both hands, brought it up hard into his chin. The bag burst open and the contents flew out, the bones to which the meat cleaved clattering on the metal floor. The knife flew away as Tank's head snapped backwards, the rest of him followed, but at the last minute he righted himself and he shot up and reached for me, blood running in red rivulets down his face. He caught me by surprise because I really thought I'd done a number on him, but you can't keep a big man down, it seems. I tried to scramble away but lost my footing on the meat scattered all around us. He followed me down, his big hands wrapping themselves around my throat. The back of my head clunked on the hard floor and a thousand cats in heat screamed inside my head, accompanied by a blitzkrieg of lights flashing behind my eyeballs. I felt myself beginning to tumble into a deep, black hole, but knew that I couldn't. I didn't have a bungee cord or a parachute, and I wasn't sure there was a safety net. The hole had some gravitational pull and I fought against it but it looked so damned welcoming. I flapped my arms, felt them hitting something big and solid, and I realised that that big and solid thing was Tank, sitting on top of me, forcing the air from my body, his thick, powerful fingers choking what was left. Still groggy, my hands scratched and scrambled at my side, searching for a weapon, anything that I might use to get the big lump off me, but it had to be fast because that black hole was beginning to draw me in. Blood pounded in my brain and I thought it might burst through my skull. My lungs screamed for air. I felt pressure build behind my eyes as he tightened his grip.

That damned cats' chorus continued to screech something that could put them to number one, with the right marketing. Tank was smiling, the bastard was actually enjoying this, and blood dripped from his wounds onto my face. It was unpleasant, but the least of my worries. My hand found something hard and sharp. I didn't know what it was, but it would have to do, so I gripped it as firmly as I could and slammed it into the side of his head. He grunted, but his hold didn't flinch. My vision clouded and he began to fade, like a frame of melting film, and that deep, dark pit called to me again. Somehow, I found the will to send my makeshift weapon – whatever it was – crashing into his face again. My other hand found something similar and I repeated the process. His fingers loosened, but still not enough. I didn't have long before he either cut off all my air or he crushed my windpipe. And I needed that. Summoning every ounce of strength I could muster, I slammed both hands together in tandem. He wobbled. I did it again. And again. It was like I was giving him a round of applause. His fingers slackened, his head dropped, and air surged back into my chest. He slid away, crumpling in a heap at my side.

A paroxysm of coughing later, I had hauled myself to my feet and was standing over him. I was woozy, my throat burned as if the acid from my stomach had finally made its way up. I sucked in some of the cold air but only made things worse, so I forced my breathing back to normal. I doubled over, my hands on my knees, still holding my weapons, and retched. Something hot and sticky flew out and landed on Tank's suit. He didn't seem to care and neither did I. Of course, had he been conscious he might've taken issue with it. I looked at my makeshift weapons and almost laughed, would have too, if the entire room hadn't lurched to the side. I wasn't out of the woods yet. Not that there were any woods there, just those damned dead animals on their hooks, swinging to and fro, fro and to. The room pitched sideways, threatened to turn upside down. Hell, I was in *The Poseidon Adventure*. Someone fetch me Gene Hackman, I thought. No, Shelley Winters, because I was going under and she was the swimmer. But she died in that movie. Shit.

I had the presence of mind to find my mobile, punch in a number and when I heard the familiar voice I said, 'Sam Price's shop.'

Then that big, gaping hole spun in front of me and I decided it would be okay to take the plunge after all.

Chapter Twenty-Eight

It was warm and dark in the hole. I liked it.

But then the temperature dropped and the black became grey, as if the sun was coming up somewhere, but there wasn't any sun and it was turning colder, which wasn't right.

As the midtones lightened, I saw I wasn't in a hole. I was in my bed. And Ginty was beside me, but she wasn't moving and there was something dark and oozing at her throat.

Something moved at the doorway and I saw the hem of a black cloak wafting out the door and long, bony fingers snaking around the edge.

Duncan, Hamish and Father Verne lay where the figure had left them. They were dead, but their eyes were open and staring. At me.

I looked at Ginty. She was staring at me too.

They were all dead and yet still alive.

And then her lips began to move, but she made no sound.

I can't hear you, I told her.

Words formed on her lips, but they carried no weight.

I looked at the others, lying lifeless on the floor. They were mouthing the same words, but I couldn't hear them.

I can't hear you, I said.

Their lips still moved. The same thing, over and over. I wanted to lean closer to Ginty, but the gaping wound in her throat scared me. I couldn't move anyway. Tank's weight still held me down. I could feel him on my chest, his hands burning at my throat. I strained to hear the words.

But then they began to fade – Ginty, Duncan, Hamish, Father

Verne – as if someone was taking an eraser to them, rubbing them away, bit by bit, limb by limb.

But still they spoke words that no-one could hear.

When I came to I'd been dragged into the office and was propped up against the wall. Someone had thrown a tartan car rug over me. I looked at it, tried to identify the plaid. I don't know one from the other, but I tried all the same. Royal Stewart, I decided. It could've been James Stewart for all I knew, but it seemed to satisfy my curiosity. The back of my head ached where it had slammed against the floor. I couldn't tell if it was bleeding, and my body was too sore to reach up and find out. My neck was stiff and the skin was taut and burning. I swallowed, carefully, and winced as it felt like something was lodged down there. The fire in my gut was gone, though. At last, I'd found a cure.

A movement at the door drew my attention. I moved my head, slowly, carefully, because every muscle in my neck and shoulders threatened to write a letter to their MP. Duncan stood there with a bottle of water. In books, guys wake up to beautiful women offering them brandy, sometimes in various stages of nakedness. Well, in the books I read, at least. I get a muscular Geordie with a shaved head and a bottle of Tesco's still water. Real life can be disappointing.

Then I remembered the dream and I shivered, as if someone had walked over my grave. Or his.

Duncan handed me the bottle. I tried to twist the top off but couldn't. He took it from me, loosened it, handed it back. I thanked him.

'Wimp,' he said. As bedside manners go, it needed work.

'You try going ten rounds with a gorilla trying to peel you like a banana and see how you feel after it,' I said, my voice like Clint Eastwood with a really bad cold. Maybe the water would lubricate it. It felt like I was drinking rocks. I took another sip. It was better. Just felt like gravel. 'Where is the gorilla, anyway?'

'Still in the freezer,' said Duncan. 'We brought you in here in case you got piles.'

'Considerate,' I said.

'That's what friends are for.'

'He still unconscious?'

He nodded. 'Out cold.'

That made me smile. 'We need to wake him.'

Duncan shook his head. 'What we need to do is get you to a hospital. You've been out for half an hour. That's not good news.'

I struggled to get up. 'No hospitals.' I don't do doctors, they just find things wrong with you. I don't mind playing doctors and nurses, though.

Duncan held me down. 'Dom, your head's been bleeding. You could have a concussion.'

'No thanks, just had one,' I said, then a thought struck me. 'Any blood or fluid coming out of my ears?'

Duncan checked, shook his head. I was relieved. Any sort of discharge from the ear or nose after a head injury wasn't good. I've seen *Thunderbolt and Lightfoot*.

I began to struggle upright. 'Help me up. We need to have a chat with Tank.'

Duncan knew there was no point in arguing with me, so he hauled me to my feet. Once upright, I wished I was back on the floor again. The cats had given up the stage inside my head to the Royal Scottish National Orchestra's percussion section, and they were giving it big licks. The room spun in time to the beat of the kettle drums and I had to grab hold of Duncan's arm to steady myself. I felt like throwing up, too.

'Dom,' said Duncan, concern evident, but I just shook my head at him. That just made the drummers angry. Hurt like hell, too.

Duncan all but carried me to the freezer where Tank was still prone on the floor. Obviously the threat of haemorrhoids was not a consideration when it came to him. Hamish was there and he gave his brother a questioning look. I caught a peripheral glimpse of a slight shake of the head from Duncan. Hamish's eyebrows gave a little shrug and he smiled.

'You did quite a job on him, bonny lad,' said Hamish. 'What the hell did you hit him with?'

I didn't have the strength to say anything so I merely waved a finger at the meat still littered on the floor. Hamish looked at it as if seeing it for the first time, then stooped to pick up two pork chops, the meat still solid on the hard bone.

'These?' He said.

I nodded. It hurt so I decided not to do it again.

'You hit him with these?' He asked again.

I nodded again. Dammit!

'What are they? Karate chops?'

I groaned inwardly. I'd gone through all this to give Hamish a punchline. Life is cruel.

'We need to wake him up,' said Duncan.

'He's coming round anyway,' said Hamish, dropping the chops again and turning to Tank. He grasped the big man's face with one hand and gave it a shake. 'Wakey, wakey, sunshine.'

Tank's eyelids fluttered and something unintelligible dropped from his tongue. Something told me it wasn't exactly the Queen's English. Unless Her Majesty swore a lot. Hamish tapped him on one cheek, then the other. It didn't seem to have any effect so he did it again, only harder. Tank's eyes opened again and he stared at us with the kind of glazed expression you get on people who watch a lot of *Made in Chelsea*. Finally they focussed on me. He said something I couldn't make it out, but I knew it wasn't complimentary.

Duncan knelt in front of him and Tank's eyes moved sluggishly from me to him. 'Tank, Dom has some questions and you're going to answer them. If you don't, or if he doesn't like the answers, Hamish and I will take extreme umbrage.' Umbrage. Duncan had been at the dictionary again. 'Do you understand?'

It took him a few moments but finally Tank nodded. I thought about kneeling too, but I didn't think I'd get back up again, so I made do with leaning against the wall. Duncan looked up at me, Hamish reached out to steady me. I was grateful because I don't think the wall was up to it. They waited for me to say something. Even Tank looked expectant. The words were slow in coming.

There was a mist gathering in the room now and I wondered why they didn't see it. I swallowed, trying to dislodge that lump in my throat. The boys with the drums in my head were having a go at the finale of the 1812 overture, complete with cannons. The mist was beginning to rise and I waved it away with a hand. It was thick and sinuous and it wrapped itself round my fingers. I stared at it.

'You see that?' I said.

Duncan frowned. 'See what?'

I looked at him, saw the concern on his face, then back at my hand. The mist was gone. Okay, that was strange. 'Nothing,' I said, and forced my concentration on Tank, who was feeling well enough now to give me a full-on glare. I knew I had questions, but for the life of me I couldn't think of them. Then I remembered something. 'Your car.'

'I told you, it was stolen.' His voice was cracked, but it sounded better than mine. Mind you, he hadn't had his hands wrapped round his throat.

'When?'

'Two days ago. Taken from outside my apartment.'

His apartment. He lived in Knightswood. They don't have apartments. They have flats.

'Did you report it to the police?'

His face, bruised and swollen as it was, folded with disdain. 'Yeah, right.'

Of course he wouldn't report it. People like Tank had as little contact with the boys in blue as possible. Okay, he was sticking to the car theft line. Could be true. Could be a lie. I wasn't in any state to try to decide which. Then I remembered what I really wanted to know.

'The jade,' I said. 'How did you hear about it?'

He fell silent. Hamish nudged him with a toe. 'Speak up, lad. Don't make me ask you.'

Tank gave him a glare that was marginally less heated than the one he reserved for me, but he knew he didn't want Hamish asking any kind of questions. That way lay more pain. 'Sam Price. He heard about it, gave us the address, told us when the owners would be out.'

I asked, 'How did he hear about it?'

Tank sighed, gave Hamish another heated look. 'A friend, he said. Someone who knew the owners.'

If I'd been in any fit state I'd have exclaimed 'Aha!' But I wasn't, so I didn't. Instead, I sort of slithered down the wall. That mist was back and it was creeping over me. The last thing I remember was Duncan and Hamish rushing towards me as I started to slide into that black hole that was opening up beneath my feet again. I didn't know what was down in that pit. Could've been a pendulum. Could've been Quatermass. Could've been Brad looking for the missing T. Whatever was there, I was going to find out.

* * *

Fragments.

Flashes.

Sounds that came and went.

I was in the back of a car. Rain hammering the windows. Wipers waving.

Then the pit.

A severe but bored woman not looking at me as she punched something into a computer. She was behind glass. Duncan was leaning forward, telling her to hurry up. Can't we do this later? She didn't reply, just kept punching. Forms to be filled, procedures to be followed. I was in a wheelchair. As my vision slumped along with my head, I saw hospital porters in grey coats, young men and women looking very busy. One carried a clipboard. There were voices, someone singing somewhere. Somewhere Over the Rainbow.

Way up high.

I was on a bed. A face: young, handsome, stethoscope round

his neck. George Clooney used to do that, back when he was a doctor. He was saying something, but all I could hear was rain battering on the roof and against the opaque window behind me. He shone a tiny light into my eyes. Flicked it away. Flicked it back. It was bright. I felt myself flinch. Judy Garland was still yearning for a better place. But Judy sounded like she'd been on the batter for days. Alcohol had dried out her voice and left it cracked and hoarse. Only it wasn't Judy. It was a man and he didn't know all the words to the song, just the first few lines. And he was singing it over and over and over.

And as I drifted away it segued into another song being played over and over and over. A female singer, saying she was sorry, so sorry.

Then it all went black again.

Hello, darkness – missed me?

Awake again. Alone. The male Judy was silent now. Maybe he'd reached the end of the rainbow. I could hear people moving around beyond the cubicle's curtains. I tried to move, but my head hurt. I decided I wouldn't be beaten so I took a deep breath and swung my legs over the side of the bed. Lay there, my head on the pillow, my legs dangling, my body twisted in the middle like a broken doll. That wouldn't do. That little voice in my head said, *Okay, Queste, you're a proud Glaswegian – you're all pretty damn tough, let's see you prove it. Get up.* I sensed the voice was mocking me. It didn't think I could do it. Well, I'd show it who was boss. I forced my upper body to rise. My head complained. My body ignored it, kept moving. My head protested. I kept moving, trying to get erect. My head whined. I told my head to get with the programme. It didn't. It hammered and banged and sent pain coursing through my entire body. I hated my head. But I managed to engineer myself upright. Well, if upright meant sitting in a slumped position with a marked tilt to the right.

I felt myself slipping away again.

I felt sick.

I contemplated stretching my feet to the floor. I looked down.

It looked like an awfully long way and I didn't have a parachute. I giggled. I don't know, it just struck me as funny. I stretched out one foot to test the water because by this time it wasn't a floor, it was a pool, deep and blue and inviting. I kept reaching but couldn't touch it. That struck me as strange. That struck me as funny. I giggled again.

The curtain pulled back and the young doctor I'd glimpsed earlier waded through the water towards me. He didn't seem to think it strange that the cubicle had turned into a swimming hole so I didn't mention it.

'Mister Queste,' he said, reaching out towards me, 'I don't recommend moving just yet.'

He was Australian. At least, I think he was Australian. In my memory his accent was all Crocodile Dundee slipping an extra shrimp on the barbie, but I didn't see him again after that so I can't be sure. But we'll go with Australian. I wondered where his hat was, the type with all the corks on strings.

He gently forced me back down onto the bed. 'You've had quite a bang on the head,' he said. *I know*, I thought, *I was there.* 'You've suffered a severe concussion. Had you been drinking or taking any sort of drugs?'

I opened my mouth to speak, found I couldn't form the words. There were people in my life who would pay good money to witness that. I tried again, managed, 'No.' *Atta boy*, I thought.

'Okay,' he said, 'we'll take some bloods and urine just to be sure. We're going to admit you, keep you in overnight for observation.'

I knew I had to speak again. 'I'm okay,' I managed. But I knew I wasn't okay. I knew I was about to take a dive into that pit again. I'd been in and out of there so often you'd think I had a woman stashed away.

'Yeah?' he said, smiling. 'And where'd you get your medical degree?'

He had me there, right enough.

'We'll keep you in, a night, two at the most. There're no

fractures, but the fact you've been phasing in and out means we need to keep an eye on you.'

'Okay,' I said. My manly pride assuaged by my earlier protestation, weak though it was. I was ready to be ministered to by some cute nurses.

He began talking again but I didn't hear a word, not really. I drifted while he spoke and let the blackness wrap around me like a blanket.

* * *

It was dark. I was awake, but not really. The rain was still falling outside. I could hear someone snoring and I hoped it wasn't me. I was in a high bed, I was surrounded by other high beds, each one occupied. I tried to move but the bedclothes were wrapped around me like a straightjacket. Maybe it really was a straightjacket. Maybe Tank had dislodged something in my head and I was a gibbering idiot. Nick Cornwell thought I wasn't far from that at the best of times. And did they use straightjackets now? I gave up trying to move and lay still. There were six beds in total in this room. Through the double glass doors I could see a soft light at the nurses' station. There was no-one there. Probably off ministering, I supposed. A vague memory of being brought here fought its way through the fog. I recalled bloods being taken and being asked to pee into a plastic bottle.

A movement at the far corner caught my eye.

Something in the darkness.

Something taking shape.

Something that was of the darkness yet not part of it.

And then I heard it.

The breathing.

The harsh, asthmatic, rhythmic breathing.

The figure had form now. I could see the cloak and the hood and the claw-like hand reaching out towards me, one bony finger pointing in my direction.

I cried out, sat up. The man in the bed beside me grumbled, said something that was far from comforting, and rolled over. No-one else stirred, suggesting I hadn't cried out too loudly. But it was enough for a nurse to slip through the doors and come to my side. She was a big woman and she had the kind of stern face that made me resolve there and then not to mess with her. She looked like she could arm wrestle Tank and still have strength enough to give Godzilla a severe thrashing.

She asked me if I was all right and I told her I'd simply had a bad dream. She felt my head with the back of her hand and seemed satisfied I wasn't fevered. She nodded, fluffed up my pillow and helped me settle down. She tucked the sheets around me, told me to rest.

'It'll be better in the morning,' she said. It wasn't meant as a comfort. It was an order.

I thanked her and closed my eyes, heard her walk away. When I heard the doors swinging shut again I opened my eyes, stared at the corner where I'd seen the shape. I knew it hadn't really been there, but it doesn't do any harm to double check.

It'll be better in the morning, she'd said. I thought about that and finally decided that no, it wouldn't be.

Chapter Twenty-Nine

Shayleen knew that the road ahead was long and hard. She was only a teenager, but she had lived, she had seen, she had experienced. She wanted to be free of the yoke of addiction, but she knew that in a quiet corner of her brain, of her soul, the demon would always slumber, and occasionally it would awaken and demand attention. That's the thing with addiction. You're never free of it. Never. The warm feeling, the security, the high promised would be something she would yearn for many years down the line. But she would have to guard against it, because all drugs are liars. Yes, when you're high you think nothing can harm you, that the world you're trying to escape is a sham and that this feeling, this right now while the brown is surging through your veins and working its magic on your mind and body, this is the real world, this is where you belong. But it's all an illusion, and it vanishes like smoke in mist when the hit wears off and you're back in the real world and your body is itching and screaming for more and you have to get out there to earn the scratch to make it better again. So you do things that no teenage girl should be doing, no woman should be doing, and you take money for it and then you let the brown smooth it all over again, make it all right, put the men and the boys and the toys they use and the things they do out of your mind. For a while. For a little while.

And you think this isn't a bad way to go. That perhaps simply fading away, becoming one with the brown, wouldn't be the worst way to check out. Because what is life anyway but a series of painful encounters and even more painful memories? As Father

Verne said, you're either clean, using or dead. That's the addict's trifecta. She had a choice. The first choice, getting clean – staying clean – meant she had a chance at life. The second two were, let's face it, the same thing. If she continued to use she'd be dead, one way or another. She'd either get some bad stuff, contract a disease or be murdered by a punter. Or a loving sibling.

She had made attempts to get clean before, but Cody had always been there to lure her away. The last time had been when she'd been in the refuge and she'd made the mistake of going to see him. She'd intended merely to tell him that she was out of it all, that she was going to get Father Verne to help her. She knew he'd try to entice her back and she thought she could stand up to him, she really did, but she couldn't. He kept her with him, pleaded with her not to leave him, told her he needed her, that he loved her, that they were family and needed to stick together because if they didn't have each other, they had nothing. And he'd offered her some brown and she'd stared at it, watched him cook it up, saw it being drawn into the hypo and it looked so inviting and the demon in her brain whispered that just one little hit wouldn't hurt, she was strong enough to take it, just one more, one more kiss, dear, and then she could be on her merry way.

But the demon was a liar. And the brown was a liar. It told you that life could be warm and happy but it wasn't. Cody was a liar, too. All addicts are liars. They lie to each other and they lie to themselves. They tell themselves they are in control but they're not. The brown is. When Cody told her he wanted her back, he probably thought he meant what he said, but really he didn't want her, he wanted what she could provide, what her body could help him get.

She was determined to win the war this time, but it was hard-going. She couldn't sleep, not for long, anyway. She couldn't hold food down, even water made her feel nauseous. Her body switched from overheating to feeling like she was in a freezer. She shivered. She sweated. She shivered again. Her muscles ached, her nose ran, her skin crawled. Whatever drugs she was being given to beat her craving were working, but only just. She still thought about it all the time, dreamed of it when she snatched sleep, longed to feel the weight of the syringe in her hand and the first glorious, euphoric rush of the brown in her system. But she knew she had to fight.

She lay in her bed, listening to the rain outside and tried to match her breathing to its rhythm in a bid to lull herself to slumber, but it was no use. Her body was alive with unpleasant sensations, her mind filled with desire for the needle and the release. She got up and padded through the quiet hallways of the refuge, her bucket in her hand. She went everywhere with that bucket, it was her best friend: her body was still purging itself, and a puke was never far away.

She saw no-one during this nocturnal constitutional. She heard some sounds from behind doors. Groaning, murmuring, snoring. One young boy was weeping to himself. She moved on, unable to control her own emotions, let alone deal with someone else's. She paused at the entrance door, locked from the inside overnight, but the key was in the lock. She looked at it, stared beyond it into the rain sweeping across the small car park, considered how easy it would be to turn that key and slip away, find Cody, get him to fix this agony of withdrawal that made her tremble and twitch and ache and burn and freeze. She could do it. It would be so very simple. Turn the key, open the door, off into the night. No-one could stop her. No-one *would* stop her. She was free to do as she wished, Father Verne had always made that clear. But that wasn't what she wished, no matter how tempting a return to that old, familiar world was. This time, she wanted to see it through. This time, she wanted to live. She tore her eyes away from the key and moved on. Always move on, she told herself, that was the secret. No going back.

And so she kept moving through the sounds of night in the refuge and the roar of the rain as it pounded the city.

Shayleen walked the corridors twice, climbed the stairs to the second floor, returned again to the ground floor. The exertion seemed to help, for she was suddenly very tired. Sleep, though, was still something only to be dreamt of. She smiled at the thought. Was that like one of those oxymorons? She smiled again, pleased that she'd thought of the word. A week ago she'd have been so out of it, she'd never've come up with it.

She reached her room again and closed the door behind her. She'd left the little bedside light on and decided to try lying in the dark; maybe that would help. She clicked it off, set the bucket down within easy reach – she hadn't thrown up for two hours, that must be a good sign – and stretched out on top of the covers. Her skin raged and she didn't want to wrap up. That would change soon, though, she knew. It always did.

She closed her eyes, tried to sleep, willed her restless mind and body to still. She concentrated on her breathing, forced it to slow and deepen. She could do this. She could beat this. She'd been through worse in her young life.

And then she heard the voice.

'Little girl…'

It was a rasp, like a file on metal.

It took on a sing-song tone. 'Little gi-irl…'

And then a scratching, nails on glass.

She opened her eyes, looked to the window.

Cody's face was pressed against the glass. It was obscured slightly by the thin net curtain, but it was still recognisably her brother. There was another scratch and the voice said, 'Little gi-irl, come and see me…'

It wasn't Cody's voice, but she got up and stepped across the room, pulled the curtain to the side. Cody's eyes were open, but they were blank and lifeless. One eyelid drooped and his mouth gaped to reveal his tongue between his lips. She saw another figure, etched in the rain, tall, powerful, hooded. He had something in his hand.

And as she looked closer, she saw that the something in his hand was Cody's head.

That was when she began to scream.

Chapter Thirty

Somehow I managed to sleep through the night without any dreams. I think they must've given me something and for that I was grateful. When I was awakened by a nurse at 7am – hospitals believing that early to bed and early to rise makes a man healthy, if nothing else – my head still pounded, but I was given a couple of painkillers so powerful they could make the dead boogie. For the first time in days, my head was fairly clear. I thought about my clothes and wondered if they were in the tall bedside cabinet beside me. I struggled to pull myself upright. The room whirled around me and I had to sit back down again. I wasn't as fit as the drugs made me believe. The same nurse who had spoken to me in the night was at my side instantly.

'Mister Queste,' she said, laying a hand on my shoulder as if to steady me. I wanted to tell her that if she could steady the room, I'd be just fine, but something told me I didn't want to show any weakness. 'You shouldn't be out of bed.'

'I need my phone. Where's my phone?'

'It'll be in the cabinet there, but you should be taking it easy. You've had quite a bang on the head. And if the consultant sees you using the phone here, he'll have a fit.'

I didn't care about the consultant's state of health. 'I need it.' I sounded firm. She glared at me and I saw she could be pretty firm too.

'Nurse,' I said, 'here's how it'll play. I'll dig my heels in, you'll digs yours in. I'll let you think you've won and you'll go away because I'm fairly certain you've got more important things to

185

deal with than me. As soon as you've gone, I'll get up – it'll be a struggle, but I'm resolute. Look, this is my resolute face.' I pointed at my face. She looked. She didn't seem impressed by my resolute face. 'But I will get up and I'll get my phone and I'll make my call. So why don't you just save us both a lot of time and effort and give me my phone?'

Her mouth tightened. 'I can see you're going to be trouble.'

'Trouble is my business,' I said. I knew I'd get to say it eventually.

Her sigh was more exasperated than resigned, but she bent over, rifled inside the cabinet and came up with both phones. I'd forgotten about the Nightcaller's phone. 'Which one?'

'Both,' I said and took them from her.

'You need two phones?'

'I've a morbid fear of battery failure.'

When I began to pull myself out of the bed, she said, 'Where do you think you're going?'

I didn't want anyone to overhear my call. 'When nature calls, it cannot be ignored.'

'I can bring you a bottle.'

'It's not that sort of call,' I said.

'We have receptacles for that too.'

'No, thanks. I gave up shitting in bed when I gave up the potty. That was twenty years ago and I've never looked back.'

'Mister Queste …'

I pointed at my resolute face again and her lips compressed in irritation, but she helped me swing my legs out of bed. I gave her the kind of dashing, devil-may-care grin that Errol Flynn and David Niven might give as fighter pilots heading off to their death and stood up. The room spun like a dervish on roller skates, but I managed to make it to the toilet without the need of a crash helmet and kneepads. I locked myself in and checked the mobiles. On my own phone there were three missed calls from Ginty and another two with numbers withheld. I couldn't face talking to Ginty, not yet. I wasn't ready to explain.

I checked the Nightcaller hot line. There were three missed calls. No number, of course. That couldn't be good.

I speed-dialled Duncan's number. He answered on the second ring.

'Dom, how you feeling, man?'

'Like someone bounced my head off a freezer floor a few times. I need you to come pick me up. Where am I, by the way?'

'You're in hospital.' That Duncan, such a wit.

'Yeah, I guessed that, with all the doctors and nurses around here. Which one?' But before he could answer I said, 'You know, doesn't matter. Just come and get me.'

'You think that's a good idea?'

A wave of nausea hit me. I leaned against the wall until it passed. Duncan's voice swam through the foam like he was looking for Nemo. 'Dom? You okay?'

'I'm fine,' I said but I didn't feel fine. 'Just come get me.'

'What if they don't let you out?'

'They'll let me out. We got our country back, remember? That means I can tell the NHS where to stuff it.'

I hung up, gathered my strength and went back to bed. I managed to climb back in without disgracing myself. I lay back, closed my eyes, and willed the world to get off the merry-go-round. Despite the spinning, for the first time in days I was able to stop and think, about murderers and green jade and small-time catchers and high-class restaurant owners and tough cops. And finally, I began to make some sense out of it all. Well, bits of it.

Just after nine, a very business-like doctor came round with two students in tow and stood at the side of my bed. One of them handed her my chart.

'And how are we today, Mister Queste?' She asked. She was small and of Pakistani origin, but her accent was Scottish.

'Don't know about you, but I'm one bed bath away from living the dream,' I said.

She didn't respond as she looked at my notes then studied me over the rims of her glasses. 'And how did we receive this head injury?'

That was a tricky one, because there was no way on God's green earth I was telling her about my encounter with Tank Milligan.

'We fell,' I said. I could tell by her look that she didn't believe me.

'That's what your friends who admitted you said.' Inwardly, I sighed with relief at my lucky reply. 'You must've bounced a few times, because you have multiple lacerations and a number of contusions at the back of the cranium and on other parts of your body. And it also looks as if you were throttling yourself when you fell. Does this often happen? You take a tumble while choking your own throat?'

She didn't wait for a reply, which was fortunate because I didn't have one. She set the clipboard on the bed and took her little pen light from the top pocket of her white coat. She leaned in, pulled one eyelid back and did her shiney thing. She checked the other eye. 'Any wooziness or blurred vision?'

'No, but I keep seeing this bright light in my eye.'

She said nothing as she put her pen light away again and held up three fingers. 'How many fingers am I holding up?'

'One more than I usually get.'

Her jaw tightened slightly. 'Are we in pain?'

'Can't speak for you, but I'm tickety-boo.' That was a lie. My head felt as if Andy Murray had been using it as a ball at Wimbledon.

One of the students stifled a grin and the doctor treated him to a dry look as she took out her pen again, took up the chart and began scribbling something. 'Any loss of hearing?'

'Pardon?'

Another grin from the young trainee and a slight snort from other. The doctor gave them a glance that told them not to encourage me. I know I was being childish but give me a break – I'd gone for hours without making one smart-arsed comment. It was making me ill.

The doctor's eyes were challenging as she looked at me over her clipboard, daring me to make another quip. 'Memory loss?'

'No. Well, maybe. What was the question again?' What can I say? I always take a dare.

'Please take this seriously, Mister Queste. Do you know what day of the week it is?'

'Why? Don't you?'

The grinning student was ready to burst but kept himself under control. The doctor waited for me to answer, her face stern. I relented and told her what day it was. She then asked the month and year. I answered properly.

'And who is the Prime Minister?'

I winced. 'Please – don't remind me!'

She sighed. 'Mister Queste, I don't think you understand how serious this could have been. Your skull could have been fractured. You could have suffered brain damage. You could at this very moment be dead or, at the very least, in a coma.'

'But I'm not.'

'No, you're not. You have a mild concussion. You are very lucky.'

'Lucky's my middle name,' I said. 'So when can I get out of here?'

She shook her head. 'We should keep you in for another day, at least.'

I shook my head back at her. It hurt but I tried not to show it. 'No can do, doc.'

She was ready to argue, 'Mister Queste…'

'Look, I'm responsive, you'd say I'm responsive, right?'

There was a slight smile at that. 'Yes, you're responsive.'

'My eyes open spontaneously, right?'

She knew where I was going with this. 'Right.'

'And I'd say my motor responses are fairly normal. Okay, my head's sore and my throat's rough, but that's to be expected. My posture's fine, no rigidity, nothing. So what would you say my GCS would be?'

189

If she was surprised at me knowing what the Glasgow Coma Scale was, she didn't show it. I, however, was quite taken aback. I didn't even know that was tucked away in my memory somewhere. Seriously, I need to do a memory dump, like a computer.

'Based on this cursory examination and the notes from my colleague in the A&E, I'd say you were a fifteen.'

That was better than I expected. Anything less than eight and I would've been in serious trouble.

'But we really should make further tests to ensure…'

And that was when the Nightcaller's phone rang. For a moment I contemplated ignoring it, I know the doctor's expression told me to ignore it, but I knew I couldn't. I held up a finger and said, 'Hold that thought. I need to take this.'

I didn't fancy the battle to get out of bed again so I answered it where I was. I reminded myself to be careful what I said.

'Where have you been?' The voice was angry, despite the mechanical manipulation. 'I told you to keep this phone with you at all times. I told you to keep it switched on. I've called three times.'

'I've been busy.'

'Mister Queste…' said the doctor. I held up my hand.

The voice asked, 'Who is that?'

'No-one.'

There was silence then. The doctor was growing annoyed and I couldn't blame her. I gave her an apologetic shrug, placed my hand over the phone's microphone and said, 'I'm sorry. This call's important.'

'Mister Queste, we're in the middle of an examination,' she said.

'You broke my rules,' said the Nightcaller. The voice was flat now. 'What's happened is on you. I may even have done you a favour.'

Then he was gone, leaving me wondering what had happened. I'd spoken to Duncan, everyone was fine. That left Ginty. The doctor rolled her eyes as I picked up my own phone.

'Sorry,' I said, but even I was beginning to get annoyed. I hit Ginty's number and heard it ring. I willed it not to jump to voice-mail. It kept ringing. She should be at work by now, I thought. It kept ringing.

The doctor sighed heavily and gave me a pointed stare but I ignored her and concentrated on the phone ringing on the other end.

'Mister Queste…' she said.

I held up a hand as the ringing stopped and I heard Ginty's voice. 'Erasmus, where the hell have you been?'

'I'll tell you later. I'm just checking you're okay.'

'Of course I'm okay, why shouldn't I be?'

Good question. I didn't have a good answer. But I was getting there. 'I'll tell you later. Have to go.'

I rang off. I'd suffer for that later, but right then I couldn't explain. I looked back at the doctor and painted my resolute face on again. 'I need to get out of here.'

She saw I meant business. 'If you leave, it is against medical opinion.'

'Fair enough.'

She stared at me, her better judgement struggling with my determination. 'Very well,' she said, 'I'll have the paperwork prepared. But you must promise me that if you experience any extreme dizziness, vomiting or impairment of vision, you will report immediately to your GP.'

I forced a smile. 'I'm from Glasgow. What you've just described is Saturday night to me.'

191

Chapter Thirty-One

Duncan and Hamish were waiting for me at the nurses' station once I'd completed all the paperwork. They had a wheelchair ready.

'Your carriage awaits, Chief Ironside,' said Hamish with a flourish.

'I can walk,' I said. Actually, I may have been a bit overly optimistic in that regard, but I was still keeping up appearances.

'You can walk all you like once you're out of the hospital,' said a staff nurse in a tone as sharp as a drill sergeant with toothache. 'But inside this building, you'll take the wheelchair.'

Resistance, as they say in *Star Trek*, was futile, so I eased myself into the wheelchair and allowed Hamish to hurl me through the corridors at warp speed.

'Slow down there, big fella,' I said, for I had no burning desire to add to my injuries. 'You're not Charlton Heston and I'm no chariot.'

'Don't be such a wimp,' he said, and pushed me even harder. I swear I felt my hair ruffle.

They'd managed to park Duncan's car very close to the main entrance so I didn't have to walk far, which was just as well. As I slumped into the back seat, I began to doubt the wisdom of my actions. I wasn't getting any younger and all this chasing around, grappling and quick-fire banter was taking its toll. I'd also been keeping things from my friends, which added further strain. A couple of days in hospital – having my meals brought to me, nurses tucking me in – would be just what the doctor ordered.

But then the boys told me what had happened at the refuge overnight and I knew I had to be out. I knew it was the Night-caller. But what kind of favour was that? Scaring a young woman half to death? Things couldn't go on like this. I couldn't go on like this. It was time to bring all this to an end.

But how?

I thought immediately of Tank and asked where he was.

'God knows,' said Duncan. 'We thought he was out cold, but he legged it while we were loading you into the car to take you to hospital.'

I felt something akin to shame at that. I thought I'd given as good as I got, but he was clearly made of sterner stuff.

Hamish twisted round to face me. 'So you've added another martial art to your arsenal? First there was self-defence with office supplies, and now butcher meat.'

I'd once defended myself in an office with a staple gun, which gave Hamish no end of amusement. He often warned people to beware of my three-hole punch. Now I'd given him more ammunition. I waited. His karate chop crack from before wouldn't be the end of it, I knew that. But he merely smiled and turned away again.

'What?' I said. 'That it? Nothing further to say?'

He shook his head. 'Hell, no. You might make mincemeat out of me.'

Hamish always makes me realise what other people have to put up with from me. I ignored him and phoned Ginty.

'Dom, what the hell are you playing at?' I couldn't tell if she was worried or angry, or both.

I told her about Tank and concussion and hospital. I decided there was no point in lying. She'd see me sooner or later and I doubted the bruises would vanish that quickly.

Her voice changed instantly to one of concern. 'Are you all right?'

'I'll live,' I said. I'm so macho.

'Where are you now?'

'On my way home. Duncan and Hamish are with me.'

'Good,' she said. 'Stay there. I'll come over.'

'I can't, I've got things to do.'

'Stay there, Dom,' she said, her voice firm. 'Or I'll really give you a going over.'

I had no doubt she was capable of that. I gave in. Truth was, I was in no condition to go anywhere. I think a day in bed was called for. With Ginty. It was only my head that was sore. Maybe my back. Certainly my shoulders and my arms. Everything below the waist was fine. At least, that's what I told myself.

* * *

Detective Constable Theresa Cohan was waiting for me at the flat. She climbed out of a car when she saw us pull up. A big detective I'd never seen before was with her. He looked tough. He looked like he could keep a gang of drunken football supporters in line with only a glare. I'd had enough of tough guys. Theresa took in the additional swelling on my face and the way I was standing as if I was in urgent need of a walker, which I was.

'We've been calling you,' she said. So that explained the withheld numbers. 'You need to come with us, Dom.'.

'Why?'

'DCI Cornwell wants to talk to you.'

'It's not convenient right now, lass,' said Duncan. 'Dom's been in an accident. He needs to rest.'

Theresa's eyes flicked to Duncan then back to me. She wanted to know what happened, but she knew I'd have some sort of smart reply ready. She decided not to give me the satisfaction. I was glad, I had nothing. 'The DCI is quite insistent.'

Duncan said, 'He can insist all he likes, lass. Dom needs to take it easy.'

The big detective stepped forward, his body language speaking volumes. Hamish was fluent in it and I felt him tense beside me. 'This isn't a negotiation,' the cop said. 'The boss wants to see him, the boss will see him. He can relax on the drive over there.'

194

Which suggested I wouldn't be doing much relaxing once I was at the station. That didn't bode well.

Duncan sized the man up, a slight smile on his lips. I'd seen that smile before, and it usually didn't end well for the person on the receiving end. A brawl in broad daylight outside my flat was not something I relished. I decided it was time to join the party.

'Theresa, what's this all about?'

She struggled with her instinct to tell me and her need to adhere to Cornwell's instructions. Her partner saw her hesitate and jutted out his jaw. 'We're not here to answer questions, Queste. Just get in the car.'

I kept my eyes on Theresa. 'Am I under arrest?'

She looked away and the other cop answered again. 'You will be if you keep pissing me off.'

Duncan laughed. It wasn't much of a laugh, more an explosion of air. 'He's a tough cop, Hamish.'

'Love tough cops, me,' said Hamish.

'Bet he watches a lot of telly.'

'Bound to.'

'Bet he's got DVDs of *The Sweeney* at home.'

'Practices his tough cop act in front of the mirror.'

'Like Jack Regan.'

The detective's eyes bounced between the brothers like he was at a tennis match. When he'd had enough of their mocking he growled, 'Shut it, you two.'

The Sutherlands grinned. I doubt the cop understood that he'd provided the punchline.

Surprisingly, I was the one being serious. Maybe I'd been damaged more than I thought. I addressed Theresa, 'Okay, so I'm not under arrest, but this really isn't a request from Nick, is it?'

She shook her head. 'No.'

'How bad is it?'

Tough guy cop rolled his eyes and took a step forward. 'Jesus…'

Theresa shot him a glance that told him to leave it. He left it, but the high colour on his cheeks told me he'd learned some head-ripping skills at Cornwell's knee. Theresa returned to me. Her voice was low. 'It's bad, Dom.'

Okay, this was serious. 'Duncan, you and Hamish wait here for Ginty, she's on her way over.'

'You don't need to go, Dom,' said Duncan.

'The hell he doesn't,' said tough guy cop, and this time Duncan squared off against him. The cop recognised the stance and matched it. 'Okay, Geordie, you go for it. I'll pound on you for a while and then we'll take you along, too.'

That brought Hamish in on the act. 'We'll see about that…'

'For God's sake, give it a rest, you lot.' The weariness in Theresa's voice told me she'd encountered her partner's belligerence before. And there was so much testosterone flying around she was in danger of an unplanned sex change.

'Leave it, Duncan,' I said. 'Something tells me I'd better go along.'

The big detective grinned as Duncan's shoulders relaxed, and he stepped forward, laid his hand on my arm. 'Let's go, Queste.'

Hamish looked as if he was ready to break the hand off, but I held him with a shake of the head. I looked at the guy's big hand. I'd had enough of being manhandled. 'I can walk all by myself, thanks. I'm toilet trained too.'

Theresa said, 'Damien.' He took his hand away, stepped back. He wasn't happy, but that wasn't my concern.

Damien, I thought as I headed to their car. I could almost hear the choir singing 'Ave Satani'.

Chapter Thirty-Two

They didn't say anything on the ride across the river and out to the west. I tried to get more out of them, but if they were any more tight-lipped their jaws would break. Theresa had said this was bad and that was – well – bad. I told myself that had she been on her own I would've gleaned some information, because no woman could withstand the old Queste charm. I often lie to myself. It makes living with me easier. I gave up asking questions and slumped in the back seat and studied the back of Damien's head, looking for 666, the number of the beast. Couldn't find it. There wasn't even 668, the neighbour of the beast. That's an old line, but I still wasn't firing on full thrusters. There was a punk rock band gigging inside my head. And I'm no fan of punk rock.

I tried to work out what was so bad that it had forced Nick to summon me unto his presence. I didn't see Tank running to the law over our little set-to, and it couldn't be related to what had happened at the refuge over the past couple of days. Nick took a special interest in me, and that would naturally extend to my friends, but that was way the hell over on the far eastern side of the city and well out of his jurisdiction.

It had to be something to do with the jade bangle, which was very much a Glasgow West case. I hadn't made much progress on that, although there was something percolating in my brain. But if it was about that, how serious could it be? Couldn't be that bad, surely? Could it? I had myself convinced that Theresa had exaggerated the gravity of my situation, whatever it was. Police can do that.

We were on the Expressway and when we by-passed the turn off that would take us to Glasgow West station I sat up. 'You missed the turn,' I said to Damien, who was driving. He didn't reply. 'Theresa, we've missed the turn. The station's back that way.'

'We're not going to the station, Dom,' she said.

'Where we going, then?'

She didn't answer. Orders, I presumed. Nick wanted to keep me guessing. He wanted to ramp up the stress, because he was like that. Well, I'd beat him. I was tired, I was hungry and I was sore all over, even below the waist. I wasn't going to let Nick Cornwell get to me, no way, no how. I sat back and tried to relax. I was Mr Cool. I was Philip Marlowe and Sam Spade. I was Simon Templar and Mike Hammer. The law didn't worry me. Nothing worried me.

My stomach began to burn.

* * *

They say Knightswood, to the north of the western part of Glasgow, has links to the Knights Templar, but I don't know if it's true. There're trees, but no wood to speak of. I've never met a guy in armour in the streets either.

I'd never been to this particular street, but I'd been to many just like it. It was long and lined by a mixture of former council houses and what estate agents called "cottage flats". They look like houses, but really they're two flats, one up, one down, with a stairway to the side leading to the upper apartment.

I saw the crowd gathering ahead and Damien pulled in before we reached it. He considerately opened the door for me and jerked his head for me to follow. He didn't wait for me. Theresa was already striding along the pavement. I hobbled along after them.

Uniformed police officers kept the people a good twenty feet away from a metal gate leading to a path that climbed a set of steep stairs to a cottage flat. The slope was covered in bushes so typical of Glasgow: squat, prickly and here to stay. Theresa and Damien showed their ID to the uniform guarding the gate and he let us through. The steps were tricky, but there was a metal handrail for me to help haul myself up. Even so, it was a steep climb and I wished I had Sherpa Tensing with me. When I got to the top I looked back, saw the marked police cars and the unmarked vehicles, the faces of curious residents, the blue and white tape that helped hold them back, the press photographers and a solitary news crew being kept well out of it by more police officers. Theresa said this was bad. She hadn't been exaggerating after all.

This was about as bad as it got.

Another constable acted as a sentinel at the foot of the stairs leading to the top flat. He had a clipboard in his hand and he noted Theresa's name and rank on it before she headed upwards, no doubt to tell Nick we were here. Damien stood beside me and tried to look important. He didn't speak to me. He was probably thinking about his Rottweilers and how to make the nanny hang herself. I was still maintaining my cool, although my stomach was really flaring now, and that punk band was pogoing.

Nick kept us waiting – that's what he does – so I spent my time watching the cavalcade that is a major investigation. Plainclothes cops milled around, some of them were even busy. The forensic teams were the most active, doing that voodoo they do so well. Across the street I could see that the door-to-door canvass had begun. Uniforms were rattling letterboxes and buzzing doorbells, asking neighbours if they'd seen, heard, noticed anything, anyone.

When DCI Cornwell finally graced me with his presence, with DI Val Roach and Theresa in his wake, his face was stern. Now, don't get me wrong, Nick's far from a bundle of laughs at the best of times, but as he moved down the stairway towards me, his broad face looked positively grim. Val didn't look much cheerier. Something told me I wasn't going to be offered any of her coffee. I thanked heavens for small mercies. Nick crooked a finger at

Damien to tell him to bring me. Damien gripped my upper arm and brought me. We all moved towards the rear garden, where the activity was slightly muted.

Nick studied the bruising on my face. 'Whatever you had the other night is spreading,' he said. 'What happened?'

'An all-night Tiddlywinks game turned boisterous,' I said.

He grunted. 'There's a lot of it around.'

I decided to get right the point. 'Who's dead, Nick?'

'How do you know someone's dead?'

I waved a hand at the circus behind us. 'All this is isn't for unpaid parking tickets.'

He conceded that, looked over my shoulder and called out a man's name. A kid who looked fresh out of school carrying a spiffy digital camera trotted over to us.

'Show this gentleman what you've got,' Nick ordered, making the word 'gentleman' sound somewhat less than gentlemanly. The young man pressed some buttons and held the camera out to me, viewscreen first. I didn't touch it. I thought I might break it. When I saw what he was showing me, I didn't even want to be anywhere near it.

'Now, I know you know who that is, Queste,' said Cornwell, 'so let's by-pass the usual Bob Hope routine.'

I didn't feel particularly like Bob Hope – unless you factor in his current state of deadness – so hadn't planned any smart remarks at this juncture. I was, to be honest, stunned. Theresa had said this was bad. I didn't know she had mastered understatement.

It was Tank Milligan, his broad face even more misshapen after I'd given it a going over with the frozen foodstuffs. That wasn't what drew my attention, though. It was the thin, blood-red line around his neck. It was deep. He was lying in a pool of his own blood, surrounded by fast food containers. We had our differences, but the guy didn't deserve that.

I may even have done you a favour.

Cornwell let me stare at the picture for a few moments longer, then thanked the photographer, who scurried away to snap some more blood and death. 'What have you got to say, Queste?'

I drew my eyes away from the horror show. 'It's Tank Milligan.'

'Thank you, but that we already knew. Not pretty, is it?'

For once we were in agreement.

'Doctor says it's some kind of garrotte. Cheese wire, maybe. Piano wire. We don't get much of that around here.' Cornwell paused to let that sink in. 'No sign of a struggle, but he'd been battered pretty badly already.' He paused to survey my own bruises. 'But you know that, don't you?'

I remained silent. Frankly, I was concentrating on not bringing up the acid that was burning a hole in my stomach.

'Curiously, whoever killed him also fed his cat.'

That made me perk up. I didn't see Tank Milligan as a cat person. Somehow I couldn't picture him with one on his knee. Or cleaning out a litter tray.

'How do you know?'

'Food in the bowl's fresh, just put out this morning. Someone fancies himself as Peter Manuel.'

Peter Manuel, one of Glasgow's home-grown serial killers. Slaughtered a family in their home, then sat for a while after feeding the cat. The Nightcaller was more than a movie fan. He knew his true crime history. Or maybe he was simply a cat lover.

Nick said, 'So, Queste, what do you know about his death?'

I took a deep breath. I glanced at Val Roach but she seemed to be letting Nick run this show. It was his patch, after all. She still didn't look at all friendly. 'You can't think I had anything to do with it?'

He leaned closer. 'Let me tell you what I think. I think you've been working with him in the theft of the jade. I think you and he had a falling out. I think you fought.' He stopped there, waited for me to say something clever.

'Bollocks,' I said, which was about as clever as I could muster.

'I'll take it further. I think you and Tank cooked up this whole discovering the body thing together, too. I think you knew he was going up there to kill Sam Price and your involvement was all a scam for your girlfriend's sake.' He waited again for my agile brain to hit him with a one-liner.

'Utter bollocks,' I said but I know I looked nervously towards Val. She gave me a stony stare.

Nick's eye glinted. 'Then put me right.'

I thought about this. I thought about it hard. Nick was throwing a scare into me, simple as that, but as usual, the smart thing to do would be to tell him the truth. I don't often do the smart thing. This time, though, I did.

'I learned about the jade when I was looking for Sam Price, you know that. I met Milligan while I was looking for Sam. Yes, we fought. But I didn't kill him.'

'He give you that face?'

'Most of it I had already, but the bruises and swelling is all his work. My body looks as if it's been in a demolition derby, too, but you'll have to take my word for that.'

'Why did you fight?'

'Because he thought I'd tipped you off about him.'

'Over the death of Sam Price?'

'Yes.'

'Did you tell him about his car on the video?'

'Yes. He said it was stolen.'

A grunt. 'Convenient.'

'That's what I said.'

'But things turned nasty.'

'I think with Tank that was always a possibility.'

Cornwell's eyebrow jerked. I took it as a sign of agreement. 'Where did the fight take place?'

'In Sam Price's shop.'

'Who won?'

'I'd say it was a draw.'

'Anyone witness it?'

'No.'

Cornwell stared at me.

'You know I didn't kill him,' I said.

He stared at me some more.

'I don't go around killing people, Nick.'

He bristled at the use of his Christian name. 'There's a first time for everything. And it's Mister Cornwell. Other officers might allow you to be so informal but they'll learn not to be so chummy. Only my friends call me Nick, and you're not on my Christmas card list.'

Theresa shifted slightly. I felt bad for her, but I was in a tight spot here. Damien smirked. Damien was an arse. Val was still not being friendly.

I asked, 'When did he die?'

Cornwell's face was so set in stone he made the Presidents on Mount Rushmore look like the Chuckle Brothers.

'Come on, Ni – Mister Cornwell,' I said, catching my customary informality in time. 'Work with me here.'

He sighed, his face loosening slightly. His jaw was still tighter than Nureyev's codpiece, though. 'He was found this morning by his mother, in his flat, around nine. He was last seen at midnight.'

His mother? I was just getting used to Tank owning a cat but now he had a mother too?

I said, 'So he was killed sometime between then?'

Damien's lip curled. 'You should've been a detective, Queste.'

I ignored him. The fire inside me doused a little but the punk band were still hammering away. 'I was in hospital from early evening. You can check. They kept me in overnight.' I told them what hospital and Cornwell twisted round towards Damien and jerked his head. The detective left to check this out.

The DCI faced me again and said, 'Let's say this is true…'

'Yes, let's,' I said. I'd found my mojo again.

'…you still know something, Queste. I feel it in my gut.'

'That could just be poor diet.'

His face creased with irritation. 'Queste,' he said, his teeth gritted, 'can we just have a conversation without your incessant nonsense?'

'Oh, I'm sorry, Chief Inspector, does my manner offend you?' My tone was sharper than I'd intended. 'I really do apologise. After all, it's not as if you've more or less accused me of murder, is it?'

He stared at me again. He stared at me for a long time. He was very still. I tried to return his gaze but he gave good stare. I felt myself wavering. I shouldn't have poked the bear without having a bucket of fish to throw at him.

I forced my voice back on an even keel. 'But you don't really believe I had anything to do with it, do you? Not deep down. You know I don't kill people.'

'Do I?'

'Yes.'

'What about your friends? The Sutherlands are hardly pillars of society.'

'Come on, you know they've got nothing to do with this. They're rough and ready, sure…'

He snorted. 'Rough and ready? They're thugs, Queste.'

'…but this isn't their style. You know it.'

The thing was, if the boys had done it, there probably wouldn't be a body for the mother to find. I didn't say that, though. I don't like to dwell too long on the shortcomings of my friends. That way lies sleepless nights, and I'd had quite enough of them lately, thank you very much.

Cornwell stepped away and flexed his shoulders. Dealing with me was a trial, he'd made that plain in the past, and now he looked as if he was limbering up. Cornwell is old school and I know he's slapped a few legs in his time. He has also boxed, and I had no doubt he could smear parts of me on the walls if he put his mind to it. I just hoped that he wasn't putting his mind to it.

He turned to face me again. 'I don't like you, Queste.'

'That's a shame, Nick. I was going to make you a bestie on Facebook, too.'

His face darkened. 'I don't like what you do and I don't like the company you keep. I don't like the way you seem to find trouble wherever you go. I don't like the way bodies pile up around you.'

I shrugged. I couldn't argue with him.

'You're up to something, Queste, but I don't know what.'

That made two of us, to be truthful.

Cornwell's look was even more challenging than usual. 'You not got anything to say?'

'You haven't asked a question.'

He gritted his teeth, rolled his head around on his neck as if he was relieving tension. 'I'm asking you what's going on, Queste. I've got stolen jewellery, I've got one body in DI Roach's territory, I've got a dead bad guy here at home, I've got reports coming in of extreme bloodletting at the refuge, I've got a DCI from the South Side asking me why you're poking your nose into the murder of a young woman.' So someone had tipped Hambling off? Could only have been Les, the would-be Andrew Lloyd Webber. 'So, what do you say, Queste? You going to tell me what the hell is going on?'

'Nick, I wish I could tell you. But I can't.'

'You mean you won't.'

Truth was, I really wanted to tell him everything I knew. I wanted to unburden myself of it all – the jade, Fast Freddie, the Nightcaller – but something inside me prevented me from doing so. Coming clean would have been the best thing to do but I've got a self-destructive personality – I allowed drugs to wreck my life and there's no guarantee I won't do the same again some day.

When I didn't reply, Cornwell shook his head. There was something almost sad in his expression. Or maybe he was just tired, most likely of me.

Finally, Val Roach spoke. 'Do you still have my card, Queste?'

'Yes.'

'I suggest you use it. And soon. If you know what's good for you.'

Her look was cold and hard. I could see we weren't pals any more.

Cornwell waved a hand. 'Get the hell out of here, Queste. I'm sick of looking at you.'

I was dismissed again. 'How about a lift back to my place?'

'Make your own way. Police Scotland isn't a taxi service.'

What a charmer. I saw an unspoken apology in Theresa's eye as I turned to leave. Nick wasn't finished, though. His parting words stopped me in my tracks.

'You're bad news, Queste. You're like some kind of plague carrier. Wherever you go, people die. I just hope that you don't infect any of the decent people around you.'

There was a kind of weariness in his tone and when I looked back I saw it in his eyes also. I tried to think of a snappy comeback but came up with nothing. What he said had hurt.

You know what they say about the truth.

Chapter Thirty-Three

I didn't leave the scene right away. I wanted to know more about what had happened, but didn't figure anyone in Police Scotland would tell me. So I pulled an old reporter's trick. If you want some gossip, listen to the people. I stood in the crowd that gathered beyond the cordon and listened. I didn't hear much, just that they knew there had been a murder. Just like in *Taggart*, only this one wouldn't be wrapped up neatly before the end credits. I wasn't sure this one would be wrapped up neatly at all.

After about fifteen minutes of trying to merge with the crowd and eavesdropping, a woman moved close to me with a golden Labrador on a leash. She was tall and as slim as my chances of winning the lottery. The dog sat quietly between us, and I patted its head as the woman slipped a cigarette between her lips and lit it with a cheap lighter. She gave me a look and smiled.

'Got to come out with the dog if I want to have one of these,' she said, a voice that was rough enough to sandpaper a wooden floor, and then jerked her head over her shoulder. '*He's* on a health kick these days. He hit fifty last month and he's feeling his mortality, if you know what I mean. Given up smoking, drinking, red meat. He's in there watching *Escape to the Country*. He'll be making his own dresses soon, the stupid bastard.'

That's Glasgow for you. Stand around long enough and a perfect stranger will tell you their life story.

'He wants me to give up the fags too, but I told him I'd give him up first. Stupid bastard.'

She drew in some smoke, held it for a while, and exhaled it like

207

ectoplasm. I presumed she was talking about her husband, or at least her bidey-in, as no-one seems to say nowadays. Now it's 'partner' or 'significant other'. I miss the old expressions, though.

She narrowed her eyes against the smoke and studied the investigative hoop-la. 'Only a matter of time before that guy got done somehow.'

I asked, 'Did you know him?'

'Only to say hello to, you know, in the street and that. You couldnae help but notice him. He was a big lad, so he was. His mammy's a nice wummin, though. She didnae deserve a boy like him.'

'What happened, do you know?' Me, playing the daft laddie.

She gave me a look that was part curiosity and the rest amusement. 'That's a right sore face you've got there. What happened? Were you in an accident?'

You should see the other fella, I thought.

'Something like that,' I said. I was all out of smart remarks. I patted the dog's head again and it looked up at me with big brown sad eyes. 'Lovely dog,' I said, trying to gain trust through complimenting the pet.

'He's a big soft sod, so he is,' she said, the cigarette dangling at the corner of her mouth as she joined me in stroking the animal's head. He enjoyed it, but his eyes were still sad. 'He'd never get walked if I didn't do it. You'd think *him* being on this health thing, he'd want the exercise, but naw. Lazy bastard.'

I smiled encouragingly. I wondered if my bruises and swelling made it look somewhat threatening. She smiled back, so I suppose I'd got it right.

'Did you know the fella that's deid?' She asked. 'He the one that gave you the bruises?'

Glasgow folk can be pure dead smart, so they can. 'What makes you think that?'

'Cos I saw him last night coming home. I live just over there,' she made a vague wave to the houses on the opposite side of the street, 'and he looked like he'd been on the wrong end of someone's fist.'

'What time was that?'

'About nineish.'

'He come out again?'

'No that I saw.'

Even though I hadn't answered her question, she seemed to be willing to talk now. 'See anyone else go in?'

'Was out with the dog about half-eleven and saw a bloke delivering take away.'

I thought about the photograph I'd seen and Tank's body surrounded by take away cartons. Chinese food.

'You never answered my question,' she said. 'You and him have a wee set-to?'

I nodded. 'I didn't do this, though.'

She sucked on the end of her cigarette. The tip flared briefly. 'Didn't think you did.'

'Why you so sure?'

'Don't think you'd be standing here with all these polis around, talking to me. Anyway, I saw you up there earlier. If they thought you did it they wouldn't be having a wee natter, would they? You'd be down the cop shop getting your shoelaces and belt taken off you.'

I couldn't fault her logic. 'Did you see Tank come out again?'

'Tank? That was his name? I just knew him as the big fella across the way.' She thought about this. 'Fits, though. He was as big as a tank, right enough.' She shook her head, dropped the spent cigarette onto the ground and flattened it with the ball of her foot. 'No, never saw him, but I heard that delivery man's motor come back, after midnight.'

Now why the hell did he come back? 'Was it a van with a logo?'

Another shake of the head. 'Car. A lot of they guys use their own motors, you know?'

'Had you seen him before?'

'No. We don't get our food delivered. When we used to get take away – before *he* started banging on about salt and saturated fats and monosodium whatsit – we picked it up ourselves. Height of laziness to get it delivered, but I suppose it gives someone a wee living.'

'Can you describe the delivery man?'

'Naw, too far away. He had on a thing with a hood anyway. It was pissing down, so it was. It was so wet the ducks were water-proofing their arses.'

I stroked the dog's head again as I thought about her information. Then another thought struck me. This was too easy. 'Why you telling me this?'

She smiled. 'I told you, I saw you talking to the detectives up there. Saw you arrive with them.' I realised this woman didn't miss much that happened in her street. 'Then I saw you come down here and stand around. You think I'm here by accident? I decided you needed to know all this.'

'Why not tell the police?'

'I don't speak to the polis, if I can help it. I'll no have them at my door. It's bad luck. You can tell them all this, save me getting involved.'

'They'll come to your door anyway. They'll do a house-to-house.'

'Doorbells don't need to be answered, neither they do.'

I wondered what sort of contact she'd had with the law in the past. Was it her or her health nut husband? Or someone in the family? As for the police being at your door bringing bad luck, that's another old suspicion, usually among people for whom a uniform at the door meant their luck had run out.

I asked, 'How do you know I'll pass it on?'

She gave the dog's lead a slight tug. He rose obediently. 'No my problem.' Then she walked away.

I let her go, wondering if I should tell Nick. I really should've. It would've been the right thing to do, even if the chances were it wouldn't lead anywhere. Yup, it was my civic duty to let the law know about the delivery man, whoever he was.

I turned and went in search of a cab.

Chapter Thirty-Four

They say taxi drivers in London can talk so much you can go in the back with your hair wet and it'll be blown dry by the end of the journey. There must be drivers like that in Glasgow, but it's not my experience. I was grateful the guy in the front of the black hack was as talkative as a silent movie because it allowed me the chance to settle in, lean my head back and try to forget about those everyday things like murder and blood and Nightcallers. I even managed it, too – for all of ten seconds.

I don't suppose I was surprised when the mobile rang. Part of me knew it would. Even so, the flames in my gut flared again.

It was him. 'Did you enjoy the little show?' Of course he knew where I'd been.

I twisted round to check for cars or vans following. It was a waste of time. We were on the Expressway, in heavy traffic. He could be in any of them. Or none of them. 'You were there, weren't you? In the street.'

'I am everywhere, don't you know that by now?'

I pictured the murder scene, tried to recall faces. Came up with nothing, no-one paying any notable attention to me. He was too clever for that. He'd be covert. He'd be hidden. In a car, maybe, watching through binoculars. I gave up.

'You didn't have to kill Tank,' I said.

'He was a threat to you.' A tinny little laugh. He was enjoying himself. 'That's what I'm here for.'

'And the girl at the refuge? Scaring her? What was that?'

'That was fun.'

'Terrifying a poor, screwed up kid half to death is fun for you?'

He sighed. 'Oh, Dom – you don't know me at all.'

'You're right. If I ever knew what went on in a mind as twisted as yours, I'd put myself out of my misery.'

'Dom!' There was an overly dramatic sense of hurt in the voice. 'And I thought we were getting on so well!'

My temper snapped then. The voice was really irritating me now. I'd been threatened, beaten and suspected of murder, so I wasn't in the best of moods.

'I've had enough of this. The thing is, I *do* know what's going on in that sick, fetid sumphole you call a mind. It's all about power, all about the fear. You like to see people run, don't you? You like to have them jumping at shadows, terrified that if they don't do what you want you'll kill someone close to them. You turned Paula Rogers into a mess, maybe even James Mortimer before her...'

'You have been doing your homework,' he said. 'I'm impressed.'

'Don't be. You're not as clever as you think.'

'Don't bet on that, Dom.'

'I will bet on that, because I always bet a sure thing. But here's the really annoying part of it all – your games? They were working with me. I was playing by your rules. I was being a good little victim. I was jumping at your shadows. All that ends now. It ends here.'

He laughed. 'You think you know me? You think you know what I'm all about? You think your mind is capable of that? You think you can dissect me with that blunt little tool?'

Another movie quote. *The Silence of the Lambs*. That was it for me.

'You like your movie quotes. Here's one for you. Peter Finch in *Network*. I'm mad as hell and I'm not going to take it any more. You get me, you sick bastard? I'm not going to take it any more. You want to play games? We'll play games. But just you and me. No-one else. You want me, you come get me, but let's play by big boy's rules. You and me. Just you and me.'

There was a long silence and I thought I'd overplayed my hand. I thought he'd hung up. I didn't care because I'd really had enough with him. I think the head at Shayleen's window was really the final straw, even before Tank wound up dead. I pressed the phone tighter to my ear and was rewarded by the faint sound of his asthmatic breathing.

'Okay, cowboy,' he said, and even through the distortion I could hear him smiling. 'You're on warning now. You know I'm coming.' He paused. 'And hell's coming with me. You hear that? Hell's…'

I hung up. Life's too short to listen to a madman mangle a quote from *Tombstone*. Some things are sacred.

Chapter Thirty-Five

The taxi driver continued to keep his own counsel, but I saw some curious looks darting in my direction from the rear view. After all, he'd heard my side of the conversation. He didn't say a word as I paid him. Good. I wasn't in the mood. The boys had told me they'd picked up my car from Partick while I was in hospital and took it back to my street. What I really wanted to do was get into my bed and sleep for a week, but my impulsive outburst meant that was never going to happen. Not until I brought all of this to an end, once and for all. There was a plan beginning to form, but I had to sort out some other things first. I called Duncan, told him about Tank, made sure Ginty and Father Verne were with him at the refuge, told them all to stay there together. He wanted to know where I was going and I told him I had business to take care of. He wasn't happy. He knew I was hiding something. He'd known for some time and it pained me, but I'd sort all that out later. The main thing was they were all together. Nothing could happen while they were all together.

I hoped.

My body ached as I steered through the streets. I had some antacids in the glove compartment and they manfully tackled the brush fire in my stomach, but didn't douse it entirely. I drove slowly, but didn't see anything dogging me. I regretted throwing down the gauntlet to the Nightcaller – if he took it up right away, I was dead meat. I could feel what strength I had beginning to wane. Even changing gear was an effort. But what was done was done. There was no point agonising over mistakes. I knew that from bitter experience.

214

The heavens had opened again as I pulled into Acapella's small car park beside Bree's nippy little sports car. I spotted Julio standing under the awning over the front door grabbing a fag break. He watched me run – well, hobble – through the rain towards the shelter. His eyes were hostile as I reached his side. That didn't bother me much.

'You should not be here,' he said.

I ignored him and made for the door, but he placed a hand on my chest. I wasn't in the mood, so I snatched his wrist, twisted it and forced his arm back. His body had no choice but to go with it. He was on the ground so fast even I was surprised. To be honest, I didn't think I had it in me.

'Don't piss me around, son,' I said. 'I'm not up to it today.'

'You are to stay away from Sylvia,' he said, his voice brittle through anger and a little pain,.

'She say that?'

'No... Mister Hambling...he say it.'

No surprise there. I checked the car park, spotted Bree's nifty little number. 'Is Mrs Hambling here?'

He didn't answer, so I clicked his arm into fourth. He yelled out, 'Yes!'

I let him go. He muttered something no doubt unrepeatable in polite society as he got up. Guilt tickled at my stomach, but I ignored it. Part of me was disappointed that Hambling wasn't there. After the day I'd had, I think I was more than ready for him. I looked at Julio, softened my voice. 'You want to protect Bree... Sylvia, don't you?'

He glared at me. I took it as a yes.

'You like her. The way you liked Laura.'

His dark eyes flashed at the mention of her name. 'You must not say her name.'

I didn't ask which name. He probably meant both. He was besotted and he didn't want filth like me soiling them in any way, even just by speaking their name. To him, it was as if I was spitting on them.

215

'But Laura didn't want you, did she? You wanted to be more than her friend, but she didn't want that. She had a boyfriend. But you cared for her, loved her even, so you went for confidante and she didn't want that either. You wanted to protect her, but you couldn't. And now you're here – how did you get this job, anyway?'

He didn't answer me. He rubbed his shoulder while his eyes fired stiletto blades at me.

'Did Mr Hambling get you the job? Did he see that you're the protective sort and place you here to keep an eye on his wife? Was that it? Did he know that you'd develop a crush on her and you'd do anything to protect her? Eh, Julio? Am I even half right?'

He didn't reply, so I didn't know if I was half right, all right or way off base. I hadn't properly thought this through, it all came out on impulse. I was doing that a lot, and it was a bad habit.

I left him standing under the awning, the rain dripping off the edges and soaking one shoulder of his white shirt, his eyes still burning hatred. I didn't think he'd be giving me any LOLs on social media any time soon.

The restaurant was closed and the lighting was dim to begin with, but the overcast skies outside made it even murkier. The bar was lit up, though, and I used it to manoeuvre through the tables to the office door. I didn't knock. The niceties of social convention were not for me. Bree was at her desk, paperwork in front of her. A green desk lamp was on, illuminating the desk top but little else. Her hands I could see clearly, her face was shadowed.

'You shouldn't be here,' she said, her voice dull and listless.

'Yes, I got that message at the door. And yet, here I am.'

She didn't ask who. She didn't need to. Her gaze dropped to the paperwork, but she wasn't really looking at it. 'You'd better leave.'

I stepped fully into the office but left the door open. 'Not until we get some things straightened out.'

'What things?'

'You. Sam Price. A jade bangle that's the stuff dreams are made of.' The Nightcaller had put me in the mood for movie quotes. I didn't have the lisp to say it like Bogart, but it seemed fitting.

She didn't deny anything. She didn't say anything or do anything. She just sat there, her face indistinct in the gloom, waited for me to carry on. I carried on.

'What puzzled me about the whole thing was how Sam Price, a Partick butcher and small-time catcher, heard about something as big as jewellery worth three quarters of a million. Once I had time to think about it, it was pretty obvious. I was annoyed I didn't see it right away. It took some enforced rest in a hospital bed to make me see straight. You used him, didn't you?'

'I loved him,' she said. I heard the truth in the flat way she said it.

'Maybe,' I said, though she had thrown me a little. 'But that's not how it started, was it? You wanted the jade, or rather the freedom its sale would bring you. Sam, poor dodgy Sam, could help with that. What is it, Bree? Hubby too quick with his hands? I can believe that of him. I've heard he's got a temper.'

I moved to the desk top, swivelled the lamp so that the light fell on her face. I had expected to see a bruise or two, maybe a cut. I had convinced myself that DCI Hambling was a wife beater. I was wrong. She was pale and drawn, certainly, and her carefully applied make-up couldn't completely disguise the dark circles under her eyes, but otherwise her face was clear.

She saw the surprise on my face. 'There are other kinds of abuse.' She fished a cigarette from a packet in front of her, lit up and sat back. 'Yes, I told Sam about the jade. Yes, he found the people who could take it. Yes, the plan was for him to sell it on so I could get away from here, get away from...'

She waved her hand, the cigarette between her fingers making a little smoke circle. It held its form all too briefly then began to waver and fade. 'Life with my husband has been...difficult. It wasn't like that at the beginning, but things change, don't they? He loves me, I have no doubt about it, but he loves me too much. He is a man who likes to own things. He doesn't even rent videos or go to the library. He needs to own the videos or the books. He likes to think his possessions are part of him. His house, his car, his clothes.' She took a draw on the cigarette. 'His wife.'

Love, I thought. That smoke circle said it all. First it's there, then it's gone.

'So, Mister Queste, you're right about everything, except one thing. The idea was to use Sam, to use his contacts, his know-how. I'd been to dinner many times with the judge and his wife. My husband is very well connected in that way. I'd seen the jade, I'd even handled it. I'd even been shown the safe, so I was able to pass on details. But as time went on, as the idea became a plan and the plan became a reality, I found I was thinking of Sam in a different way. And I was thinking about him a lot. That surprised me, to be honest. I thought I'd never think of a man in that way again. But Sam...well, he had a way with him. I knew he was crooked, but he was fun and he was tender and he didn't look at me as if I was a possession, something to be stored, to be trotted out whenever the need arises. He had no ambition, except to be happy and enjoy life.'

'And convert stolen goods into readies,' I said, and her head dropped a fraction.

'Yes,' she said quietly, 'that.'

Yes, that.

Her head raised again. 'But he wouldn't open my mail or check my mobile for calls or vet whoever came into contact with me or chase away any friends he deemed unsuitable. And he wouldn't make me think of ways to kill him.'

If she was expecting a response, she didn't get one. I've heard it before, from other women whose lives have been made a misery by the man they thought they loved at one time. I recalled a case I investigated for my lawyer pal, Eamonn O'Connor. He got a woman off because we could prove a pattern of abuse over a period of years, and finally she simply snapped and lashed out, killed him with a pair of scissors. Justice was done that day for sure.

'Being with Sam, snatching what time I could, put those

thoughts out of my head.' Bree paused and I knew those thoughts were back. I saw her struggle with them, force them down. 'There's something else Sam wouldn't do. He wouldn't place a spy in my restaurant to keep an eye on me.'

'That'd be Julio,' I said.

She inclined her head slightly. 'That'd be Julio. He's a nice enough boy, he'd do anything for me, he really would, but he's also Greg's man. Sam must've come here once too often and Julio told him.'

'What happened?'

'Greg told me never to see him again. I think he went to see Sam too. Warned him off.'

The sore face I'd been told about. So that was Hambling's doing. 'But Sam wouldn't take a telling.'

Her head wobbled in the shadows. The cigarette between her lips flared briefly then died. Made me think of love again. 'We decided to be more careful. Sam didn't come here. If there was a delivery, he had one of his employees handle it. But we still met, in secret, when we could.'

I began to wonder about Greg Hambling. He liked to buy videos, she'd said. Was that simply an example of his particular brand of control freakery, or was he a big movie fan?

'What about the jade, Bree? Where is it?'

She stubbed the cigarette out. 'I don't know, I really don't. Sam took it, was supposed to move it, but then he changed, became distant, as I said. He wouldn't talk to me, he wouldn't see me. I thought Greg's warning had finally taken. And then Sam vanished.'

And the rest I knew. So I was right about it all – okay, I thought she was simply using Sam, but I can't be right all the time.

She was staring at me. 'Who killed Sam, Mr Queste?'

I returned her look. 'I don't know, Bree. But whoever he is, I'm going to get him.'

If he didn't get me first.

219

Chapter Thirty-Six

I should've known Julio would phone Hambling. Maybe part of me wanted it. I've mentioned that self-destructive streak before. I almost made a clean getaway, but just as I was about to pull out of the car park, a big blue Renault Megane GT with this year's plates blocked my way. One of his possessions, and obviously lovingly cared for. It wouldn't fall in love with a cheap little butcher from Partick. Its headlights might be turned by a fancy convertible, though. You never knew.

He climbed out of the driver's seat and strode towards me through the rain, a police issue scowl on his face. I rolled down my window, was about to say something witty when he interrupted me. 'Are you hard of hearing or just forgetful?'

'I don't remember.'

His jaw stiffened further. I didn't think it was possible. He leaned in closer and I saw there was something cold and dangerous lurking in his eyes. 'I told you to stay away from my wife.'

'Yes, you did.'

'Then why are you here?'

'I'm a rebel.'

He exhaled through his nose. 'What's to prevent me from lifting you right here and now?'

'And the charge would be what, exactly?'

'I'd think of something on the way.'

'Better make it good, then, because I've got a habit of panicking when I'm arrested on false pretences. My mouth runs away from me – and I'm usually such a taciturn chap. I might say things you don't want your pals down at the police club to be talking about over their G&Ts, or whatever the well-dressed policerati are imbibing these days.'

His face wrinkled with disgust. 'And what would a snooping little shit like you have to tell them?'

I made a show of thinking about this. 'Oh, I don't know. Let's say there's this woman, married to – oh – a senior police detective who's so paranoid about losing her that he all but stifles her. She can't move, can't think without him keeping tabs on her. And let's say she meets a guy and let's say something happens, something she didn't want, didn't expect but it happened all the same. She fell for this guy. And let's say her husband finds out about it, goes to see this guy, gives him a slap, leaves him with a black eye and a swollen jaw. And let's say the husband – did I mention he has anger issues? –well, let's just say he's not too careful about who sees him.'

'You're saying a lot that can't be proved.'

'As I said, he's not too careful about who sees it. Maybe he knows the slapee isn't one to go to the law, being a bit on the shady side. But see, maybe there's this other fellow who enters the picture – a handsome chap, witty, wise, debonair in a Simon Templar kind of way...'

'Jesus, you're fond of your own voice.'

'...who's very fond of his own voice. He can listen to it all day. Anyway, he finds the man who saw the man who slapped the man, in the house that Jack built. And that handsome, witty, wise, debonair fellow may just let all that slip out if he was, say, under pressure in a police office. It wouldn't play well for the husband, would it? His wife playing around, his anger getting the better of his fists, and if the guy he slapped around later ended up dead too? Well, wouldn't look too good for him over there at Police Scotland HQ, would it? Might not sit well with those who decide on promotions and advancement and who gets the key to which executive toilet.'

He took a steadying breath, but his hand tightened on the

open window of my car. His eyes still burned with cold rage as he studied me. I wondered if he'd reach in and haul me through that open window. He didn't. Finally I saw his eyes soften and his fingers unclench. He straightened and looked towards the restaurant door, where Bree was watching us.

'You don't understand any of it,' he said, and maybe it was the weather, but I thought I heard something liquid catch at his voice.

'I probably don't. People like me never do. But if I don't, neither will your bosses.'

'She's my wife...'

I didn't say anything. I'd said enough, I thought.

'I love her so much...'

'Then my advice is change or let her go. Before something bad happens. Before one or other of you is being questioned by another DCI somewhere. And one or other of you is lying on a slab.'

He didn't say anything more to me. He exchanged a look with his wife that I couldn't read and then moved his car out of my way. I drove on, glanced once in my wing mirror. Bree was still standing in the doorway, he was in his car. Neither of them moved. I wondered if they ever would.

Chapter Thirty-Seven

It was growing dark as I reached the refuge. I hoped there was food there, because my stomach was as empty as my bank account. Apart from the now ever-present acid reflux, of course. It occurred to me that I should find a less stressful occupation, like skydiving without a parachute. At least then I'd know how it was going to turn out. A dark van pulled out of the tiny car park as I pulled in. I wondered who it was, but couldn't see the driver's face. It skidded onto Edinburgh Road, its tyres spitting up the rain from the tarmac. I was too tired and too sore to think much more about it. I didn't even have the energy to run from the car to the refuge door. I just let the rain get me. It was soothing, actually. I stopped, raised my face to it like Tim Robbins in *The Shawshank Redemption*. I'd have raised my arms too, but I saw Duncan watching me from the door and couldn't face the ribbing I'd get.

'We were about to send out search parties,' said Duncan as I moved into the dry entranceway.

'I had some business to take care of.'

'What kind of business?'

We began to walk towards the kitchen. 'I'll tell you everything, once I've got some food inside me. I could bite a baby's bum through a wicker chair.'

'You're just in time, then. The food you ordered has just arrived.'

That stopped me in my tracks. 'What food?'

'Guy's just been. He said you phoned in an order ahead. Chicken…'

Home delivery. I hadn't made the order. And Tank had food delivered before he was killed. Something told me this chicken wasn't the Colonel's recipe. I sprinted to the kitchen, Duncan behind me asking what the hell was going on.

I burst into the kitchen to find Ginty, Father Verne and Hamish around the small table, the food containers in front of them. Hamish was opening a polystyrene box and he smiled when he saw me. 'Dom, good to see you – but the food's really welcome…'

'Has anyone eaten anything?'

Puzzled, they shook their heads. 'It's just arrived,' said Ginty, then noted my grim look. 'Why? What's wrong?'

I moved to Hamish's side. 'I didn't order any food.'

Hamish was bemused. 'Then who did?'

I looked into the container in his hand. Chips. And something else.

'I don't think you want to eat that,' I said.

Hamish followed my gaze, saw what I saw, and dropped the box like it was red hot. It landed on the table, spilled some of the contents, including one of the four fingers that had been resting on top of the fries. It had the letter D tattooed on it. The other three had R, U and G. They had each been severed cleanly, snipped off rather than sawn.

Father Verne crossed himself, Ginty's hand shot to her mouth as if to stifle a scream. Hamish took an involuntary step back, as if he'd found a rat in there. Duncan was calm as he moved forward, studied the body parts with interest.

'Cut off with secateurs or garden shears, something like that,' he said. 'Takes a bit of muscle but it's quick and clean, if the body's already dead.'

I didn't ask how he knew. There are some things I'm better off not knowing.

Hamish had recovered from his initial shock to join his brother in a closer look.

'First it was Cody's head at the window, now it's his fingers in the chips,' he said. 'I'll take a guess and say he's dead.'

'Yup,' said Duncan, straightening.

Hamish leaned further forward. 'I'll say this, though – for once advertising is right.' He straightened, gave us all a grin, but a weak one, and it was forced. 'Those chips really are finger-lickin good.'

Chapter Thirty-Eight

The police took the fingers away for examination. The DNA would match the blood found outside. We knew it was Cody, and we told them that. A polite, very pleasant pair of detectives questioned us all. They spoke to Shayleen about what she'd seen at her window. Hamish had accepted the order and they grilled him for a description of the delivery man, but he hadn't really paid much attention. Male, average height, well built, not young, face obscured a bit by the hoodie he was wearing. That was really all. They were in the refuge for hours, because these things take time, and they were exceptionally professional, courteous and completely lacking in any of the tough guy schooling I'd come to expect from Scotland's finest.

That, however, would not last. I knew my name would be in the system again and Nick would be on my case. Someone else dead. Maybe I was a plague.

Once they had left, we sat in the common room where the residents usually gathered to watch TV. The big black flatscreen was silent, though, and the residents, some uncomfortable with the presence of the law, were all in their rooms. Duncan and Hamish had fried us up some bacon and eggs. Surprisingly, everyone except Duncan ate like it was our last meal on earth. That was an analogy I wished hadn't entered my head. We sat with the plates on our knee, the notion of eating at the table that had recently played host to Cody's disembodied digits somehow far from appealing. Ginty was beside me on the settee, Hamish had one armchair, Father Verne another. Only Duncan was standing, beside the gas fire, his plate resting on the broad mantelpiece, his food barely touched. He was staring at me. He knew I knew something. And it was time I told them.

'Well,' I said, clearing my throat, 'I'll bet you're wondering why I've asked you all here.'

'What's going on, Dom?' Duncan, getting down to business.

So I told them. Everything. It was time. It was way past time, to be honest. Silence was no longer an option. That's what they'd been muttering in my dream.

You should have told us.

Cody had died because he didn't know what he'd blundered into. So had Tank. You can't defend yourself against a threat you didn't know existed. The Nightcaller had said that he'd kill someone if I talked, and I hadn't. But he killed anyway. Now it was important that my friends knew what they were up against, because there was strength in numbers.

But here's another thing that had finally dawned on me. To survive, we needed an edge. The Nightcaller's edge was that he was faceless and as nutty as a squirrel's larder. James Mortimer, Paula Rogers and Sam Price knew they were under threat, but they didn't have an edge they could use. They made the mistake of playing the game by the Nightcaller's rules. It had taken me too long to understand that I had an edge too.

The Sutherland brothers.

I had the vague stirrings of a plan, but they needed to know everything to make it work. They needed to be on their guard.

But as I came clean, I felt Ginty move away from me, placing as much distance between us as she could. I didn't comment on it. I knew what it was about. I'd kept secrets.

Duncan said, 'So let's go over the story so far.'

Oh good, I thought, a bit of exposition. It always help to focus the mind. Much of what I'd told them was supposition, and sometimes hearing that from someone else either strengthens the premise or simply shows it up to be the delusion of an over-active imagination. But I think I'd got it right this time.

'Okay,' Duncan said, beginning to pace now, 'we've got three murders, all committed by this Nightcaller of yours – you couldn't have thought of a better nickname?'

'I was under pressure, give me a break.'

'Anyway, the only connection James Mortimer, Paula Rogers and Ginty's cousin have is that they've been killed by the same person. How did that work again?'

I wanted to reach out and squeeze Ginty's hand, but I didn't. I even avoided looking at her as I spoke. 'The whole thing is freaky, so here goes. I'm guessing here, but James Mortimer was a classical music fan and Paula was a cellist. She performed in concerts in the college, and it's possible that James attended one or more. I think the Nightcaller follows his victims around for a while, seeing what they do, who they interact with, and selects his next victim from there. It could be anyone – he said it to me himself…'

'Tinker, Tailor, etc,' said Father Verne.

'Exactly. It's all random and each fresh victim really doesn't have any solid connection to the last. So he selects Paula, more or less at random, out of all the people that Mortimer has any kind of contact with. He starts sending Paula the cuttings to soften her up, maybe kills her uncle in a hit and run to drive his point home. Then he kills her.'

Ginty finally spoke. 'But what's her connection to Sam?'

When I looked at her, I saw there was a coldness in her eyes. There was only about six inches between us, but she seemed so very far away. 'Another guess. Julio. He was her friend, her confidante. He began to follow him, he led him to Bree's restaurant.'

Hamish asked, 'But why not target either Julio or Bree?'

'Too close to Paula. Julio was her pal, Bree was married to the cop in charge of the investigation. Bree led him to Sam.'

'Because they were having an affair?' Father Verne again.

'Maybe, maybe not. Sam made deliveries, or one of his employees did. It's possible he latched onto that, decided there were sufficient degrees of separation to make Sam his next victim, so he sent him the cuttings about Paula's death and the whole process began again.'

Duncan said, 'And then from Sam to you.'

'Yes, only he didn't need to send me cuttings. I found the body.'

'He was taking a risk.'

'All part of the game,' I said. 'Maybe he saw me as a challenge.'

Father Verne cleared his throat slightly. 'Well, we certainly all find you very challenging.'

Something between a cough and a growl rumbled in Ginty's throat. Yup, I was in trouble.

Hamish was taking all this in. 'So was James Mortimer the first, then?'

I shrugged. 'I don't know. I've not had the chance to look into that. But I'd lay odds that he wasn't the first. Something tells me this has been going on for some time. Victims more or less at random, ostensibly unconnected to one another, each killed in different ways so as not to set any computerised alarm bells ringing.'

There was a silence as we all thought about it.

Ginty said, 'I think we should tell the police.'

Duncan and Hamish looked at her, their faces blank. Bringing the police in was, as ever, furthest from their minds. The Night-caller had threatened them and their friends. That made it their business. They'd settle it their way. It was the code of the west. Of Scotland. Even though they were from the east of England.

Duncan strengthened the moment by reaching behind him and producing an automatic pistol. 'The police will just want to arrest this freak. I've got something more permanent in mind.'

That's what I was afraid of, and I said so. They all waited for me to say something further. I stood up, walked around, told them what I had planned. When I was finished, Duncan sighed.

'Dom, do you know what the most annoying thing is in horror films?'

'The found footage genre?'

He ignored me. 'It's when people go off on their own, knowing there's a killer around.'

Hamish added, 'Or when they go off into the woods to have sex, knowing there's a killer around.'

Duncan ignored his brother too. Sometimes I think we test his patience to the limit. 'What you're suggesting is bloody crazy, Dom. We should fort up here…'

'No,' I said, 'Pulling a *Rio Bravo* won't do any good. He'll kill someone else, and this has to stop. He wants me, he's not really interested in any of you, except as a way to get to me. I need you all to stay here together. Safety in numbers.' I paused to let this register. I caught Ginty's eye, saw the anger rising. I needed to lighten the mood. 'If it makes you feel better, I'll get you a mouth organ and you can sit around and sing cowboy songs.'

Ginty rose suddenly and said, 'Dom, I need a word.'

She walked out of the room before I could argue.

Oh, boy…

Chapter Thirty-Nine

She waited for me in the kitchen, pacing up and down on the far side of the small table, as if it was a wall I'd have to breach. Her shoulders were hunched and she was rubbing her hands together absently, as if she was warming them up for some serious slapping. I stood for a moment and then decided I'd best close the door for this. I knew what was coming. I knew I deserved it.

'You're a bloody pain in the arse, Dominic Queste,' she said. I didn't need to ask why. 'You've kept all this from me? This guy phoning you? Tormenting you? All this time?'

I made a weak attempt at defence. 'It's not been that long, really, and I was worried...'

'Worried, my backside! You were doing what you always do. Being the big man. Being the tough guy. Going it alone.'

I would've contradicted her, but I knew she was right.

'You know your problem?' she asked, and I thought, *only one*? 'You think your life is a bloody film. You think you're Clint Eastwood, or John Wayne or Robert Mitchum. You think you're the handsome stranger who rides into town and cleans it up single-handed. You think you're Philip bloody Marlowe, sorting everything out by himself. Well, Dom, you're not. You're just a guy, and here's a news flash, you're not that handsome.'

Okay, that was uncalled for.

'Also, you think you're bloody immortal, but I hate to break it you, you're mortal. Look at you, look at the state of you, and all because you wanted to go it alone.'

I couldn't argue with that either. I didn't feel particularly immortal. She fell silent and I thought perhaps her anger was spent. But she was just catching her breath.

'But you know what the worst thing is?' Her eyes were really flaring now and her teeth were gritted. I'd never seen this side of her before and let me tell you, it scared the life out of me. 'The worst thing is that you didn't trust any of us enough. You didn't trust me!'

She realised her voice has risen slightly and she turned away, calmed herself down. When she turned back the volume control had been hit, but the anger was still there. 'You've got friends out there who would do anything for you and you cut them out. That bastard could've gone after any one of them, any one of us, and we wouldn't have known about it until it was too late.'

She had come to the same conclusion I had, but it had taken her significantly less time. It was only then that I understood how much I'd screwed up. I realised I hadn't mentioned the video the Nightcaller had shot of her, but I decided against raising it now. It wasn't cowardice, it was… Oh, hell, it was cowardice. I had a big streak of yellow down my back that could be patrolled by parking wardens.

It didn't matter that I thought I was doing the right thing. It didn't matter that I really thought I was protecting them by not involving them. Her words were making me look at myself in ways I didn't like. We're all the central character in our own little movies, but did I have a hero complex? I thought about what I was going to do. Was that what my plan was all about? Or was I really doing it to protect the others? The answer was simple. I didn't know.

'And now?' she said. 'What's your big plan now?'

'It's the only way…'

She spoke as if I hadn't said a thing. 'You're going to swan off, on your own, and face him, on your own. On your own!'

'I won't be on my own,' I said, but she waved that away as if it didn't matter. Which I suppose it didn't.

She took a deep breath and let it out in waves. 'Secrets,' she said. 'Secrets and men being manly. Never good, Dom. Only leads to one thing. Someone gets hurt. You know what Tiger was like.'

'I'm not your ex-husband, Ginty. I'm nothing like him.'

'The Tiger I knew was nothing like the Tiger you knew. He kept things from me too, and I watched him change. I watched the things he did – the things he kept from me, the disappointments of life, the shame at what he had become. I watched it eat away at him until there was nothing left of the man I married. I can't go through that again, Dom. I can't.'

She waited for me to say something. I searched desperately for the words to justify my position, if only slightly, but everything I came up with sounded lame, even to me. She stared at me, I think willing me to reassure her that everything would be perfect, that we'd walk into the sunset together and live happily ever after. But I couldn't.

My silence finally made her turn sharply and walk out of the kitchen. I didn't follow.

Chapter Forty

The rain blew itself out through the night and the morning was bright, though the air had a bite to it. I woke to find someone had used my spine to make the mark of Zorro. I'd slept as well as I could in one of the armchairs in the common room, the refuge being full. Father Verne had gallantly given up his own bed to Ginty but had staked a claim on the couch, citing his seniority, eminent domain and something about a Papal decree. It was empty, so that meant he was up and around. Duncan and Hamish were in two other armchairs. They looked more comfortable than I had been. Sleeping somewhere other than my own bed is an art I've never completely mastered. Not without the aid of controlled substances.

I eased myself out of my cramped position and arched my back in an attempt to untangle my muscles. The morning sun seeped through the curtains and I knew I had to be on my way. The clothes I was wearing were beginning to learn how to walk by themselves, so I knew I'd have to get back to my flat to pack a few items. I was outside the refuge taking the air when Father Verne appeared at my side with a roll and sausage wrapped in a square of kitchen roll. He handed it to me without a word and watched the early morning traffic slide past on Edinburgh Road as I ate it. He'd even put brown sauce on it. The man's a saint.

Finally, he asked, 'Dominic, you have a talent for getting into more scrapes than antiseptic – you do know that, don't you?'

'It's a gift, Father,' I said.

'You know this is a stupid idea.'

I swallowed hard. 'You think so?'

He looked at me, his eyes twinkling. 'Don't you?'

I shrugged, bit off another chunk of bread and steak lorne. 'Does everyone think that way?'

'Oh, yes.'

Okay, I thought, good to know. 'I'm doing it for the best of reasons.'

'You have good intentions.'

'That's right.'

'You know what they say about the road to hell.'

'Father, I've been there. I've no doubt I'll go back.'

A bird flew by, a blackbird. I threw the remains of my bread roll onto the grass and we watched it circle back and swoop to snatch it in its yellow beak. Father Verne's voice was soft when he spoke again. 'Dom, we're all going to hell. But some of us may be alone when we get there, which is the real punishment.'

'I think Duncan and Hamish understand why I'm doing it. They might not agree, but they understand.'

'Yes they do, and so do I. But I'm not talking about me.'

I got his meaning then. 'Ginty. She's spoken to you?'

He nodded. It didn't surprise me – he had a way of making people open up. 'You could lose her over this. She's realised what your life is like, and if you don't change it, she'll be gone.'

'I'm not a bad man.'

'No, you're not. But you're not exactly what you'd call good either.'

The problem with people knowing you well is that they know you well. When I was using, I did things that could've landed me in jail. It was only luck that they hadn't. Even now I'm clean, I've done things that don't bear too much scrutiny. I try not to think too much about them, the principle *out of sight, out of mind* being my motto.

Father Verne said, 'None of us – you, the boys, me – can be called good men, Dom. We may stand on the side of the angels, but they keep their distance. And we've been lucky, very lucky,

235

that so far we're still standing. But that can't last. The important thing is, though, we chose to do what we do, to live the life we lead. When Mary Ellis died in my arms during Mass that day I chose to begin all this…' He waved his arms at the building behind us. 'I chose my mission. Duncan and Hamish chose to help me…'

'With a little persuasion from you.'

His lips thinned into a rueful little smile. 'Yes, I helped them along, but in the end it was their decision to cast off their former lives and begin this new one with me. You made that choice too.' He stopped, but I knew there was more. 'Ginty didn't ask for you to come to her door that day, didn't ask for her cousin to be murdered, but you did and he did, and now she's here too. She's become part of this through no fault of her own. The question is, can you keep her safe?'

'The Nightcaller won't get her. I'll see to that.'

'Maybe. Maybe what you're planning really is the only way. But what if this is the fight you won't win? What if it's the next one? How many fights, Dom, how many? Before we lose?'

'So what are you saying, Father?'

'I'm saying that we're all on the road to hell with our good intentions. You, me, Duncan, Hamish. This is our path. We chose it. Ginty has to decide whether she wants to follow us down it. You have to choose whether or not to lead her.'

He began to walk back to the refuge door. Then he stopped and faced me again. 'And whatever you're going to do about this Nightcaller individual? Get it done. And get it done fast. I want my common room back.'

Chapter Forty-One

I walked to my car, settled in, thought about Father Verne's words, thought about Ginty, thought about what I was heading off to do. It was risky, but I saw no other way. I had to draw the Nightcaller away. I had to prevent Duncan and Hamish from doing something there's no coming back from. I had to deal with the Nightcaller first, then sort out the rest of my life. Because with that crazy bastard in it, I might not have a rest of my life. I thought about going to Ginty, talking to her, but that streak of cowardice was still in control.

I didn't see Duncan approach. A lot of people have made that mistake with Duncan. Thank God he's a pal.

'I need to do this alone, Duncan,' I said.

'I know,' he said.

'I need you and Hamish to keep an eye on everyone here,' I said, feeling I had to explain again.

'I know,' he said again.

I squinted against the pale sunlight. 'You not going to talk me out of it?'

'Nope.'

'Tell me I'm doing the wrong thing?'

'You are, but I won't waste my breath.'

'Tell me I'm an arse?'

'Well, you are an arse, but you don't need to hear that from me.'

'So why you here?'

'Came out here last night, while you were sleeping. I left you something you'll need. I didn't want to hand it to you in broad daylight and I didn't think you'd take it from me inside.'

I didn't need to look. I shook my head, prepared an argument, but he leaned in further and ended it before it began.

'This guy, Dom – he's a mad dog. And you know what to do with mad dogs.'

'Send them out in the midday sun with Englishmen?'

'If you can, put an end to him,' said Duncan, then turned away, walked back to the refuge. He didn't look back.

I sat for a moment, imagining I could feel the cold and heavy presence of the weapon beneath me. I wondered if I would be able to pull the trigger if I had to. If my life or someone else's life was threatened, would I do it? In the movies and on TV and especially video games it looks so easy: you point, you squeeze the trigger, bad guy goes down. Real life isn't quite so simple, for one reason – it's real life. That's not some extra I'd be firing blanks at, not some collection of computer codes and pixels, it'd be a living, breathing person. Would I be able to kill? I heard Alan Ladd speaking in *Shane*. There's no living with a killing. Right or wrong, it's a brand.

Duncan was right. The Nightcaller was a mad dog. He couldn't be cured. He could only be put down.

But was I the person to do it?

I started the car but before I could pull out, my phone rang. It was Sam's sister, Mary. I felt something sharp dig at me as I wondered if the Nightcaller had somehow turned on her.

'I'm sorry to trouble you, Mr Queste,' she said, no trace of tension in her voice.

I relaxed, but only slightly. 'It's no trouble. What can I do for you?'

'I was contacted this morning by one of Sam's neighbours. She'd…' A slight catch. No tension, but the grief was yet raw. 'She'd heard what happened. She apologised, but she's been away, you see.'

'Okay,' I said, wondering where this was leading.

'She's a nice lassie, is Joanne. Lives on her own. Her and Sam were quite friendly, in a neighbourly sort of way, you know what I mean?'

'Yes.'

'Anyway, she came by this morning, paid her respects, you know? And she dropped off an envelope Sam had left with her.'

I was suddenly alert.

'Sam had given it to her maybe two weeks ago, said that if anything should ever happen to him she should give this to me and I'd know what to do with it.'

'What's in the envelope, Mary?'

'Keys and a wee note telling me to check some storage place. Do you know what that's about?'

I smiled. Sam, you crafty bugger. 'Yes, Mary, I know.'

'Well, should I go and see what's in there? The note says I was to give it all back. What did he mean, give it all back?'

I didn't want Mary involved any more than she should be. 'I'll tell you what to do, Mary. Phone Detective Constable Theresa Cohan at the West End police station. The number's in the book. Don't speak to anyone but her. Tell her about the keys and give them to her. She'll sort it.'

'Okay, if you think that's the best thing to do.' I heard relief in her voice. Mary knew her brother. She knew she didn't really want to be anywhere near whatever was in that storage unit. As I said, Mary was a nice woman.

'It was good to see Joanne, right enough, even under these... Well, you know I mean. I'd had many a night in Sam's flat. She'd come over from her flat and we'd open a bottle of wine and have a right laugh. I miss that. I miss...'

Her voice trailed away. I knew she was thinking about her brother and I felt uncomfortable, as if I was responsible. I hadn't caused any of this, I knew that, but I still felt she blamed me. She had to blame someone, I suppose. Then something she said clicked.

'You said the neighbour came over from her flat?'

'Aye.'

'She didn't live upstairs?'

'No, Joanne has the flat opposite Sam's...'

Joanne. The name on the plate said 'J. Stewart'. The 'J' wasn't for Jack, it was for Joanne.

I'd been face-to-face with the Nightcaller and hadn't known it.

Chapter Forty-Two

The sunlight broke through the low clouds and hit the surface of the water like a spotlight. The loch was choppy, grey and so cold I felt my balls shrivel just looking at it. Mist hung around the tops of the hills and drifted sinuously through the pine forest. Even when the weather's as welcoming as a chainsaw-wielding Texan in a leather apron, some parts of Scotland can be simply breathtaking. The air was fresh and clear, and the only sounds I could hear were the water slapping against the stone banking in front of me, the slight breeze through the tree tops and the screech of a buzzard looking for breakfast. I wondered if it was the same buzzard I'd heard when I was at Yew Tree Cottage. Unlikely, I decided, as I was about ten miles to the east and I really didn't think buzzards had that wide a hunting ground. But then, what did I know? I'm not David Attenborough.

The toaster popped and I stepped into the hallway from the open door of the cottage and turned left into the kitchen. The cottage itself wasn't large, but the kitchen was spacious and fully-equipped. Washing machine, dishwasher, microwave, large kitchen table. I'd even cooked on the four-ring electric stove. I didn't have a choice, really. I was six miles from the nearest village and it didn't have a take away. The sight of those fingers resting on top of the chips had cured me of any yen for fast food for a while anyway.

I'd been in the cottage for a week and had heard nothing from the Nightcaller. Or Jack Stewart. Or whatever the hell his real name was. I couldn't believe I'd been standing not three feet away from him, had chatted to him, joked with him. I couldn't believe

I'd actually liked him. Who knew psychotic killers didn't all run around in black cloaks and Scream masks?

I checked both mobiles, my own and the one he'd given me. The only thing I'd specified when I asked Val Roach to find this place was that it have a decent signal. It wasn't great – no 4G, no 3G, barely a G at all – but I could send and receive calls and texts. Duncan had texted and called a few times, just to check I was still in the land of the living. He told me Theresa found the storage unit to be a veritable Aladdin's cave, with all sorts of stolen goods stored away, including the jade bangle. Everything was to be returned to their rightful owner.

He also told me they'd broken the news to Freddie. There was some foul language and the usual dire threats. Duncan and Hamish assured him that if he took any further steps, there would be consequences. Freddie knew this to be true. He'd calm down, chalk it up to experience.

Ginty was still pretty steamed. My slipping away without a word hadn't helped matters. That was something I'd have to deal with when I got back to Glasgow. If I got back to Glasgow. I didn't want to think about that.

There were no new calls registered on either device, which was both good and bad. Good because it meant nothing had happened back home. Bad because it meant I really didn't know what the hell the bastard was up to. I'd been so sure he would follow me up here; that was the whole plan. Stake myself out like a Judas Goat, wait until he pounced, and then Val could nab him. I'd told Ginty I wouldn't be alone, and I hadn't been for the entire week. Val had struggled to sell the idea to her bosses, but finally they gave in and a team was assigned.

The cottage was pretty remote, which was ideal. The nearest road was half a mile up a rough track that curled up the hill from the lochside through a stretch of mature hardwoods. The track ended right outside the cottage's front door. A deep river flowed out of the loch to the right and behind me was a forest of pine-wood leading to a craggy hillside. It didn't have a phone, it didn't have internet, that it had mobile reception was nothing short of a miracle. It was, I thought, the ideal place for a last stand. Even though I wasn't too keen on looking at it that way.

I carried my freshly buttered toast and a refill of coffee back outside. The weather was far from balmy, but it was dry and I liked the place. There was a wooden picnic table complete with benches on the stone patio outside the living room picture window and I sat down, hunched into my fleece jacket and munched my breakfast. The breeze was really stirring up the surface of the water now and I searched for the rowing boat that had been out there all week. I assumed the two people ostensibly fishing had been police officers. The boat had an outboard fitted, and when it all went down they could be at the bank in minutes. But there was no sign of them. There were more officers on the roadway and in the woods. I'd spoken to Val on the phone and she'd told me I wouldn't see them, but they'd be there.

The mist was thickening again, falling to kiss the water and turn the trees on the far side of the river into ghosts. It had also turned decidedly chilly now that the weak sunlight was blanketed, so I finished my toast, carried the plate and my empty cup back inside. I felt something tingling on my back and I stopped, turned, stared across the water at the forest opposite. The trees were becoming more wraith-like as the mist drifted in. I scanned the water's edge, stepped outside, studied the rutted track that pierced the thick woods behind the cottage and headed up the hillside. I listened, heard nothing but the wind and the water and the buzzard's lonely call.

And then –

Singing. A woman's voice, not too loud, maybe from a phone, but I couldn't tell where it was coming from. It floated from the thickening mist, bounced from the trees and the water, vibrated in the air, swirled and spun and eddied.

Brenda Lee. Still sorry after all this time.

My heart hammered as I moved into the cottage, found my own phone again, thumbed a message to Val's mobile.

HE'S HERE.

And then the song stopped.

I moved back to the open door again, really feeling the chill for the first time. Everything seemed so silent now, even the wind had dropped and the water was flat and still. I zipped up my fleece, stepped down the small flight of steps, eyes straining through the white mist for sight of Jack Stewart. I knew he was out there, somewhere. I could feel his eyes on me. I came to a halt at the gate, remained still, waited. He'd do something, I knew it. He couldn't help himself, not now. He'd hung around for a week. Now was his time.

Then –

'Daaaw-minic..!'

The sing-song call floated through the air. I cocked my head to pinpoint its direction, but like the song, it seemed to drift around me with the mist.

'Daaaaw-minic..!'

It wasn't close, I knew that. My focus narrowed on the track leading to the rear.

'Daaaw-minic! I'm here, Dominic…'

It was Jack Stewart's voice. I'd only had that one conversation, but I recognised it well enough. He no longer scrambled it, he had no need.

'Come and get me, Dominic…'

I still had my phone in my hand and I checked it for Val's reply, but the screen was blank. Where the hell was she and her team? They should've come as soon as I texted. I stared out to the water but heard no motor spluttering into life. I checked the track leading to the roadway but saw no figures, heard no vehicles.

'I'm waiting, Dominic…' The voice seemed further away. He was moving.

I moved back to the cottage doorway. If I was right and he was in the woods behind me, he couldn't see me there. I called Val's number, but it rang out. Shit! Where the hell was she?

'Come and get me…Daaaw-minic!'

I knew what I should do. I should go back inside, barricade myself in, wait it out, wait for the cavalry. That's what I should've done. Discretion, valour, all that jazz. But it was time this ended. It was time.

My car keys were in the fleece pocket. I absently pressed the button to unlock the door, my attention still focussed on the mist hanging around me, fished the gun Duncan had left me from under the seat and set off along the trail.

A man's gotta do…

Chapter Forty-Three

The trail was uneven and damp underfoot, while the wet mist beaded on my jacket and stroked my face like clammy cobwebs. The trees crowded around me; conifers, still green, cocking a snook at the seasons. If trees could cock a snook. Whatever the hell a snook is.

It was even quieter in the forest, which I didn't think was possible, the silence broken only by the occasional trickle of a stream on either side and, regularly, running across the trail. I had good, sturdy hiking boots on, so when I couldn't leap across I simply splashed through. Wet feet were the least of my worries.

The gun was heavy in the pocket of my fleece and it bounced against my side with each step. Step-bounce, step-bounce. I'd put the weapon out if sight, even though I didn't think I'd meet anyone up here. Apart from him, of course. I fully intended to meet him. It was comforting to know that the gun was there, but again I wondered if I'd be able to use it while hoping I wouldn't have to. With luck, the police were close behind me, or even ahead of me. I checked my phone, but the signal had completely died. Probably the trees. I'd trekked this way two or three times during my stay, but never when the mist was so thick that it made everything seem alien. And threatening. I could only see about three feet around me. Anything could be lurking there. Or anyone. I consoled myself with the thought that if I couldn't see him, he couldn't see me. He could hear me, though, because I'm not in the slightest way fit and the incline was quite steep: I was breathing like the little engine that could. Something cold trickled down the small of my back, but I couldn't tell if it was the exertion or if the damp air had penetrated my clothing.

A small waterfall had cut a deep trench across the path, the water launching itself from the hillside towards the river below. I had to leap across it. I managed it, but the gun bumped against my side again, reminding me it was there.

'Daaaaw-minic!' The voice was muffled, but that didn't disguise its mocking tone. God, I hated this guy. 'Hope you're coming up to see me. Got a surprise for you!'

Butterflies revved up in my gut to take off in formation as I gripped the gun through the material of my fleece. And I've got a surprise for you, I thought. I'd decided I could do it, if I had to. Wing him, maybe, but I know that only works in movies. I'd fired weapons before, generally as a warning, into the ceiling, the floor. Never at a person. Never at something that could bleed, could fall down, could die. I didn't know guns, just knew how to point and fire, to make the end with the hole go bang. But as I listened to the voice floating down from somewhere above me, to the laughter that rippled through it, I told myself that I could do it if I had to.

The incline was much steeper after I crossed the waterfall and I was walking hard against a steep rock face. Somewhere up ahead I knew I'd come to a flat outcrop, high above the valley and the river that sliced through it. From there you could look right down the valley across an undulating carpet of green and gold towards Rannoch and Glencoe, but I doubted I'd see that far with this mist. Beyond it, the woods and the gorse thickened before they petered out to an expanse of open heath pitted with muddy bogs. He'd be waiting at the outcrop. Above me, somewhere in the mist, the rocks grew to ragged peaks separated by deep incisions. In days of yore, members of the MacGregor clan used to hide out in those hollows from government troops and rival clans. They called the MacGregors the Children of the Mist because they could merge with it so easily. They had plenty of practice up here. I knew before the day was over, I'd wish I was a MacGregor.

The path levelled as I reached the flat patch that jutted over the valley. The drop here was steep and somewhere below were the tops of tall trees descending to the river, its waters foaming white against jagged boulders that stood against it midstream. I couldn't see that today, but I could hear the angry water rage and roil against the rocks. All I could see today was the grey mist, about three feet of damp grass and the cliff face ahead of me. No Jack Stewart.

I came to a halt, not willing to move any further. It was slippery underfoot, even in my walking boots, and I had no desire to take a header over the edge. There would be very little chance of surviving that fall.

I stood very still and waited. The wind had died completely now. There was just the sound and fury below, and me wrapped in the mist. Waiting.

I grew impatient. 'Okay, Jack, you've got me here – what now?'

I moved around in a circle, searching the gloom for his shadows, listening for his footfalls, breathing. A cough would've been nice.

'Come on,' I said. 'What are you waiting for?'

The mist hung around me yet moved at the same time. Pockets drifted while the rest remained static, as if there were little currents within. I kept turning, slowly. I hadn't drawn the gun. It still nestled at my hip, but I'd unzipped the pocket and my hand rested over it. I hadn't practised my quick draw since I was a kid in front of the mirror, but I didn't want to show my hand just yet.

'Come on, Jack,' I said, injecting as much confidence into my voice as I could. 'I thought you wanted to play?'

'I do, Dom.'

The voice came from behind me and I swung round, but all I saw was the mist.

'I like to play.'

This time it was to my left. I jerked to face it, but again, nothing.

I told myself that if I couldn't see him, he couldn't see me. He knew where I was because I'd been calling out. I almost convinced myself, too. All the same, I decided to say nothing more until we were face-to-face.

'Don't you want to know what your surprise is, Dom?'

Back to my right again. I slid my hand into my pocket, hoped I'd be able to pull the gun without snagging on the material.

When I didn't respond, I heard a chuckle. He was moving, somewhere ahead of me, just beyond the curtain of mist. If I concentrated, I could hear him shuffling in the wet grass. I just couldn't see him.

'What's wrong, friend? Cat got your tongue?'

He'd stopped. Another chuckle.

'Not very sporting of you, going quiet.'

I held my breath, remained frozen, my hand tightening on the gun butt in my pocket. Come on, you bastard, show yourself. Just for a minute, I'll show you what a surprise is.

Then the voice all but breathed in my ear.

'I can seeee you…'

I whirled, jerked the gun free, raised it, but he was gone. I thought I saw something dark fold itself into the mist, but couldn't be sure. He was nippy on his feet for an elderly man.

'Oooh, a gun,' he said. He was moving again, over to my right, towards the rock wall again. 'Make you feel like a big man, Dom, holding that?'

I took a few tentative steps forward, closer to where I thought he was. And away from the edge. I wouldn't put it past him to rush me and take us both over.

'They say a gun's the symbolic extension of the penis,' he said, as if we were having a chat over a drink. 'You need a little bit of symbolic extension, Dom?'

I took a few more steps, the gun held two-handed ahead of me. I was so scared that I'd forgotten all my quibbles about using a firearm. Just give me a glimpse, I thought, that's all I ask. Peek out of the mist for a second, I'll symbolically extend you all the way to hell.

The rock face loomed dark and hard in front of me and I

stopped, listened. I heard movement to my right so I faced it, still ready to fire. Footsteps on grass. Louder than before. Much louder. I wondered if it was the police team, finally catching up, but it was too slow, too irregular. The cops would come in like gangbusters, all shouted warnings and intimidation. This wasn't like that. This was like someone dragging something.

And then I saw the figures loom out of the murk. One was Jack Stewart.

The other was Val Roach, held in front of him like a shield.

Chapter Forty-Four

I couldn't see it, but could tell from the way he was holding her with one hand and the other hidden that he had a weapon at her back. My guess was a knife. He liked blades. She was very erect, her arms tight against her back because he had bound them, but her feet dragged and there was a stream of blood at her temple. She looked groggy, but she saw me. He came to a halt and smiled.

'Nice to see you again, Dom,' he said, as if we were meeting in the park. He was wrapped in a brown waterproof coat that draped to his calves. He had a good, thick pair of leather boots on his feet. And he had a wide-brimmed hat on his head. 'You know Miss Piggy here, don't you?' His hidden hand moved slightly and Val jerked. Yes, he had a blade there, jammed into her back. She was wearing a thick parka, zipped to the neck. Her jeans were wet and muddy at the knees. 'Bet you're surprised, eh? Didn't expect to see her like this?'

'Let her go,' I said, staring down the barrel of the gun, hoping for a shot, but he was too close to her and I was no marksman.

He laughed. 'I knew you'd say that. I told her you'd say that, didn't I, Miss Piggy?' He pressed his mouth close to her ear. 'Tell him how predictable he is.'

Val didn't say anything. She struggled a bit, but the crack on the head had weakened her. All the same, he pressed the weapon into her back and she winced. Yes, a blade.

He smiled. 'She's shy, I think.' He gave me a little look, his head cocked. 'You're going to call me a bastard now.'

I gritted my teeth. I actually was going to call him a bastard.

'Oh, Dom,' he said, 'don't try to be the strong, silent type. It ill becomes you.' He waited for me to say something, didn't seem at all offended when I didn't. 'Ah, well. No matter. It's that point of the game where we all show our cards, isn't it? You've shown me yours. Surprised at you, Dom, packing heat. That's how you'd think of it, isn't it? All those books and films of yours. Private eyes, cowboys, tough guys. Going heeled. Toting a piece. Loaded for bear.' He pulled Val tighter to him. 'And you thought the police would save you, didn't you? You thought they'd charge in, armed to the teeth, bristling with weaponry, ready to take me in or take me down. Maybe they're out there. Maybe they're waiting for the order.' He looked over his shoulder and yelled, 'Come and get me, coppers! You'll never take me alive. Top of the world, Ma!' He tilted his head as if was listening, then he shrugged. 'Sorry, Dom. Guess they're not there after all. Guess your little plan went all tits up, as they say. See, here's the thing about police forces all over the world, they have budgets. And those budgets are stretched. And Police Scotland? Well, such a little country, such a little force. Money's tight. Manpower's tight. They can't afford to keep a team of good men and women hanging around the countryside for too long. I knew this. And all I had to do was wait. So guess what?'

He paused for an answer. I didn't give him the satisfaction.

He shrugged again. 'I waited. And as old Hannibal Lecter said, all good things come to those who wait, Clarice. You don't mind me calling you Clarice, do you? I feel as if we have a similar relationship. Even though we're both big, strapping laddies.'

I said, 'Why don't you let her go and us two big, strapping laddies can get this finished?'

'In good time, Clarice, in good time. I've not finished my expositionary bit yet. You want to deprive me of my big scene? It's all been about you so far – allow me my moment in the sun.' He looked up into the cold grey that surrounded us. 'So to speak. Now, where was I?' He made a show of thinking about it. 'Ah yes – they called them off this morning, the police squad. Pulled

251

them out faster than you can say "Evening, all". Juliet Bravo here was coming to tell you when I intercepted her. That right, Miss Piggy?' He leaned closer to her, but she didn't reply. He sighed. 'You know, she's a bore. I hate boring people.'

His shoulder jerked as he rammed the knife into her back. Her back arched and a strangled cry rumbled in her throat, and then Stewart threw her to the side, sending her crashing into the rock face. She hit it hard, bounced off and crumpled to the ground. I swung the gun again but I was too late, he'd floated back into the protection of the mist. I edged my way forward, knelt, the gun held straight in one hand while I felt her neck for a pulse. She was still alive at least, but out cold. I loosened the rope knotted at her wrists as I kept my eyes on the mist around me.

'You and me now, Dom,' he said, somewhere off to my right. I tried to follow the voice with the barrel of the gun, but it was useless. 'Bet you want to shoot me now, eh? Bet it's so bad you can taste it. Well, you'll get your chance soon enough, so be ready.'

I rose, both hands back on the gun, and edged in the voice's direction, my back hard against the rock.

Stewart kept up his commentary. 'You'll be wondering about me, eh, Dom? You'll have all sorts of questions. Like how many have I killed? Why do I do it? How do I get away with it? Who am I, really? 'Cos – spoiler alert, Dom – Jack Stewart isn't my name. Want to know what it is?'

I didn't reply. I concentrated on the voice.

'Still not talking, eh? Well, I'll tell you anyway.' He paused. 'I am Legion, for we are many.' He laughed. 'I'm the dybbuk of the Hebrews. I'm the bogey-man, the thing under the bed, the shadow in the cupboard. I'm the face at the window, the tingle at the back of your neck and the thing you see in the corner of your eye. I am rage. I am darkness. I am death.'

He waited. I waited. Then he laughed again. 'No, all bullshit. Seriously, Dom, I'm just a guy, a bloke, a geezer, a dude.' He stretched out the vowel sound on the last word. 'With one very special uniquity. Is that a word, uniquity? Or have I just made it up? Good though, isn't it? Uniquity.' He savoured it, pleased with himself. 'Anyway, my uniquity is that I kill people. And I'm very good at it. Been doing it for years, never came close to being caught. All over the world, too – I'm a much-travelled man, Dom.'

I edged through the mist, trying to pinpoint where he was, hoping he was so intent in his monologue that he wouldn't hear me.

'So why do I kill? Would you believe me if I said it was because my parents were unfeeling, cold, distant? I never knew a loving relationship until I was in my early twenties, when I met a woman who just wanted to possess me? Would you believe that?' He paused again, waiting for a reply. He was disappointed. He didn't sound it, though, as he went on with his one-sided conversation. 'No, quite right. More bullshit. How about I was abused as a child and I took out my anger on small animals first, then graduated to larger prey? No? Not buying that either? Quite right. Bullshit, too. The fact is I had a perfectly normal, loving childhood and I married a beautiful girl who loved me and I loved her back. She had no clue that while I was hitting every point of the compass to bring in the bacon, I was perfecting my other skills. I was an engineer, if you're interested, and really good at it too.' He stopped. 'My wife's gone now, by the way. I didn't kill her, she was taken by natural causes.' His laugh was more rueful this time. 'Natural causes. Polite way of saying she got sick, withered and died without ever suspecting that I had killed more people than Burton and Eastwood in *Where Eagles Dare*. That's another wee movie reference there for you, Dom, to make you feel at home.'

I was wandering blind. He kept moving around, I could tell because his voice would fade, become less distinct as it swirled with the mist around me, as if he was turning this way and that, trying to find me, hopefully as disoriented as I was. We could do this all day, blundering around until one of us got lucky. I so needed that to be me. I stopped and decided to let him come to me.

'Why the song, Jack?' I asked.

'Ah! He speaks!' The voice was clearer now as he zeroed in on me. 'A new wrinkle, that. Just came to me on the spur of the moment. He had it on a mix CD and I thought it would be something else for the police to scratch their head over. Later, of course, when I got to know you a bit better, I thought you might appreciate it. The use of music, particularly a vintage song. Of course, in retrospect it should've been 'Sea of Love' – just to keep our cinematic theme going. You do know what I'm talking about, don't you?'

Of course I did. Al Pacino, Ellen Barkin, a killer who left the song playing at the scene.

He didn't need me to answer, though. 'So I'm assuming you've put some of it together: how I pick my victims, blah, blah, blah. James Mortimer was the first, by the way, in case you were wondering. Well, the first in Glasgow for some time, anyway. Years, in fact. The random nature of my work throws the law. The fact that I kill with differing methods really baffles them. They like patterns, routines, modus operandi. I did get sloppy this time round, though. Maybe I'm getting old. I let that girl scratch me. They'll never find a match because I'm not in the system, but it does mean I can't come back here again, to Scotland. Shame that: it's home. But they might match samples from other crime scenes in the future and my secret will be out. They won't know it's me, of course, but they will know there's a serial killer on the loose.'

He stopped talking and I tensed, expecting him to lunge towards me.

'Serial killer,' he said, thoughtfully. 'So preferable to the old phrase – psychotic killer. Or homicidal maniac. That's not very politically correct at all.'

The mist must have fully cleared from the valley floor, because a stutter of gunfire reached us from wherever they were shooting down the valley.

'Hear that, Dom?' He said. 'Fun and games. Life and death. I'm just like those men, really. I like to hunt. I like to stalk and track and trail. And then, when the time is right, I strike. The way I see

254

it, you're either the hunter or the hunted in this life. Predator or prey. I know what I am. What are you?

The mist was beginning to lift, at least I thought I could see more of the space around me. I strained to see ahead of me, where his voice was coming from.

'Not talking again? Well, I'll tell you, Dom. You're the prey…'

Something began to take shape, dark against the grey. A long coat. A wide-brimmed hat. He was only about six feet away from me. I aimed the gun at centre mass. Duncan was right, he needed to be put down like a mad dog. He didn't move. He must've been able to see me. His face began to clear. He was smiling. He was waiting.

'There you are,' he said.

I stood firm to soak in the recoil and pulled the trigger. Once, twice, again and again.

Each time all I heard was a click…

Chapter Forty-Five

He didn't even flinch as I pulled the trigger. All he did was smile.

'Oh, dear,' he said. 'Not working? You firing blanks? That the symbolic extension of anything, Dom?'

Then he held out his left hand and I could see the ammunition clip nestling in his palm. I checked the gun. The clip was gone. Duncan would've known by the weight. I didn't. I flashed to me opening my car door, knowing now that I hadn't heard it unlock. I hadn't been paying attention. Idiot.

He saw me looking at the useless weapon in my hand. 'Doesn't work without bullets, Dom,' he said. 'I saw your friend, the bald Geordie, leave it in your car. I've got to admit that I didn't see you as a pistolero, but I didn't want to take any chances. You should know by now that I can break into just about anything. Houses, cars. I've stolen a lot of cars over the years. I'm really good at it, too. I make *Gone in 60 Seconds* look like *The Long Weekend*. That's another movie reference for you, I hope you appreciate all my effort.'

I didn't show him any appreciation. He didn't seem to mind. 'You can toss that to the side now, it won't work. However…' He swung his right hand up to let me see the automatic he held. 'This one will. I took it from the Gentle Touch over there. I don't think she'll be needing it any more. I think she'll be walking the beat with the angels by now.'

I darted a look towards the rock face, saw Val's shape, dark in the thinning mist. I didn't throw the gun away.

His eyes didn't move from me. 'We really didn't need her.

This...' He waved the hand holding the clip to my gun. 'This is Thunderdome, Dom. Two men enter, one man leaves.' He brought the gun level, aimed it directly at me. 'Guess who that's going to be?'

Thoughts of throwing myself to the side flitted through my mind, but I knew it wouldn't do any good. I didn't know if he was proficient with a firearm, but presuming Val's police-issue weapon was fully loaded, he'd have more than enough bullets to get me. I couldn't rush him, either. Six feet is a long, l-o-n-g way when there's hot lead flying in your direction. But I knew I had to do something.

'How did you manage to kill Tank without a struggle?'

He smiled and the gun lowered, but only a little. 'Ah! He was a big lad, and I didn't think I could take him when he was compos mentis. Back in the day, maybe, and while I keep myself trim, I'm no longer in the first flush. So I played to his essentially corrupt nature. Told him the fast food had been ordered for his address and already paid for. He didn't even bat an eyelid, just took it from me. So predictable.'

'You put something in the food?'

'Yes, slipped him a mickey, as you'd no doubt say. Then I went back and simply finished him off. I thought that, given the way he was – the suit, the hat, the whole Mafioso persona – the piano wire was a fitting touch.'

'And what about the cat?'

He frowned. 'The cat?'

'Yes,' I said, 'you fed the cat. What was that about?'

'She was hungry. And I like cats. They're so amoral. They'll kill anything – and have fun doing it. They don't need to be hungry, they'll simply kill for pleasure. And turn it into an art.'

'Like you.'

That smile again. 'Now you're catching on, sport. Really, old friend, I'd love to stand here chewing the fat all day, but it's time I was moving. Don't stay too long in one place, that's my secret. Don't do anything the same way twice. Don't dilly-dally.' He levelled the gun again. 'Ladies and gentlemen, girls and boys – dyin' time's here…'

The figure slammed into him from what was left of the mist. He had been too intent on me, too convinced he'd finished the job to notice that Val had pulled herself to her feet. I saw it when I looked over and knew I had to play for time, keep him talking. He loved to talk. She hit him at waist level with her shoulder, like an American football player tackling an opponent. He grunted as the air was forced out of him and the ammo clip from my gun flew from his hand, but he retained his grip of her automatic. He lost his footing on the wet grass and hit the ground hard, but he twisted immediately and let off a shot. Val was already leaping out of the way and it went wild. He raised to one knee as Val threw herself to the ground and rolled, kept rolling, trying to put as much distance between them as possible. He grasped the gun in both hands. Took careful aim. Val could roll all she liked, but he'd get her.

'Don't,' I said, and something in my voice made him pause and look in my direction. I had the gun aimed directly at him, held steadily in both hands. He squinted as he looked around the grass for the clip.

'I didn't see you pick it up,' he said. Val had stopped rolling, but his gun was still on her.

'You were otherwise engaged,' I said.

His gaze finally settled on me. His smile returned. 'I think you're bluffing.'

'I wouldn't bank on it.'

Val raised herself to one knee, mirroring his pose, and his head jerked back in her direction. She froze. 'Well now,' he said, 'we've got ourselves a Mexican standoff, don't we? What now, Dom? We sit here like this until one of us gives up?'

'I've got all day, not that it'll take that long. I took the liberty of phoning my friends before I set off up here. It'll only take them a couple of hours to get here, not even that long, the way Duncan drives. Believe me, Jack, you don't want them to get you.'

His head inclined slightly, conceding that. 'My name's not Jack. You know that, don't you?'

'I know,' I said, keeping the gun squarely on him.

'It just fitted. Not only the nameplate – yes, I saw you clocked it – but Jack, so evocative. Jack be nimble, Jack be quick. Jack of all trades. Springheel Jack. Jack the Ripper.' Neither of us moved. He still had his gun on Val. She knew there was nowhere to run and remained like a statue as she watched and listened. He gave her a look, then back to me, saw my gun was steady. Then back to Val. He thought about the situation. 'I could kill Miss Piggy before you get off a shot.'

'Maybe.'

'I might even get you too. You don't know how good I am with a gun.'

That had occurred to me. 'You might. You might not.'

'And you might miss.'

That fact had occurred to me too. 'I might. You might get me first. You might get lucky. You know what you have to ask yourself, don't you?' I said, unable to resist. 'Do you feel lucky?'

He smiled as if he genuinely appreciated the line. 'Touché, Dom, touché.' He breathed in deeply. 'My, my, don't we have ourselves a situation?'

'Not if you put your gun down. Then we can all be pals again.'

A little smile played on his lips. 'I could, but here's the thing – I still don't think you got the clip.'

I didn't say anything. He looked back at me, studied my face, looking for some signal that I was bluffing.

'You didn't get the clip, did you?' he said. 'I didn't see you move. You didn't have time to find it. I think it might even have gone over the edge. No, Dom, you didn't get the clip.'

And then he moved, suddenly but with grace, swinging the gun in my direction, bringing the barrel level, and he smiled with the certainty that I hadn't found the clip as his finger tightened on the trigger.

I fired once. A tiny scarlet bloom flowered at his shoulder and he twitched to his left, fell back onto his backside. He looked at the hole in his fancy coat and the blood seeping through, then back at me, the smile dripping away as the realisation reached his eyes.

'I got the clip,' I said.

He began to snarl, and the snarl became a growl and then a bellow, and he jerked the gun up once more and I fired again. I kept firing as I walked slowly towards him, watching his body jolt and judder as each bullet struck him as if someone offstage was yanking at wires.

I tugged the trigger long after the clip was empty and he lay on his back, staring at the blue sky that was beginning to form out of the white that had surrounded us. I kept at it until Val eased the weapon from my hands. Even then, I could still feel its weight, still feel the pull of the gun as it fired again and again.

Chapter Forty-Six

We never did find out his real name. There was nothing on his body that led to an identification. The car he'd used, found in a lay-by two miles away, was stolen. He'd told us he was good at breaking into cars. He hadn't been lying when he said his fingerprints and his DNA weren't on file. He'd told us he'd been married, that he'd been an engineer and maybe that would lead somewhere in the future, but for now he was a bloody ghost, a spectre. He'd said he was the dybbuk, and I guess that's what he was. The assumption was that he'd taken on different identities over the years, possessed them, if you like. His photograph would be circulated and maybe, some way down the line, the mystery would be solved. Maybe not. I knew where I'd put my money.

Val told her bosses that I'd used the killer's own gun to kill him because her life was in imminent danger. She didn't have to do that, but she did. It prevented any awkward questions about where the unlicensed weapon actually came from.

Her stab vest had protected her from the worst of the knife thrust. He'd managed to penetrate it and pierce her body, but she would be fine. The blow to the head he'd dealt her, not to mention the subsequent slam against the rock face, had done more damage, and she'd been out of it for a while. Even when I saw her hauling herself to her feet, she wasn't quite sure where she was. She'd gone for him without thinking, which was probably just as well, because if she had thought about it she more than likely wouldn't have done it.

I liked her.

They kept me in Perth for a while, answering questions. There would an inquiry, more questions, but as far as they were concerned I'd saved one of their officers. For once, I was treated with respect. I was patted on the back. I was shaken by the hand. I was given coffee and cake and even a whisky. Talisker. The good stuff. They stopped short of carrying me through the streets on their shoulders.

I thanked them and accepted all their praise and their back patting and their handshakes and their coffee, cake and whisky. I was courteous. I was humble. I didn't make any smart remarks. Outwardly I was cool and calm and confident. Inside I felt something small and nasty gnaw at me. Shane was right. There's no living with a killing. Even when a man needed killing.

I knew I wouldn't be the same again.

As I was leaving, Val saw me to my car. She had a bandage on her head and her arm was in a sling. Turned out she'd damaged a tendon during her flying tackle. She held my door open and we stared at each other for a moment. Nothing was said: there was nothing left to say. Then we hugged, not too tight, because she was injured.

We still held each other as I said, 'Nick never hugs me.'

'I don't think he's a hugger,' she said.

'Thank heaven for small mercies.'

We broke. She gave me a smile. 'You take care of yourself, Dom. Stay out of trouble.'

'I don't go looking for it,' I said.

'But it finds you.'

'Every time,' I said, and climbed into my car. She watched me back out of the car park and head back to Glasgow.

I slipped some John Barry into the CD player. A greatest hits selection. It soothed me, made the glare of approaching headlights, the cars roaring up my tailpipe to overtake, the rain that began to batter down as I hit the northern outskirts of the city all more bearable.

My phone rang as I merged onto the M8. It was dark now and the rush hour was an exhaust-fumed memory. I did my customary check for police vehicles, held the phone in one hand under the driving wheel, hit accept and then the loudspeaker.

'My hero,' said Alicia.

I should've known the jungle drums would've reached her by now. I heard a match strike at her end. 'You smoking tobacco again, Alicia?'

'Yeah. Life's too short for that vaping carry on. So when you coming in to give me the story?'

'Not tonight, Alicia. I'm worn out.'

'You wouldn't be thinking of taking it to someone else, would you?' Paranoia. In the newspaper world, they hand it out along with reporter's notebooks, cheap pens and the need to mainline caffeine.

'Relax. The story's all yours, just like I promised. Tit for tat.'

Hannibal Lecter's line came into my head, but it wasn't Sir Anthony speaking, it was the Nightcaller's voice – *quid pro quo, Clarice...*

'From what I hear, if I get this story, I'll give you more than tit, believe me. Tomorrow, Dom, early. Bring donuts.'

And then she was gone. For the first time that day, my smile was genuine.

✳ ✳ ✳

I didn't go to the refuge and I didn't go to Duncan and Hamish's flat and I didn't go home. I went straight to Ginty's flat. I knew she wasn't at the refuge and I suppose I should've called first. She didn't answer her door. We had to talk, but it would have to wait. The truth is, I was relieved.

My phone rang as I hit the pavement.

'Dom.' Ginty's voice. It was quiet, almost a whisper. I glanced at her windows, but the blinds were half drawn and the room beyond in darkness. 'I didn't answer the door,' she said. I imagined her standing in her living room, in the shadow, watching me through the slatted blinds as I stood in the soft rain under the street lamp.

'You going to let me in, Ginty?'

She avoided that question. 'I'm glad you're okay. I'm glad you're safe. This time.'

This time. Another time, it'll be different. *What about the fight we lose?* Father Verne had asked. Maybe she hadn't avoided the question.

'Let me in, Ginty,' I said, still facing the windows. She could see me. I knew she could.

'No,' she said. 'If I'm close to you, I'll chicken out and I need to be strong. I can't live this way, Dom. Not again. Not knowing who is going to come at you. Not knowing if you're going to come home ever again. And you, keeping things from me because you think you're protecting me.'

'I was…'

'I know, but I don't want to be protected.' She amended that. 'I don't want to be in the position that I need to be protected. Do you understand? And I told you – I can't go through this again. I can't watch you change.'

'I won't change.' I said the words, but even I didn't swallow it. I knew I'd already changed. She said nothing. I said nothing. I waited, knowing there was nowhere for the conversation to go. Ginty knew that too.

'Goodbye, Erasmus,' she said, and hung up.

I thought about calling her back, but I didn't. I thought about knocking at her door again, but I didn't. I thought about standing there until she weakened and spoke to me again, but I didn't. Instead I turned and walked down a pavement that was slick with rain. I should've had a trench coat and a fedora. There should've been saxophone music. Something faintly jazzy. Something sad. But there wasn't.

As I walked alone I knew for certain that, in my world, happy ever afters were an endangered species.

THE END

264

Acknowledgements

Grateful thanks go to Dr Sharlene Butler, who guided me in relation to Dominic Queste's hospital examination. Any errors are mine, not hers, and patients can relax.

Thanks are also due to an incredibly supportive group of crime writers in Scotland and beyond, in particular Alex Gray, Caro Ramsay, Lin Anderson, Theresa Talbot, Michael J Malone, Neil Broadfoot, Mason Cross, Mark Leggatt, Gordon GJ Brown, Matt Bendoris and Quintin Jardine, who all championed the first book above and beyond.

Also, my gratitude must go to Craig Robertson, Alexandra Sokoloff, Martina Cole, SJI Holliday, James Oswald, Denzil Meyrick and Marsali Taylor for their support and guidance.

Similarly, the reviewers and book bloggers who took Dom to their hearts, particularly Sharon Bairden, Noelle Holton, Gordon McGhie, Crime Fiction Lover, Scots Whay Hae, Craig Sisterson, Shari Low, Crime Time, Undiscovered Scotland, The Times Book Club and Crime Review UK. If I've missed anyone, please accept my abject apologies.

Many thanks to the organisers of festivals and events who have kindly placed me on the bill in order to talk utter nonsense. In 2016 I appeared at the first Bute Noir, Bloody Scotland, Aye Write, the Grantown Festival, rhe West End and Byres Road Festivals, Tidelines Festival, the online ScotLitFest and the Scottish Association of Writers conference, and continued the world tour of parts of Scotland with the Crime Factor squad of

Broadfoot, Brown, Leggatt and Peter Burnett. There were also appearances in libraries, which are always fun to do.

To my Carry on Sleuthing castmates, Caro, Michael, Theresa and Neil – thanks for taking a pig's ear and turning it into, if not a silk purse, then at least something similar. I'm still not sure how similar or even what it is, but you made it. I'm not taking all the blame.

Authors wouldn't be anywhere without the booksellers. They let me make a fool of myself before audiences and, hopefully, place my books in prominent positions (face out, always face out). I can't name them all, but Caron Macpherson, David McCormack, Kenny Bryan – all of Waterstones – and Karen Latto at Print Point and Marjory Marshall of the Bookmark in Grantown-on-Spey deserve special mention.

I've been fortunate in my fiction to have had the same editor and long may that continue. Louise Hutcheson does a wonderful job and my thanks go to her, as well as Sara Hunt and everyone at Contraband.

Thanks also to Gary McLaughlin for risking his camera lens by taking author shots and Graham Turnbull for keeping www.douglasskelton.com online.

As before, special thanks got to Iain K Burns for everything he's done over the past few years and, again, Stephen Wilkie.

There – I think I've crawled to just about everyone I can think of. If I've missed anyone out, hopefully there will be further titles to make up for it.